THE RELIVE BOX AND OTHER STORIES

ALSO BY T. CORAGHESSAN BOYLE

NOVELS

SHORT STORIES

ANTHOLOGIES

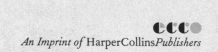

An Imprint of HarperCollins*Publishers*

THE
RELIVE
BOX

AND OTHER STORIES

T. CORAGHESSAN BOYLE

THE RELIVE BOX AND OTHER STORIES. Copyright © 2017 by T. Coraghessan Boyle. All rights reserved. Printed in the United States of America. No part of this book may be used or reproduced in any manner whatsoever without written permission except in the case of brief quotations embodied in critical articles and reviews. For information address HarperCollins Publishers, 195 Broadway, New York, NY 10007.

HarperCollins books may be purchased for educational, business, or sales promotional use. For information please e-mail the Special Markets Department at SPsales@harpercollins.com.

A hardcover edition of this book was published in 2017 by Ecco, an imprint of HarperCollins Publishers.

FIRST ECCO PAPERBACK EDITION PUBLISHED 2018.

Designed by Michelle Crowe

Library of Congress Cataloging-in-Publication Data has been applied for.

ISBN 978-0-06-267345-9

18 19 20 21 22   LSC   10 9 8 7 6 5 4 3 2 1

For Milo, Alexis and Olivia

I love not Man the less, but Nature more.

−George Gordon Byron, *Childe Harold's Pilgrimage*

Man hands on misery to man.
  It deepens like a coastal shelf.
Get out as early as you can,
  And don't have any kids yourself.

−Philip Larkin, "This Be the Verse"

CONTENTS

ACKNOWLEDGMENTS

Grateful acknowledgment is made to the following magazines, in which these stories first appeared: *The Iowa Review,* "The Designee"; *The Kenyon Review,* "The Five-Pound Burrito" and "Surtsey"; *McSweeney's,* "The Argentine Ant"; *Narrative,* "She's the Bomb," "Warrior Jesus" and "You Don't Miss Your Water ('Til the Well Runs Dry)"; *The New Yorker,* "The Relive Box," "Are We Not Men?" and "The Fugitive"; *Playboy,* "Theft and Other Issues."

"Are We Not Men?" also appeared in *The Best American Short Stories 2017,* edited by Meg Wolitzer (Boston: Houghton Mifflin Harcourt, 2017), "The Relive Box" in *The Best American Science Fiction and Fantasy 2015,* edited by Joe Hill (Boston: Houghton Mifflin Harcourt, 2015) and "The Five-Pound Burrito" in *The Pushcart Prize, XLI: Best of the Small Presses,* edited by Bill Henderson (Wainscott, NY: The Pushcart Press, 2017).

THE RELIVE BOX AND OTHER STORIES

THE RELIVE BOX

Katie wanted to relive Katie at nine, before her mother left, and I could appreciate that, but we only had one console at the time and I really didn't want to go there. It was coming up on the holidays, absolutely grim outside, nine-thirty at night—on a school night—and she'd have to be up at six to catch the bus in the dark. She'd already missed too much school, staying home on any pretext and reliving the whole time I was at work, so there really were no limits, and who was being a bad father here? A single father unable to discipline his fifteen-year-old daughter, let alone inculcate a work ethic in her? Me. I was. And I felt bad about it. I wanted to put my foot down and at the same time give her something, make a concession, a peace offering. But even more I wanted the box myself, wanted it so baldly it was showing in my face, I'm sure, and she needed to get ready for school, needed sleep, needed to stop reliving and worry about the now, the now and the future. "Why don't you wait till the weekend," I said.

She was wearing those tights all the girls wear like painted-on skin, standing in the doorway to the living room, perching on one foot the way she did when she was doing her dance exercises. Her face belonged to her mother, my ex, Christine, who hadn't been there for her for six years and counting. "I want to relive now," she said, diminishing her voice to the shaky hesitant plaint that was calculated to make me melt and give in to whatever she wanted, but it wasn't going to work this time, no way. She was going to bed and I was going back to a rainy February night in 1982, a sold-out show at the Roxy, a band I loved then, and the girl I was mad crazy for before she broke my heart and Christine came along to break it all over again.

"Why don't you go up and text your friends or something," I said.

"I don't want to text my friends. I want to be with my mom."

This was a plaint too and it cut even deeper. She was deprived, that was the theme here, and the whole thing, as any impartial observer could see in a heartbeat, verged on child abuse. "I know, honey, I know. But it's not healthy. You're spending too much time there."

"You're just selfish, that's all," she said, and here was the shift to a new tone, the tone of animus and opposition, the subtext being that I never thought of anybody but myself. "You want to what, relive when you were like my age or something? Let me guess: you're going to go back and relive yourself doing homework, right? As an example for your daughter?"

The room was a mess. The next day was the day the maid came, so I was standing amidst the debris of the past week, a healthy percentage of it—abandoned sweat socks, energy-drink cans, various crumpled foil pouches that had once contained biscotti, popcorn or Salami Bites—generated by the child standing there before me. "I don't like your sarcasm," I said.

Her face was pinched so that her lips were reduced to the smallest little O-ring of disgust. "What *do* you like?"

"A clean house. A little peace and quiet. Some privacy, for Christ's sake—is that too much to ask?"

"I want to be with Mom."

"Go text your friends."

"I don't have any friends."

"Make some."

And this, thrown over her shoulder preparatory to the furious pounding retreat up the stairs and the slamming of her bedroom door: "You're a pig!"

And my response, which had become ritualized ever since I'd sprung for the $5,000 second-generation Halcom X1520 Relive Box with the In-Flesh Retinal Projection Stream and altered forever the dynamic between me and my only child: "I know."

Most people, when they got their first Relive Box, went straight for sex, which was only natural. In fact, it was a selling point in the TV ads, which featured shimmering adolescents walking hand in hand along a generic strip of beach or leaning in for a tender kiss over the ball return at the bowling alley. Who wouldn't want to go back there? Who wouldn't want to relive innocence, the nascent stirrings of love and desire or the first time you removed her clothes and she removed yours? What of girlfriends (or boyfriends, as the case may be), wives, ex-wives, one-night stands, the casual encounter that got you halfway there and flitted out of reach on the wings of an unfulfilled promise? I was no different. The sex part of it obsessed me through those first couple of months and if I drifted into work each morning feeling drained (and not just figuratively), I knew it was a problem and that it was adversely affecting my job performance, and even, if I didn't cut back, threatening my job itself. Still, to relive Christine when we first met, to relive her in bed, in candlelight, clinging fast to me and whispering my name over and over in the throes of her passion, was too great a temptation. Or even just sitting there across from me in the Moroccan restaurant where I took her for our first date, her eyes like portals, like consoles themselves, as she leaned into the table and drank up every word and witticism that came out of my mouth. Or to go further back, before my wife entered the picture, to Rennie Porter, the girl I took to the senior prom and spent two delicious hours rubbing up against in the backseat of my father's Buick Regal, every second of which I'd relived six or seven times now. And to Lisa, Lisa Denardo, the girl I met that night at the Roxy, hoping I was going to score.

I started coming in late to work. Giving everybody, even my boss, the zombie stare. I got my first warning. Then my second. And my boss—Kevin Moos, a decent-enough guy five years younger than me who didn't have an X1520, or not that he was letting on—sat me down in his office and told me, in no uncertain terms, that there wouldn't be a third.

But it was a miserable night and I was depressed. And bored. So bored you could have drilled holes in the back of my head and taken core samples and I wouldn't have known the difference. I'd already denied my daughter, who was thumping around upstairs with the cumulative weight of ten daughters, and the next day was Friday, TGIF, end of the week, the slimmest of workdays when just about everybody alive thinks about slipping out early. I figured even if I did relive for more than the two hours I was going to strictly limit myself to, even if I woke up exhausted, I could always find a way to make it to lunch and just let things coast after that. So I went into the kitchen and fixed myself a gin and tonic because that was what I'd been drinking that night at the Roxy and carried it into the room at the end of the hall that had once been a bedroom and was now (Katie's joke, not mine) the reliving room.

The console sat squarely on the low table that was the only piece of furniture in the room aside from the straight-backed chair I'd set in front of it the day I brought the thing home. It wasn't much bigger than the gaming consoles I'd had to make do with in the old days, a slick black metal cube with a single recessed glass slit running across the face of it from one side to the other. It activated the minute I took my seat. "Hello, Wes," it said in the voice I'd selected, male, with the slightest bump of an accent to make it seem less synthetic. "Welcome back."

I lifted the drink to my lips to steady myself—think of a conductor raising his baton—and cleared my throat. "February 28, 1982," I said, "9:45 p.m. Play."

The box flashed the date and time and then suddenly I was there, the club exploding into life like a comet touching down, light and noise and movement obliterating the now, the house gone, my daughter gone, the world of getting and doing and bosses and work vanished in an instant. I was standing at the bar with my best friend, Zach Ronalds, who turned up his shirt collar and wore his hair in a Joe Strummer pompadour just like me, only his hair was black and mine choirboy blond (I'd dye it within the week), and I was trying to get the bartender's attention so I could order us G&Ts with my fake ID. The band, more New Wave than punk, hadn't started yet, and the only thing to look at onstage was the opening act packing up their equipment while hypervigilant girls in vampire makeup and torn fishnet stockings washed round them in a human tide that ebbed and flowed on the waves of music crashing through the speakers. It was bliss. Bliss because I knew now that this night, alone out of all the long succession of dull nugatory nights building up to it, would be special, that this was the night I'd meet Lisa and take her home with me. To my parents' house in Pasadena, where I had a room of my own above the detached garage and could come and go as I pleased. My room. The place where I greased up my hair and stared at myself in the mirror and waited for something to happen, something like this, like what was coming in seven and a half real-time minutes.

Zach said what sounded like "Look at that skank," but since he had his face turned away from me and the music was cranked to the sonic level of a rocket launch (give credit to the X1520's parametric speaker/audio beam technology, which is infinitely more refined than the first generation's), I wasn't quite sure, though I must have heard him that night, my ears younger then, less damaged by scenes like this one, because I took hold of his arm and said, "Who? Her?"

What I said now, though, was "Reset, reverse ten seconds," and everything stalled, vanished and started up once more, and here I was trying all over again to get the bartender's attention and listening hard when Zach, leaning casually against the bar on two splayed elbows, opened his mouth to speak. "Look at that skank," he said, undeniably, there it was, coloring everything in the moment because he was snap-judging Lisa, with her coat-hanger shoulders, Kabuki makeup and shining black lips, and I said, "Who? Her?," already attracted because in my eyes she wasn't a skank at all or if she was, she was a skank from some other realm altogether and I couldn't from that moment on think of anything but getting her to talk to me.

Now, the frustrating thing about the current relive technology is that you can't be an actor in the scene, only an observer, like Scrooge reliving his boarding school agonies with the Ghost of Christmas Past at his elbow, so whatever howlers your adolescent self might have uttered are right there, hanging in the air, uned-ited. You can fast-forward, and I suppose most people do—skip the chatter; get to the sex—but personally, after going straight to the carnal moments the first five or six times I relived a scene, I liked to go back and hear what I had to say, what she had to say, however banal it might sound now. What I did that night—

and I'd already relived this moment twice in the past week—was catch hold of the bartender and order not two but three G&Ts, though I only had something like eighteen dollars in my wallet, set one on the bar for Zach and cross the floor to where she was standing just beneath the stage in what would be the mosh pit half an hour later. She saw me coming, saw the drinks—two drinks—and looked away, covering herself because she was sure I was toting that extra drink for somebody else, a girlfriend or best bud lurking in the drift of shadow the stage lights drew up out of the murky walls.

I tapped her shoulder. She turned her face to me.

"Pause," I said.

Everything stopped. I was in a 3-D painting now and so was she and for the longest time I just kept things there, studying her face. She was eighteen years old, a commander of style, beautiful enough underneath the paint and gel and eyeliner and all the rest to make me feel faint even now, and her eyes weren't wary, weren't *used*, but candid, ready, rich with expectation. I held my drink just under my nose, inhaling the smell of juniper berries to tweak the memory, and said, "Play."

"You look thirsty," I said.

The music boomed. Behind me, at the bar, Zach was giving me a look of disbelief, like *What-the?*, because this was a violation of our club-going protocol. We didn't talk to the girls, and especially not the skanks, because we were there for the *music*, at least that was what we told ourselves. (Second time around I did pause this part, just for the expression on his face—Zach, poor Zach, who never did find himself a girlfriend as far as I know and who's probably someplace reliving every club he's ever been in and every date he's ever had just to feel sorry for himself.)

She leveled her eyes on me, gave it a beat, then took the cold glass from my hand. "How did you guess?" she said.

What followed was the usual exchange of information about

bands, books, neighborhood, high school, college, and then I was bragging about the bands I'd seen lately and she was countering with the band members she knew personally, like John Doe and the drummer for the Germs, and letting her eyes reveal just how personal that was, which only managed to inflame me till I wanted nothing more on this earth than to pin her in a corner and kiss the black lipstick right off her. What I said then, unaware that my carefully sculpted pompadour was collapsing across my brow in something very much like a bowl cut (or worse—*anathema*— a Beatles shag), was "You want to dance?"

She gave me a look. Shot her eyes to the stage and back, then around the room. A few people were dancing to the canned music, most of them jerking and gyrating to their own drugged-out beat, and there was no sign—yet—of the band we'd come to hear. "To this?"

"Yeah," I said, and I looked so—what was it?—*needy*, though at the time I must have thought I was chiseled out of a block of pure cool. "Come on," I said, and I reached out a hand to her.

I watched the decision firm in her eyes, deep in this moment that would give rise to all the rest, to the part I was about to fast-forward to because I had to get up in the morning. For work. And no excuses. *But watch, watch what comes next* . . .

She took my hand, the soft friction of her touch alive still somewhere in my cell memory, and then she was leading me out onto the dance floor.

She was leading. And I was following.

Will it surprise you to know that I exceeded my self-imposed two-hour limit? That after the sex I fast-forwarded to our first date, which was really just an agreed-upon meeting at Tower Records (March 2, 1982, 4:30 p.m.), and took us thereafter up to Barney's Beanery for cheeseburgers and beers and shots of peppermint schnapps (!), which she paid for because her father was a rich executive at Warner Brothers? Or that it made me feel so good I couldn't resist skipping ahead three months to when she was as integral to my flesh as the Black Flag T-shirt that never left my back except in the shower? Lisa. Lisa Denardo. With her cat's tongue and tight torquing body that was a girl's and a woman's at the same time and her perfect, evenly spaced set of glistening white teeth (perfect, that is, but for the incisor she'd had a dentist in Tijuana remove in the spirit of punk solidarity). The scene I hit on was early the following summer, summer break of my sophomore year in college, when I gave up on my parents' garage and Lisa and I moved into an off-campus apartment on Vermont and decided to paint the walls, ceiling and floors the color of midnight in the Carlsbad Caverns. June 6, 1982, 2:44 p.m. The glisten of black paint, a too-bright sun caught in the windows and Lisa saying, "Think we should paint the glass too?" I was oblivious to anything but her and me and the way I looked and the way she looked, a streak of paint on her left forearm and another, scimitar-shaped, just over one eyebrow, when suddenly everything went neutral and I was back in the reliving room staring into the furious face of my daughter.

But let me explain the technology here a moment, for those of you who don't already know. This isn't a computer screen or a TV or a hologram or anything anybody else can see—we're talking retinal projection, two laser beams fixed on two eyeballs. Anybody coming into the room (daughter, wife, boss) will simply see you sitting there in a chair with your retinas lit like furnaces. Step in front of the projector—as my daughter did now—and the image vanishes.

"Stop," I said, and I wasn't talking to her.

But there she was, her hair brushed out for school and her jaw clenched, looking hate at me. "I can't believe you," she said. "Do you have any idea what time it is?"

Bleary, depleted—and guilty, deeply guilty, the narcissist

caught in the act and caring about nothing or nobody but his own reliving self—I just gawked at her, the light she'd flicked on when she came into the room transfixing me in the chair. I shook my head.

"It's 6:45, a.m. In the morning. The *morning*, Dad."

I started to say something but the words were tangled up inside of me because Lisa was saying—had just said—"You're not going to make me stay here and watch the paint dry, are you, because I'm thinking maybe we could drive out to the beach or something, just to cool down," and I said, or was going to say, "There's like maybe half a pint of gas in the car."

"What?" Katie demanded. "Were you with Mom again? Is that it? Like you can be with her and I can't?"

"No," I said, "no, that wasn't it, it wasn't your mom at all—"

A tremor ran through her. "Yeah, right. So what was it, then? Some girlfriend, somebody you were gaga over when you were in college? Or high school? Or what, *junior* high?"

"I must have fallen asleep," I said. "Really. I just zoned out."

She knew I was lying. She'd come looking for me, dutiful child, motherless child, and found me not up and about and bustling around the kitchen preparing to fuss over her and see her off to school the way I used to, but pinned here in this chair like an exhibit in a museum, blind to anything but the past, my past and nobody else's, not hers or her mother's, or the country's or the world's, but just mine.

I heard the door slam. Heard the thump of her angry feet in the hallway, the distant muffled crash of the front door, and then the house was quiet. I looked at the slit in the box. "Play," I said.

By the time I got to work I was an hour and a half late, but on this day—miracle of miracles—Kevin was even later, and when he did show up I was ensconced in my cubicle, dutifully rattling keys on my keyboard. He didn't say anything, just brushed by me and buried himself in his office, but I could see he was wearing the same vacant pre-now look I was, and it didn't take much of an intuitive leap to guess the reason. In fact, since the new model had come on the market, I'd noticed the same randy faraway gaze in the eyes of half a dozen of my fellow employees, including Linda Blanco, the receptionist, who'd stopped buttoning the top three buttons of her blouse and wore shorter and shorter skirts every day. Instead of breathing "Moos and Associates, how may I help you?" into the receiver, now she just said, "Reset."

Was this a recipe for disaster? Was our whole society on the verge of breaking down? Was the NSA going to step in? Were they going to pass laws? Ban the box? I didn't know. I didn't care. I had a daughter to worry about. Thing was, all I could think of was getting home to relive, straight home, and if the image of a carton of milk or a loaf of bread flitted into my head I batted it away. Takeout. We could always get takeout. I was in a crucial phase with Lisa, heading inexorably for the grimmer scenes, the disagreements—petty at first, then monumental, unbridgeable, like the day I got home from my makeup class in Calculus and found her sitting at the kitchen table with a stoner whose name I never did catch and didn't want to know, not then or now—and I needed to get through it, to analyze it whether it hurt or not, because it was there and I had to relive it. I couldn't help myself. I just kept picking at it like a scab.

Ultimately, this was all about Christine, of course, about when I began to fail instead of succeed, to lose instead of win. I needed Lisa to remind me of a time before that, to help me trace my missteps and assign blame, because as intoxicating as it was to relive the birds-atwitter moments with Christine, there was always something nagging at me in any given scene, some twitch of her face or a comment she threw out that should have raised flags at the time but never did. All right. Fine. I was going to go there, I was, and relive the minutiae of our relationship, the ecstasy and agony both, the moments of mindless contentment and the swelling tide of antipathy that drove us apart, but first things first, and as I fought my way home on the freeway that afternoon, all I could think about was Lisa.

In the old days, before we got the box, my daughter and I had a Friday-afternoon ritual whereby I would stop in at the Italian place down the street from the house, have a drink and chat up whoever was there, then call Katie and have her come join me for a father-daughter dinner so I could have some face-time with her, read into her and suss out her thoughts and feelings as she grew into a young woman herself, but we didn't do that anymore. There wasn't time. The best I could offer—lately, especially—was take-out or a microwave pizza and a limp salad choked down in the cold confines of the kitchen while we separately calculated how long we had to put up with the pretense before slipping off to relive.

There were no lights on in the house as I pulled into the drive-way and that was odd, because Katie should have been home from school by now—and she hadn't texted me or phoned to say she'd be staying late. I climbed out of the car feeling stiff all over—I needed to get more exercise, I knew that, and I resolved to do it too, as soon as I got my head above water—and as I came up the walk I saw the sad frosted artificial wreath hanging crookedly there in the center panel of the front door. Katie must have dug it out of the box of ornaments in the garage on her own initiative, to do something by way of Christmas, and that gave me pause, that stopped me right there, the thought of it, of my daughter having to make the effort all by herself. That crushed me. It did. And as I put the key in the lock and pushed the door open I knew things were going to have to change. Dinner. I'd take her out to dinner and forget about Lisa. At least for now.

"Katie?" I called. "You home?"

No response. I shrugged out of my coat and went on into the

kitchen, thinking to make myself a drink. There were traces of her here, her backpack flung down on the floor, an open bag of Doritos spilling across the counter, a diet Sprite, half-full, on the breadboard. I called her name again, standing stock-still in the middle of the room and listening for the slightest hint of sound or movement as my voice echoed through the house. I was about to pull out my phone and call her when I thought of the reliving room, and it was a sinking thought, not a selfish one, because if she was in there, reliving—and she was, I knew she was—what did that say about her social life? Didn't teenage girls go out anymore? Didn't they gather in packs at the mall or go to movies or post things on Facebook, or, forgive me, go out on dates? Group dates, even? How else were they going to experience the inchoate beginnings of what the Relive Box people were pushing in the first place?

I shoved into the room, which was dark but for the lights of her eyes, and just stood there watching her for a long moment as I adjusted to the gloom. She sat riveted, her body present but her mind elsewhere, and if I was embarrassed—for her, and for me too, her father, invading her privacy when she was most vulnerable—the embarrassment gave way to a sorrow so oceanic I thought I would drown in it. I studied her face. Watched her smile and grimace and go cold and smile again. What could she possibly be reliving when she'd lived so little? Family vacations? Christmases past? The biannual trips to Hong Kong to be with her mother and stepfather? I couldn't fathom it. I didn't like it. It had to stop. I turned on the overhead light and stepped in front of the projector.

She blinked at me and she didn't recognize me, didn't know me at all because I was in the now and she was in the past. "Katie," I said, "that's enough now. come on." I held out my arms to her even as recognition came back into her eyes and she made a vague gesture of irritation, of pushing away.

"Katie," I said, "let's go out to dinner. Just the two of us. Like we used to."

"I'm not hungry," she said. "And it's not fair. You can use it all you want, like day and night, but whenever I want it—" and she broke off, tears starting in her eyes.

"Come on," I said. "It'll be fun."

The look she gave me was unsparing. I was trying to deflect it, trying to think of something to say, when she came up out of the chair so suddenly it startled me, and though I tried to take hold of her arm, to pull her to me whether she fought it or not, she was too quick for me. Before I could react, she was at the door, pausing only to scorch me with another glare. "I don't believe you," she spat, before vanishing down the hall.

I should have followed her, should have tried to make things right—or better anyway—but I didn't. The box was right there. It had shut down when she leapt up from the chair and whatever she'd been reliving was buried back inside it, accessible to no one, though you can bet there are hackers out there right now trying to subvert the retinal-recognition feature. For a long moment I stared at the open door, fighting myself, then I went over and pulled it softly shut. I realized I didn't need a drink or dinner either. I sat down in the chair. "Hello, Wes," the box said. "Welcome back."

We didn't have a Christmas tree that year and neither of us really cared all that much, I think—if we wanted to look at spangle-draped trees we could relive holidays past, happier ones, or in my case, I could go back to my childhood and relive my father's whiskey in a glass and my mother's long-suffering face blossoming over the greedy joy of her golden boy, her only child, tearing open his presents as a weak bleached-out California sun haunted the windows and the turkey crackled in the oven. Katie went off (reluctantly, I thought) on a skiing vacation to Mammoth with the family of her best friend, Allison, who she hardly saw anymore, not outside of school, not in the now, and I went back to

Lisa, because if I was going to get to Christine in any serious way—beyond the sex, that is, beyond the holiday greetings and picture-postcard moments—Lisa was my bridge.

As soon as I'd dropped Katie at Allison's house and exchanged a few previously scripted salutations with Allison's grinning parents and her grinning twin brothers, I stopped at a convenience store for a case of eight-ounce bottles of spring water and the biggest box of power bars I could find and went straight home to the reliving room. The night before I'd been close to the crucial scene with Lisa, one that was as fixed in my memory as the blowup with Christine a quarter century later, but elusive as to the date and time. I'd been up all night—*again*—fast-forwarding, reversing, jumping locales and facial expressions, Lisa's first piercing, the evolution of my haircut, but I hadn't been able to pinpoint the exact moment, not yet. I set the water on the floor on my left side, the power bars on my right. "May 9, 1983," I said, "4:00 a.m."

The numbers flashed and then I was in darkness, zero visibility, confused as to where I was until the illuminated dial of a clock radio began to bleed through and I could make out the dim outline of myself lying in bed in the back room of that apartment with the black walls and black ceiling and black floor. Lisa was there beside me, an irregular hump in the darkness, snoring with a harsh gag and stutter. She was stoned. And drunk. Half an hour earlier she'd been in the bathroom, heaving over the toilet, and I realized I'd come too far. "Reset," I said, "reverse ninety minutes."

Sudden light, blinding after the darkness, and I was alone in the living room of the apartment, studying, or trying to. My hair hung limp, my muscles were barely there, but I was young and reasonably good-looking, even excusing any bias. I saw that my Black Flag T-shirt had faded to gray from too much sun and too many washings, and the book in my lap looked as familiar as something I might have been buried with in a previous life, but then this *was* my previous life. I watched myself turn a page, crane my neck toward the door, get up to flip over the album that was providing the soundtrack. "Reset," I said, "fast-forward ten minutes," and here it was, what I'd been searching for: a sudden crash, the front door flinging back, Lisa and the stoner whose name I didn't want to know fumbling their way in, both of them as slow as syrup with the cumulative effect of downers and alcohol, and though the box didn't have an olfactory feature, I swear I could smell the tequila on them. They'd gone clubbing, midweek, and I couldn't go because of finals, but Lisa could because she didn't have finals and she didn't have work either. I jumped up out of the chair, spilling the book, and shouted something I couldn't quite make out, so I said, "Reset, reverse five seconds."

"You fucker!" was what I'd shouted, and now I shouted it again prior to slapping something out of the guy's hand, a beer bottle, and all at once I had him in a hammerlock and Lisa was beating at my back with her birdclaw fists and I was wrestling the guy out the door, cursing over the soundtrack ("Should I Stay or Should I Go," one of those flatline ironies that almost makes you believe everything in this life's been programmed). I saw now that he was bigger than I was, probably stronger too, but the drugs had taken the volition out of him and in the next moment he was outside the door and the three bolts were hammered home. By me. Who now turned in a rage to Lisa.

"Stop," I said. "Freeze." Lisa hung there, defiant and guilty at the same time, pretty, breathtakingly pretty, despite the slack mouth and drugged-out eyes. I should have left it there, should have forgotten it and gone on to those first cornucopian weeks and months and even years with Christine, but I couldn't help myself. "Play," I said, and Lisa raised a hand to swat at me, but she was too unsteady and knocked the lamp over instead.

"Did you fuck him?" I demanded.

There was a long pause, so long I almost fast-forwarded, and then she said, "Yeah. Yeah, I fucked him. And I'll tell you something"—her words glutinous, the syllables coalescing on her tongue—"you're no punk. And he is. He's the real deal. And you? You're, you're—"

I should have stopped it right there.

"—you're *prissy*."

"Prissy?" I couldn't believe it. Not then and not now.

She made a broad stoned gesture, weaving on her feet. "Anal retentive. Like who left the dishes in the sink or who didn't take out the garbage or what about the cockroaches—"

"Stop," I said. "Reset. June 19, 1994, 11:02 p.m."

I was in another bedroom now, one with walls the color of cream, and I was in another bed, this time with Christine, and I'd timed the memory to the very minute, post-coital, in the afterglow, and Christine, with her soft aspirated whisper of a voice, was saying, "I love you, Wes, you know that, don't you?"

"Stop," I said. "Reverse five seconds."

She said it again. And I stopped again. And reversed again. And she said it again. And again.

Time has no meaning when you're reliving. I don't know how long I kept it up, how long I kept surfing through those moments of Christine—not the sexual ones, but the loving ones, the companionable ones, the ordinary day-to-day moments when you could see in her eyes that she loved me more than anybody alive and was never going to stop loving me, never. Dinner at the kitchen table, any dinner, any night. Just to be there. My wife. My daughter. The way the light flooded the windows and poured liquid gold over the hardwood floors of our starter house in Canoga Park. Katie's first birthday. Her first word ("Cake!"). The look on Christine's face as she curled up with Katie in bed and read her *Where the Wild Things Are*. Her voice as she hoarsened it for Max: "I'll eat you up!"

Enough analysis, enough hurt. I was no masochist.

At some point, I had to get up from that chair in the now and evacuate a living bladder, the house silent, spectral, unreal. I didn't live here. I didn't live in the now with its deadening nine-to-five job I was in danger of losing and the daughter I was failing and a wife who'd left me—and her own daughter—for Winston Chen, choreographer of martial arts movies in Hong Kong who was loving and kind and funny and not the control freak I was (*Prissy*, anyone? *Anal retentive?*). The house echoed with my footsteps, a stage set and nothing more. I went to the kitchen and dug the biggest pot I could find out from under the sink, brought it back to the reliving room and set it on the floor between my legs to save me the trouble of getting up next time around.

Time passed. Relived time and lived time too. There were two windows in the room, shades drawn so as not to interfere with the business of the moment, and sometimes a faint glow appeared around the margins of them, an effect I noticed when I was searching for a particular scene and couldn't quite pin it down. Sometimes the glow was gone. Sometimes it wasn't. What happened then, and I might have been two days in or three or five, I couldn't really say, was that things began to cloy. I'd relived an exclusive diet of the transcendent, the joyful, the insouciant, the best of Christine, the best of Lisa and all the key moments of the women who came between and after, and I'd gone back to the Intermediate Algebra test, the very instant, pencil to paper, when I knew I'd scored a perfect one hundred percent, and to the time I'd squirted a ball to right field with two outs, two strikes, ninth inning and my Little League team (the Condors, yellow tees, white lettering) down by three, and watched it rise majestically over the glove of the spastic red-haired kid sucking back allergic snot and roll all the way to the wall. Triumph after triumph, goodness abounding—till it stuck in my throat.

"Reset," I said. "January 2, 2009, 4:30 p.m."

I found myself in the kitchen of our second house, this house, the one we'd moved to because it was outside the L.A. city limits and had schools we felt comfortable with sending Katie to. That was what mattered: the schools. Christine and I both insisted on it, and if it lengthened our commutes, so be it. This house. The one I was reliving in now. Everything gleamed around me, counters polished, the glass of the cabinets as transparent as air because details mattered then, everything in its place whether Christine was there or not—especially if she wasn't there, and where was she? Or where had she been? China. With her boss. On film business. Her bags were just inside the front door, where she'd dropped them forty-five minutes ago after I picked her up at the airport and we'd had our talk in the car, the talk I was going to relive when I got done here, because it was all about pain now, about reality, and this scene was the capper, the coup de grâce. You want wounds? You want to take a razor blade to the meat of your inner thigh just to see if you can still feel? Well, here it was.

Christine entered the scene now, coming down the stairs from Katie's room, her eyes wet, or damp anyway, and her face composed. And there I was, pushing myself up from the table, my beginner's bald spot a glint of exposed flesh under the glare of the overhead light. I spoke first. "You tell her?"

Christine was dressed in her business attire, black stockings, heels, skirt to the knee, tailored jacket. She looked exhausted, and not simply from the fifteen-hour flight but from what she'd had to tell me. And our daughter. (How I'd like to be able to relive *that*, to hear how she'd even broached the subject, let alone how she'd smoke-screened her own selfishness and betrayal with some specious concern for Katie's well-being—let's not rock the boat and you'll be better off here with your father and your school and your teachers and it's not the end but just the beginning, buck up, you'll see.)

Christine's voice was barely audible. "I don't like this any better than you do."

"Then why do it?"

A long pause. Too long. "Stop," I said.

I couldn't do this. My heart was hammering. My eyes felt as if they were being squeezed in a vise. I could barely swallow. I reached down for a bottle of water and a power bar, unscrewed the cap, tore open the wrapper, drank, chewed. She was going to say, "This isn't working," and I was going to say, "*Working?* What the fuck are you talking about? What does work have to do with it? I thought this was about love. I thought it was about commitment." I knew I wasn't going to get violent, though I should have, should have chased her out to the cab that was even then waiting at the curb and slammed my way in and flown all the way to Hong Kong to confront Winston Chen, the martial arts genius who could have crippled me with his bare feet.

"Reset," I said. "August 1975, any day, any time."

There was a hum from the box. "Incomplete command. Please select date and time."

I was twelve years old, the summer we went to Vermont, to a lake there where the mist came up off the water like the fumes of a dream and the deer mice lived under the refrigerator, and I didn't have a date or time fixed in my mind—I just needed to get away from Christine, that was all. I picked the first thing that came into my head.

"August 19," I said, "11:30 a.m. Play."

A blacktop road. Sun like a nuclear blast. A kid, running. I recognized myself—I'd been to this summer before, one I remembered as idyllic, messing around in boats, fishing, swimming, wandering the woods with one of the local kids, Billy Scharf, everything neutral, copacetic, life lived in the moment. But why was I running? And why did I have that look on my face, a look that fused determination and helplessness both? Up the drive now, up the steps to the house, shouting for my parents, "Mom! Dad!"

I began to get a bad feeling.

I saw my father get up off the wicker sofa on the porch, my vigorous young father who was dressed in a T-shirt and jeans and didn't have even a trace of gray in his hair, my father who always made everything right. But not this time. "What's the matter?" he said. "What is it?"

And my mother coming through the screen door to the porch, a towel in one hand and her hair snarled wet from the lake. And me. I was fighting back tears, my legs and arms like sticks, striped polo shirt, faded shorts. "It's," I said, "it's—"

"Stop," I said. "Reset." It was my dog, Queenie, that was what it was, dead on the road that morning, and who'd left the gate ajar so she could get out in the first place? Even though he'd been warned about it a hundred times?

I was in a dark room. There was a pot between my legs and it was giving off a fierce odor. I needed to go deeper, needed out of this. I spouted random dates, saw myself driving to work, stuck in traffic with ten thousand other fools who could only wish they had a fast-forward app, saw myself in my thirties, post-Lisa, pre-Christine, obsessing over Halo, and I stayed there through all the toppling hours, reliving myself in the game, boxes within boxes, until finally I thought of God, or what passes for God in my life, the mystery beyond words, beyond lasers and silicon chips. I gave a date nine months before I was born, "December 30, 1962, 6:00 a.m.," when I was, what—a zygote?—but the box gave me nothing, neither visual nor audio. And that was wrong, deeply wrong. There should have been a heartbeat. My mother's heartbeat, the first thing we hear—or feel, feel before we even have ears.

"Stop," I said. "Reset." A wave of rising exhilaration swept over me even as the words came to my lips, "September 30, 1963,

2:35 a.m.," and the drumbeat started up, *ba-boom, ba-boom,* but no visual, not yet, the minutes ticking by, *ba-boom, ba-boom,* and then I was there, in the light of this world, and my mother in her stained hospital gown and the man with the monobrow and flashing glasses, the stranger, the doctor, saying what he was going to say by way of congratulations and relief. A boy. It's a boy.

Then it all went dead and there was somebody standing there in front of me, and I didn't recognize her, not at first, how could I? "Dad," she was saying, "Dad, are you there?"

I blinked. Tried to focus.

"No," I said finally, shaking my head in slow emphasis, the word itself, the denial, heavy as a stone in my mouth. "I'm not here. I'm not. I'm not."

SHE'S THE BOMB

Ru ok?

          QQ

Srsly? ur crying?

          I want to kill myself

Dont say that

          I'm saying it

If we had a helicopter, or better yet, a drone, we could hover over Hailey Phegler's shoulder at this juncture and watch her text, but we don't, so we won't. Instead, since fiction allows us to do this, we'll go directly inside her head and attempt to assess the grinding awfulness of this moment, which has stranded her, in cap and gown, among the 332 prospective graduates of the College of Arts and Sciences at Hibernia College in Hibernia, New York, where the trees are just beginning to unfold their leaves after the long winnowing blast of an upstate winter. She is beyond distraught—she is panicking. Breathing in such short gasps her thumbs actually tremble over the keypad.

When she glances up from her phone in a tic of annoyance, the first person she locks eyes with is Stephanie Joiner, who was in her Introduction to Poetry class last spring and who has zero style and a brain the size of a Snickers bar, but who's here nonetheless, in cap and gown and with her hair combed out and sprayed with shellac, all set to graduate.

"Hi," Stephanie says, coming right up to her so Hailey has to hide her screen, which produces an awkward moment. Somebody, wasted already, shouts "Free at last!" and a low undercurrent of giggly laughter washes through the crowd. "Oh my god," Stephanie chirps, and is she actually going to take her hand, or what, hug her? "I mean, it's been like ice ages, right?" Her contacts have a weird tint, too blue by half, but her eyes are like lasers. "I didn't even know you were still—" she starts, but she doesn't want to go there and cuts herself off. There's a moment of self-congratulatory beaming, the lasers slicing right into her, before Stephanie says, "Congrats, you!" And then, after a quick shuffle of her clunky white platforms that only show off how thick her ankles are, she adds the refrain "We made it! Can you believe it?"

Every word is a nail, and this girl, this nobody with her pasted-on smile, is a human nailgun, and this place, the First Niagara Bank Center quad, with its rearing white tent erected by underpaid illegal immigrants, is the worst place Hailey has ever been in her life. She wants to lash out. Wants to swing her purse like a whatever you call it—a *mace*—and just obliterate the smile from Stephanie Joiner's face, but she hasn't got time for that, so she holds up her phone by way of excuse, turns her back on her and shoots off another text to her best friend, Janelle Esposito, in Annandale-on-Hudson, whose graduation at Bard isn't till the following weekend.

Pls get me out of here!

Wish i could

I'm desprt

Chill it will work out

No, no, no b/c my mothers
here

I thought she wasnt
coming?

I have 2 do something

Like what? like tell her?

I'd rather die

Ur dressed the part ur
walking whos going to
know?

My mom didnt see my
name on the list

So? they make mistakes.

I'm going 2 like off myself

Stop it

Srsly i never thought
i'd wish for a school
shooting . . .

???

Srsly

Her mother, since as long as she could remember, was always harping on her. And what was her main theme? You're a procrastinator, that's what she said. Elementary school, junior high, high school and now college. *You're a procrastinator.* All right, guilty as charged, but then who isn't? The problem wasn't her, really, it was Nathaniel Hawthorne. Back in September, when she couldn't put off her American Lit requirement anymore, she'd signed up for Professor Dugan's course and the first book was *The Scarlet Letter,* which might as well have been written in Mandarin Chinese for all she could make sense of it. *But there is a fatality, a feeling so irresistible and inevitable that it has the force of doom, which almost invariably compels human beings to linger around and haunt, ghostlike, the spot where some great and marked event has given the color to their lifetime; and still the more irresistibly, the darker the tinge that saddens it.*

No joke, it was just plain boring and so she procrastinated as far as actually reading it went and then, even with the help of Write My Paper Here and Best Term-Paper Service, trying to do the paper on it, and then one thing led to another and she stopped going to Professor Dugan's class because of the embarrassment factor, and once she'd stopped she had to pull the plug on her other courses too, even her poetry workshop, because the classes were all in Fenster Hall and she couldn't risk running across Professor Dugan, who would stink-eye her through his Coke-bottle lenses and wonder why she hadn't been to class and when he could expect her Hawthorne paper, if, like, ever? Plus, it was around then that she met Connor Hayes and fell hard and just wanted to be with him through those warm drifting endless Indian summer afternoons when the sun threw the shadows of the trees across the quad in a thousand rippling variations and the two main student bars—Elsie's and The Study Hall—were offering Happy Hour all day every day until further notice. And there were the other bars in the outlying towns Connor loved to take her to on the back of his turquoise Triumph motorcycle so they could watch their beers sizzle on the bartop and eat peanuts in the shell and snuggle and laugh and feel as if life actually opened out instead of boxing you in with Nathaniel Hawthorne and who, Jonathan Edwards? Jesus. School was bad enough as it was, but Professor Dugan's class just broke her spirit, crushed her, really—it was all so useless, so *stupid*—and then Connor came along and that was that.

What did she tell her mother? Nothing. School was fine, everything was fine, and if she sounded a little down it was just because she was working so hard. "That's fine, honey," her mother told her over the phone, "just don't put too much pressure on yourself—remember, no matter how dark it may seem now, there's a light at the end of the tunnel. Think of May. May'll be here before you know it."

"Hi, Hail." She's standing there in the crowd of students, frowning at her phone, and there's somebody else squeezing in on her now, somebody calling her name, tall, a guy, and she looks up into the face of Toll Hauser, who used to be Connor's best bud before Connor dumped her and he dumped Connor so he could ask her out without too many complications, and that was okay, because she liked him even if she wasn't all that attracted to him, but really, over the last month she'd been in such a mounting panic she could barely get out of bed, eating nothing but shrimp ramen and sleeping fourteen hours a day, and so she kept putting him off. Six-five, skinny, the gown hanging on him like a shroud, like something Hawthorne would wear in his day, Toll has the mortarboard raked down over one eye, which gives him a kind of comical look that might have cheered her up under any other circumstances, but just leaves her speechless now. "Cool to see you made it," he says, flapping the arms of the gown as if he's going to lift off and soar around the tent. "You must've worked your butt off on those incompletes . . ."

"Yeah," she says, and the word—the single syllable—is like the pit of some sour fruit she's tried to swallow whole.

"You all right?" He's bending over now, his face almost level with hers, his arms dangling and his shoulders tentpoling in back. "I mean, you look . . . you start the party already?"

"I'm okay," she says, each word like a finger locking into place around her throat. "It's just—my mother, you know?"

"Tell me about it." He flashes that smile of his, his best feature, really, but he isn't Connor and never will be and he's just making her tenser, delaying her, because it's now or never and she really can't see any other way out. Both his parents are here too, he tells her, nattering on, and three of his grandparents, plus his kid sister and his aunt and uncle and like half a dozen cousins, and he's not complaining but all he really wants to do is go down to Elsie's with everybody else and get shit-faced. He says something more, a whole lot more, but she's not listening because she's too keyed up, the words she can't say, the words she's going to say into her phone in the next sixty seconds going off like alarm bells in her head. After a minute, people swarming all around them and some dean or somebody trying to get their attention so they can take their seats before the doors open to the general public, she realizes he's still staring at her and she can't help herself because she just wants this over with and when she snaps *What?* at him he actually steps back a foot.

"I was just saying, will I see you there? At Elsie's? Or have you got some family thing?"

She doesn't answer because she's not there anymore, moving now, the scholarly folds of her robe snatching and billowing, pushing through the crowd of people she mostly recognizes, heading for the exit where they set up the Porta-Pottys so she can have a little privacy, the words she can't say looping over and over like a short-circuit in her brain: *There's a bomb in the Bank Center quad. A bomb, you hear me?*

So i did it

                              Did what?

Called in a bomb

                              ???

U there?

                              Ur joking

OMG my heart is like
  10000 beats a second

What ru saying?

I'm saying i did it

Are you serious? i'm
like, stunned

Real life

Real life? hail, what are
you thinking?

I told you i was desprt

That's when things really accelerate, the dean or whoever
he is, the president maybe, going to the microphone on the dais
and thumping it with one thick finger so the blast of static makes
everybody look up, and then he's saying, "Attention, please—
seniors, everyone!" The chatter of the crowd falls off, and at the
same time, as if all that noise has somehow been suppressing it,
the smell of perfume rises up like some fog that's choking her all
of a sudden, Vera Wang, Dolce & Gabbana, Juicy Couture, and
her stomach clenches so fast and hard and tight she thinks she's
going to be sick right there in the middle of the temporary floor-
ing the immigrants magically laid down overnight. "There's a
situation here that's just come to our attention," the dean hisses
through the speakers, his face a pinched white sack straining at the
knot of his bow tie, "and believe me, we're going to get to the bottom of this, and I do not find this amusing, people, not at all—"

And what is she feeling? A complete revolution, three hundred sixty degrees, suddenly as high as she's ever been in her life,
her whole body throbbing with the endorphins rushing through
her, and she can already see it, dinner with her mom and Aunt
Ceecie, who's come all the way up from North Carolina for the
occasion. What a crime somebody had to spoil the day, she'll
say over her first margarita, rocks, no salt, some prankster, some
idiot, but so they send my degree in the mail, what matters is
we're all here together, right? Right, Mom? Right?

"The fact is," the dean says, "somebody called in a bomb threat—" An instant of stunned amazement, and then the tumult breaks out, people gasping, shouting, cursing, as if the whole quad's one big pit filled right to the top with bilge water and everybody's drowning together. The faces around her are worse than ugly, pathetic really, people just chewing at the air, flailing their arms, digging out their cell phones to mindlessly record whatever this is or might be. "So what we're going to have to do," the dean goes on, "and I'm sorry, but we have no choice in the matter, is—"

Cancel the ceremony, she shouts inside the reverberant walls of her own skull, *cancel it and go back to your dorm rooms and your parents and loved ones or whoever—*

"—change the venue to the Threlkeld Arena." The dean has to raise his voice now, because even with the microphone the noise under that tent is too much for him to cope with no matter how much he's fighting to project an aura of calm for the sake of everybody present. "Which means we will convene there in exactly"— she watches in disbelief as he throws back the billowing sleeve of his robe to check his watch—"one hour and fifteen minutes from now. So, everybody"—more shouts, groans, tumult—"the new time will be seven p.m. sharp. Is that clear?"

Ru kidding me?

        Beyond belief

What ru going 2 do now?

        I dont know my moms
        berserk

Tell her?

        U cant be serious!? like
        tell her i lied & then
        what, called in a bomb?

Not the bomb u cant tell
anybody ever they'll put
u in jail

                                        Shit dont tell me that,
                                        shit, shit, shit!!!

        U have 2 tell your mom
          sooner or later so u need
          2 tell her now

                                        No way

        Way

                                        Sorry got 2 go

There are five thousand people out there waiting to get into the tent, which is something like fifteen friends and relatives for every graduate, and they are definitely not happy about having to traipse all the way across campus to Threlkeld, which, unbeknownst to her, the college always reserves as a backup venue in case of a tornado or lightning storm or any other unforeseen event. Like a bomb threat. Or what, nuclear holocaust. Which, to her mind, would be better than this—anything would be better than this.

She's squeezed in tight with the mass of graduates making for the back exit, the dean and a dozen other functionaries, like Ms. Krentz, the PE teacher who coaches women's soccer and has a face like an over-inflated soccer ball, insisting they all stay together for safety's sake in case the threat is real, which in ninety-nine percent of the cases it isn't, but the college can't take that risk. Obviously. So Hailey's boxed in and sweating—it must be ninety degrees—and her heart is going so hard she thinks she's having a heart attack and here they are out in the sunshine with the trees everywhere and the sweet cool smell of the air and Stephanie Joiner comes out of nowhere like a guided missile to stick her face in hers and crow, "Can you believe it? I mean"—loping along in her big white heels that are like rowboats on the green river of the lawn—"what a shitty thing for somebody to do."

"You don't think it's real, then?"

Stephanie looks almost insulted. "You kidding me? It's just some asshole, some frat rat that thinks he's being cute—"

"What about the terrorists?"

"Terrorists? What are you talking about? In Hibernia? There isn't a Muslim within three hundred miles of here."

"Well, they're not *all* Muslims," she says, matching her stride for stride when all she wants is to get away someplace private because she knows what she has to do, of course she does, and that's make another phone call to public safety because there're bombs all over the place, don't they realize that? In Threlkeld especially. "I mean, what about Columbine? Or what, that elementary school in where was it, Connecticut?"

Stephanie—how did she manage to glom onto her? doesn't she have any friends?—just swings her head round to glare at her without breaking stride, tramp, tramp, tramp. "I'm not going to debate you. It's a prank. Bet you anything."

"Terrorists," she insists, or tries to, but she doesn't sound very convincing, because after all, Stephanie's right, whether she knows it or not. What do they shout, the terrorists? *Allahu Akbar!* Why doesn't some dude in a beard come running across campus shouting *Allahu Akbar* and save her the trouble? Tramp, tramp, tramp. It would be almost funny if she wasn't having a heart attack. Everybody's murmuring and bitching, the whole black-clad crowd of them trudging across the lawn like cattle with Ms. Krentz and a dozen other profs herding them along because the college is running scared now and they all have to stick together, the sun, the trees, the mass of parents somewhere behind them, and all at once she breaks free and makes for the nearest building, Morey Hall, the engineering building she's been in maybe once in her life and she's furious suddenly, because why won't they listen to her?

She needs privacy. She's having a heart attack. She's got her phone in her hand. But here's Ms. Krentz double-timing across the grass to cut her off, calling out to her from fifty feet away, "No, no—you're all to stick together." And then, adding lamely, "Till we get this sorted out. Dean's orders."

It's a moment. Ms. Krentz is right there, pulling up short. "Come on," she says, and she couldn't recognize her, could she? It's been three years since Hailey took PE, and she was hardly a shining light, especially since she couldn't for the life of her figure out how to dismount the parallel bars without crashing on her ass about sixty percent of the time. "I know this is hard, but we need to—"

"I have to use the restroom."

Ms. Krentz—she wears her hair long, unlike any other PE teacher on this planet, and if her face wasn't so puffy she might almost have been attractive, or once maybe—gives her a look of incredulity. "You can't hold it till we get there?"

"It's an emergency?"

Everyone's shuffling past and giving them sidelong looks, as if things aren't unusual enough as it is, and Ms. Krentz just lets it go. "Be careful, okay?" she says, then turns round and starts back across the lawn.

Inside the restroom at the far end of a cool wax-smelling hall with arched ceilings and framed photos of men in lab coats and glasses glinting from the walls, Hailey locks the door and ducks into the farthest stall down and then locks that door too, steadies her phone in one trembling hand and punches in the number. Someone answers on the first ring—a man, the same man she talked to half an hour ago, his voice tense and low. "Hello?"

"I told you," she says. "I warned you. There's bombs all over the place, in Threlkeld too. You need to clear out graduation or things are going to get"—and here she hesitates, all the bad lines from all the bad movies she's ever seen cartwheeling through her brain—"get ugly," she says finally, and cuts the connection.

Thanksgiving break had been the worst, till now anyway, going home and having to act as if everything was okay and listen to her mother go on about how proud she was of her, the first one in their family to graduate college and could she possibly know how much that meant to her? She actually brought a bunch of books home with her and locked herself in her room with her laptop to keep up the pretense when she wasn't out making the rounds with her girlfriends from high school and some of the guys too, who were all home from their various schools, and she kept up the pretense with them too. Her mother kept asking if she had enough money for books, tuition, housing, and she kept saying she was okay, living off-campus now with these two other girls and telling her how much she appreciated the checks, which were fine, they really were. Did she like lying to her mother's face? No. But she kept meaning to make up the classwork, at least that first semester, but then, after winter break, Connor unceremoniously dumped her to go out with Chrissie Fortgang, a blond stuck-up bitch whose father owned half the building supply stores in upstate New York and Vermont too, and she went into a depression that just kept spiraling down till she hated herself and couldn't get out of bed and for a while there (in February, February was the low point) even stopped going out to Elsie's and The Study Hall. It was like she was in a cell in a prison somewhere, and if she did go out to the bars there was no joy in it because she knew it was inevitable she'd see Connor there, with or without Chrissie Fortgang, and she felt she just couldn't handle that. Spring, which always used to make her feel as if her whole life just got kickstarted and she could do anything there was in the world, slammed down on her like the lid of a coffin, and she didn't go home for spring break because she couldn't face her mother and she didn't go anywhere else either. Just stayed in her room, hating herself, while her two roommates went to Saint Thomas and soaked up the sun.

She was so miserable that week she even tried Hawthorne again, as if that would help her, as if she could roll that big stone of Professor Dugan's class off her chest and then maybe go to summer school or something, just catch a break, but that didn't happen because Hawthorne was as impenetrable—*boring*—as ever and how he could be some sort of big American writer was beyond her, even in his day when things were so slow and rural and people didn't have as much choice in their lives.

Had I one friend,—or were it my worst enemy!—to whom, when sickened with the praises of all other men, I could daily betake myself, and be known as the vilest of all sinners, methinks my soul might keep itself alive thereby. Even thus much of truth would save me! But now, it is all falsehood!—all emptiness!—all death!

Right. So die already.

U there?

      I'm here but i'm afraid to ask—u ok?

Not

      U really called in again?

What else was i supposed to do?

      Thats crazy

They dont, i mean they're not, like nothings happening & my moms in the stands

      Dont panic

You know what, i wish i did have a bomb

This is the worst moment of her life, maybe of anybody's life, ever, though right there at the dark margins of her imagination she can picture a whole vast world of refugees and genocide victims and starvation and disease spinning away from her out beyond the towering high ceiling of the basketball arena and the safety and privilege it encloses, but you've got to put it in perspective. None of that matters now, not the kittens in the kill shelters she used to circulate petitions over when she was in high school or the welfare mothers or the Zika babies or anything else—she'd sacrifice them all in a heartbeat, right now, right here and now, if those idiots would only take her seriously. Just for today, that's all she asks, just this once. They're the public safety department, aren't they? What are they, deaf? Don't they care? What if some maniac really did call in a threat? What then?

She is seated now, one of 332 prospective graduates in the crisp white folding chairs that scallop the backs of their black gowns as far as she can see in front of her, and so far nothing is happening. There's a smell of body heat, cologne, that perfume again. Gum maybe. Everyone's chewing gum because the atmosphere's so tense, the crowd in the bleachers buzzing softly, like the yellow jackets that used to hover in the meadow out back of the house on hot, still summer days, the students around her looking vacant and sober, any party atmosphere just squashed dead now. She wants to text. She has to text. It's like breathing. Janelle's the only person in the world that knows what she's feeling right now and she needs her more than anything, but she can't text now, she won't, this is it, the final drop of the final blade, and why aren't they canceling it, why isn't the dean—?

But there he is, rising up out of the first row with a whole troop of dignitaries, older people, white hair and red ears, jewelry, sashes, and that woman, she must be the politician that's supposed to deliver the commencement speech, though nobody's ever heard of her, and—

But again. Always a but, always an interruption.

At first she didn't notice the two men in uniform, not public safety, but cops, real cops, making their way up the row in the opposite direction of the dignitaries, heightened security, that's what it is, and still she doesn't get it. Not yet. Not until they keep on coming, walking abreast, their heads up and eyes alert, as if they're looking for something, and they finally stop at the aisle where she's sitting, six seats in from the left.

In the days of Connor, the first days and weeks especially, she felt freer than she ever had in her whole life, because she was in love, yes, but not just with him, with the idea of him too. School had been the one constant in her life since the dawn of consciousness, preschool, kindergarten, elementary school, junior high, senior high, college, on and on till she hit the wall in Dugan's class, and Connor—who'd dropped out junior year to sail through the Panama Canal to Puerto Vallarta and back round again and never did bother to reenroll, or at least he was taking his time about it—was contra to all that. He gave her those slow syrupy days, gave her the wind in her face and the smell of the grass and the flowers and the wild rocket ride of a beer and shot for breakfast, though of course he was a bastard and had been all along and she hated him. But back then? There was this one outfit she used to wear—black Topshop jeans, suede ankle boots and a tight tee that read HOME-MADE across her tits—and every time he saw her in it he'd give her a slow smile and say, "Hey, Hail, you're the bomb, you know it?"

If there's irony in that, she's not the one to appreciate it. You can't afford irony when your mother looks at you like she wants to cut you up in small pieces and feed you to the sharks, when you have a lawyer and have to go to court and when the memory of that night at graduation when they traced her calls and came up the aisle and took her away in handcuffs is like a slow drip of acid every minute of every day she has her eyes open.

The good news? She's not getting any jail time, or any more

than the one night she already served before her aunt Ceecie bailed her out because her mother wouldn't. She's currently working as a sales clerk at Nordstrom Rack in Poughquasic Falls to pay down the $10,000 fine the judge imposed on her and she's got two and a half years left of the three years' probation they gave her, with community service thrown in for good measure. Nobody at Hibernia will ever speak to her again, not that that's a bad thing, especially. And Poughquasic Falls, which is fifteen miles south of Hibernia, is just far enough away so she doesn't have to really see any of them. She's down on herself, of course, so far down she sometimes thinks she'll never climb back up, but she's trying, each day that crawls by taking her that much further from that arena and the nightmares that shook her awake every night for the first month. She's got a dirt-cheap efficiency above the thrift store, a neighborhood bar she can almost tolerate, and she's just started seeing this guy who likes to shoot pool there on weekends (he drives a Ford Saturn and if he's ever even heard of a Triumph motorcycle it's only because it's part of the background noise of society).

So there's this one day, maybe ten days before Christmas, the store a madhouse, and she glances up from the cash register and who does she see standing there in back of her current customer but Stephanie Joiner. Stephanie doesn't notice her at first because she's got her head down, mentally adding up the price tags, so Hailey has a moment to prepare herself, fighting down the sick feeling rising in her throat. If anything, Stephanie looks even worse than in college, her hair cut short as if she's the penitent and not Hailey, and she's wearing a white parka that makes her look like the Doughboy. That helps. But still, once the woman in front of her—middle-aged, dandruff like sleet in her hair, taking forever to dig out her credit card and ID—bundles up her packages and steps aside, there's Stephanie, looking as if she's in *Saw II* or something.

"Jingle Bell Rock" rattles out of hidden speakers. The whole store smells of that Christmasy cinnamon deodorizer the floor manager likes to go around spraying every fifteen minutes and the overhead lights are harsh, blunting everybody's eyes and making death masks of their faces. For a long moment Stephanie just stands there, clinging to her armful of ugly skirts and uglier sweaters, then, without a word, she marches over to the next cash register and gets in the back of the line. And then it's the next customer and the next one after that.

Guess who i saw in the store like ten minutes ago?

> Who?

Stephanie joiner

> Who's that?

Like really i might as well have a letter A stitched on my sweater

> What ru talking about?

Or a B, maybe a B

> ??? who's stephanie?

I don't know just some girl

> So who is she?

Actually?

> Yeah

She's nobody

> So why mention her?

I dont know maybe b/c i'm nobody too

> Dont say that

I'm saying it

ARE WE NOT MEN?

The dog was the color of a maraschino cherry and what it had in its jaws I couldn't quite make out at first, not until it parked itself under the hydrangeas and began throttling the thing. This little episode would have played itself out without my even noticing, except that I'd gone to the stove to put the kettle on for a cup of tea and happened to glance out the window at the front lawn. The lawn, a deep lush blue-green that managed to hint at both the turquoise of the sea and the viridian of a Kentucky meadow, was something I took special pride in, and any wandering dog, no matter its chromatics, was an irritation to me. The seed had been pricey—a blend of chewings fescue, bahia and zoysia incorporating a gene from a species of algae that allowed it to glow under the porchlight at night—and while it was both disease- and drought-resistant it didn't take well to foot traffic, especially four-footed traffic.

I stepped out on the porch and clapped my hands, thinking to shoo the dog away, but it didn't move. Actually, it did, but only to flex its shoulders and tighten its jaws around its prey, which I now saw was my neighbor Allison's pet micropig. The pig itself—doe-eyed and no bigger than a Pekingese—didn't seem to be struggling, or not any longer, and even as I came down off the porch looking to grab the first thing I could find to brandish at the dog, I felt my heart thundering. Allison was one of those pet owners who tend to anthropomorphize their animals and that pig was the center of her unmarried and unboyfriended life—she would be shattered, absolutely, and who was going to break the news to her? I felt a surge of anger. How had the stupid thing got out of the house anyway, and for that matter, whose dog was this? I didn't own a garden rake and there were no sticks on the lawn (the street trees were an edited variety that didn't drop anything, not twigs, seeds or leaves, no matter the season) so I stormed across the grass empty-handed, shouting the first thing that came to mind, which was "Bad! Bad dog!"

I wasn't thinking. And the effect wasn't what I would have hoped for even if I had been: the dog dropped the pig, all right, which was clearly beyond revivification at this point, but in the same motion it lurched up and clamped its jaws on my left forearm, growling continuously, as if my forearm were a stick it had fetched in a friendly game between us. Curiously, there was no pain—and no blood either—just a firm insistent pressure, the saliva hot and wet on my skin as I pulled in one direction and the dog, all the while regarding me out of a pair of dull uniform eyes, pulled in the other. "Let go!" I demanded, but the dog didn't let go. "Bad dog!" I repeated. I tugged. The dog tugged back.

There was no one on the street, no one in the next yard over, no one in the house behind me to come to my aid. I was dressed in the T-shirt, shorts and slippers I'd pulled on not ten minutes earlier when I'd got out of bed, and here I was caught up in this maddening interspecies pas de deux at eight in the morning of an otherwise ordinary day, already exhausted. The dog, this cherry-red hairless freak with the armored skull and bulging muscula-ture of a pit bull, showed no sign of giving in: it had got my arm and it meant to keep it. After a minute of this, I went down on one knee to ease the tension in my back, a gesture that only seemed to excite the animal all the more, its nails tearing up divots as it fought for purchase, trying, it occurred to me now, to bring me down to its level. Before I knew what I was doing I balled up my free hand and punched the thing in the head three times in quick succession.

The effect was instantaneous: the dog dropped my arm and let out a yelp, backing off to hover at the edge of the lawn and eye me warily, as if now, all at once, the rules of the game had changed. In the next moment, just as I realized I was, in fact, bleeding, a voice cried out behind me, "Hey, I saw that!"

A girl was striding across the lawn toward me, a preternaturally tall girl I at first took to be a teenager but was actually a child of eleven or twelve. As soon as she appeared, the dog fell in step with her and everything became clear. She marched directly up to me, glaring, and said, "You hit my dog."

I was in no mood. "I'm bleeding," I said, holding out my arm in evidence. "You see this? Your dog bit me. You ought to keep him chained up."

"That's not true—Ruby would never bite anybody. She was just . . . playing, is all."

I wasn't about to debate her. This was my property, my arm, and that lump of flesh lying there bleeding into the grass was Allison's dead pet. I pointed to it.

"Oh," she said, her voice dropping, "I'm *so* sorry, I didn't . . . is it yours?"

"My neighbor's." I gestured to the house just visible over the hedge. "She's going to be devastated. This pig"—I wanted to call it by name, personalize it, but couldn't summon its name for the life of me—"is all she has. And it wasn't cheap either." I glanced at the dog, its pinkish gaze and incarnadine flanks. "As I'm sure you can appreciate."

The girl, who stood three or four inches taller than me and whose own eyes were an almost iridescent shade of violet that didn't exist in nature, or at least hadn't until recently, gave me an unflinching look. "Maybe she doesn't have to know."

"What do you mean she doesn't have to know? The thing's dead—look at it."

"Maybe it was run over by a car."

"I don't believe it—you want me to lie to her?"

The girl shrugged. The dog, panting, settled down on its haunches. "I already said I'm sorry. Ruby got out the front gate when my mother went to work—and I came right after her, you saw me—"

"What about this?" I demanded, holding up my arm, which wasn't so much punctured as abraded, since most of the new breeds had had their canines and carnassials genetically modified to prevent any real damage in situations like this. "It has its shots, right?"

"She's a *Cherry Pit,*" the girl said, giving me a look of disgust. "Germline immunity comes with the package. I mean, everybody knows that."

It was a Tuesday and I was working from home, as I did every Tuesday and Thursday. I worked in IT, like practically everybody else on the planet, and I found I actually got more done at home than when I went into the office. My coworkers were a trial, what with their moods, opinions, facial tics and all the rest—not that I didn't like them, it was just that they always seemed to manage to get in the way at crunch time. Or maybe I didn't like them, maybe that was it. At any rate, after the little contretemps with the girl and her dog, I went back in the house, smeared an antibiotic ointment on my forearm, took my tea and a handful of protein wafers to my desk and sat down at the computer. If I gave the dead pig a thought, it was only in relation to Allison, who'd want to see the corpse, I supposed, which brought up the question of what to do with it—let it lie where it was or stuff it in a trash bag and refrigerate it till she got home from the office? I thought of calling my wife—Connie was regional manager of Bank USA, by necessity a master of interpersonal relations, and she would know what to do—but then it was hardly worth bothering her at work over something so trivial. I could have buried the corpse, I suppose, or tossed it in the trash and played dumb, but in the end I wound up doing nothing.

It was past three by the time I thought to take a lunch break and because it was such a fine day I brought my sandwich and a glass of iced tea out onto the front porch. By this juncture I'd forgotten all about the pig, the dog and the grief that was brewing for Allison, but as soon as I stepped out the door it all came back to me: the trees were alive with crowparrots variously screeching, cawing and chattering amongst themselves, and they were there for a very specific reason. (I don't know if you have crowparrots in your neighborhood yet, incidentally, but believe me, they're coming. They were the inspiration of one of the molecular embryologists at the university here who felt that inserting genes of the common crow into the invasive parrot population would put an end to the parrots' raids on our orchards and vineyards, giving them a taste for garbage and carrion instead of fruit on the vine and having the added benefit of displacing the native crows, which had pretty well eliminated songbirds from our backyards. The only problem was the noise factor—something in the mix seemed to have redoubled not only the volume but the complexity of the birds' calls so half the time you needed earplugs if you wanted to enjoy pretty much any outdoor activity.)

Which was the case now. The birds were everywhere, cursing fluidly (*Bad bird! Fuck, fuck, fuck!*) and flapping their spangled wings in one another's faces. Alarmed, I came down off the porch and for the second time that day scrambled across the lawn to the flowerbed, where a scrum of birds had settled on the remains of Allison's pet. I flailed my arms and they lifted off reluctantly into the sky, screeching *Turdbird!* and the fractured call that awakened me practically every morning: *Cock-k-k-k-sucker!* As for the pig (which I should have dragged into the garage, I realized that now), its eyes were gone and its faintly bluish hide was striped with bright red gashes. Truthfully? I didn't want to touch the thing—it was filthy. The birds were filthy. Who knew what zoonoses they were carrying? So I was just standing there, in a quandary, when Allison's car pulled into the driveway next door, scattering light.

Allison was in her early thirties, with a top-heavy figure and a barely tamed kink of ginger hair she kept wrapped up in various scarves, which gave her an exotic look, as if she were displaced here in the suburbs. She was sad-faced and sweet, the victim of one catastrophic relationship after another, and I couldn't help feeling protective toward her, a single woman alone in that big house her mother had left her when she died. So when she came across the lawn, already tearing up, I felt I'd somehow let her down, and before I knew what I was doing I'd stripped off my shirt and draped it over the corpse.

"Is that her?" she asked, looking down at the hastily covered bundle at my feet. "No," she said, "don't tell me," and then her eyes jumped to mine and she was repeating my name, "Roy, Roy, Roy," as if wringing it in her throat. *Fuck you!* the crowparrots cried from the trees. *Fuck, fuck, fuck!* In the next moment she flung herself into my arms, clutching me to her so desperately I could hardly breathe.

"I don't want to see," she said in a small voice, each syllable a hot puff of breath on the bare skin of my chest. I could smell her hair, the shampoo she used, the taint of sweat under her arms.

"The poor thing," she murmured and lifted her face so I could see the tears blurring her eyes. "I loved her, Roy, I really *loved* her."

This called up a scene from the past, a dinner party at Allison's, Connie and me, another couple and Allison and her last inamorata, a big-headed boor who worked for Animal Control, incinerating strays and transgenic misfits. Allison had kept the pig in her lap throughout the meal, feeding it from her plate, and afterward, while we sat around the living room cradling brandies and Benedictine, she propped the thing up at the piano, where it picked out "Twinkle, Twinkle, Little Star" with its modified hooves.

"No," I said, agreeing with her, "you don't want to look."

"It was a dog, right? That's what"—and here she had to break off a moment to gather herself. "That's what Terry Wolfson said when she called me at work—"

I was going to offer up some platitude about how the animal hadn't suffered, though for all I knew the dog had gummed it relentlessly, the way it had gummed my arm, when a voice called "Hello?" from the street behind us and we broke awkwardly apart. Coming up the walk was the tall girl, tottering on a pair of platform heels, and she had the dog with her, this time on a leash. I felt a stab of annoyance—hadn't she caused enough trouble already?—and embarrassment, that too. It wasn't like me to go shirtless in public—or to be caught in a full-body embrace with my unmarried next door neighbor either, for that matter.

If she could read my face, the girl gave no indication of it. She came right up to us, the dog trotting along docilely at her side. Her violet gaze swept from me to the lump on the ground beneath the bloodied T-shirt and finally to Allison. "*Je suis désolée, madame,*" she said. "*Pardonne-moi. Mon chien ne savait pas ce qu'il faisait—il est un bon chien, vraiment.*"

This girl, this child, loomed over us, her features animated.

She was wearing eyeliner, lipstick and blusher, as if she were ten years older and on her way to a nightclub, and her hair—blond, with a natural curl—spread like a tent over her shoulders and dangled all the way down to the small of her back. "What are you saying?" I demanded. "And why are you speaking French?"

"Because I can. *Puedo hablar en español también und Ich kann auch in Deutsch sprechen.* My IQ is 162 and I can run the hundred meters in 9.58 seconds."

"Wonderful," I said, exchanging a look with Allison. "Terrific. Really. But what are you doing here, what do you want?"

Your mother! the birds cried. *Up yours!*

The girl shifted from one foot to the other, looking awkward, like the child she was. "I just wanted to please, *please* beg you not to report Ruby to Animal Control, because my father says they'll come and put her down. She's a good dog, she really is, and she never did anything like this before, and we never, never, ever let her run loose. It was just a—"

"Freak occurrence?" I said.

"Right," she said. "An anomaly. An accident."

Allison's jaw tightened. The dog looked tranquilly up at us out of its pink eyes as if all this were none of its concern. A bugless breeze rustled the trees along the street. "And what am I supposed to say?" Allison put in. "How am I supposed to feel? What do you want, forgiveness? Well, I'm sorry, but I just can't do it, not now." She gave the girl a fierce look. "You love your dog?"

The girl nodded.

"Well, I love—*loved*—Shushawna too." She choked up. "More than anything in the world."

We all took a minute to gaze down on the carcass, then the girl lifted her eyes. "My father says we'll pay all damages. Here," she said, digging into her purse and producing a pair of business cards, one of which she handed to me and the other to Allison. "Any medical treatment you may need, we'll take care of, one hundred percent," she assured me, eyeing my arm doubtfully before turning to Allison. "And replace your pet too, if you want, *madame*. It was a micropig, right, from Recombicorp? Or if you want—my father authorized me to say this—we could get you a Cherry Pit, like Ruby, or even a dogcat, if that sounds like a good idea at all—"

It was a painful moment. I could feel for Allison and the girl too, though Connie and I didn't have any pets, not even one of the new hypoallergenic breeds, and we didn't have children either, though we'd discussed it often enough. There was a larger sadness at play here, the sadness of attachment and loss and the way the world wreaks its changes whether we're ready for them or not. We would have gotten through the moment, I think, coming to some sort of understanding—Allison wasn't vindictive and I wasn't about to raise a fuss—but that same breeze swept across the lawn to flip back the edge of the T-shirt and expose the eyeless head of the pig and that was all it took. Allison let out a gasp, and the dog—that crimson freak—jerked the leash out of the girl's hand and went right for it.

When Connie came home, I was in the kitchen mixing a drink. The front door slammed (Connie was always in a hurry, no wasted motion, and though I'd asked her a hundred times not to slam the door, she was constitutionally incapable of taking the extra two seconds to ease it shut). An instant later her briefcase slapped down on the hallway table with the force of a thunderclap, her heels drilled the parquet floor—*tat-tat-tat-tat*—and then she was there, in the kitchen, saying, "Make me one too, would you, honey? Or no: wine. Do we have any wine?"

I didn't ask her how her day had gone—all her days were the same, pedal-to-the-metal, one *situation* after another, all of which she dealt with like a five-star general driving the enemy into the sea. I didn't give her a hug or blow her a kiss either. We weren't that sort of couple—to her mind (and mine too, to be honest) it would have been just more wasted motion. Wordlessly, I turned to the cabinet, took a glass down from the cupboard, poured her a glass of the Sancerre she liked and handed it to her. Though I had the window open to catch the breeze, there was no sound of the birds, which must have flown off to haunt somebody else's yard.

"Allison's pet pig was killed today," I said, "right out on our front lawn. By one of those transgenic pit bulls, one of the crimson ones they're always pushing on TV?"

Her eyebrows lifted. She swirled the wine in her glass, took a sip.

"And I got bit," I added, holding up my arm, where a deep purplish bruise had wrapped itself around the skin just below the elbow.

What she said next didn't follow, but then we often talked in non sequitur, she conducting a certain kind of call-and-response conversation in her head and I in mine, the responses never quite matching up. She didn't comment on my injury or the dog or Allison or the turmoil I'd gone through. She just set her glass down on the counter, patted her lips where the wine had moistened them and said, "I want a baby."

I suppose I should back up here a moment to give you an idea of where this was coming from. We'd been married twelve years now and we'd both agreed that at some point we'd like to start a family, but we kept putting it off for one reason or another— our careers, finances, fear of the way a child would impact our lifestyle, the usual kind of thing. But with a twist. What sort of child, that was the question. Previous generations had only to fret over whether the expectant mother would bear a boy or girl or if the child would inherit Aunt Bethany's nose or Uncle Yuri's monobrow, but that wasn't the case anymore, not since CRISPR gene-editing technology hit the ground running twenty years back. Now, not only could you choose the sex of the child at conception, you could choose its other features too, as if having a child were like going to the car dealership and picking the options to add onto the basic model. The sole function of sex these days had become recreational; babies were conceived in the laboratory. That was the way it was and that was the way it would be, until, as a species, we evolved into something else. The result was a nation—a world—of children like the tall girl with the bright red dog.

To my way of thinking, this was intrusive and unnatural, but to Connie's it was a no-brainer. "Are you out of your mind?" she'd say. "You really want your kid—*our* kid—to be the bonehead of the class? Or what, take career training, cosmetology, *auto mechanics*, for Christ's sake?"

Now, tipping back her glass and downing the wine in a single belligerent gulp, she announced, "I'm thirty-eight years old and I'm putting my foot down. I've made an appointment at GenLab for ten a.m. Thursday, and I'm sacrificing a day of work for it too. Either you come with me"—she was glaring at me now—"or I swear I'm going to go out and get a sperm donor."

Nobody likes an ultimatum. Especially when you're talking about a major life-changing event, the kind of thing *both* people involved have to enter into in absolute harmony. It didn't go well. She thought she could bully me as if I were one of her underlings at work; I thought she couldn't. She thought she'd had the final word on the subject; I thought different. I said some things I wound up regretting later, snatched up my drink and slammed through the kitchen door and out into the backyard, where for once no birds were cursing from the trees and even the bees seemed muted as they went about their business. What came next was dependent on that silence, because otherwise I never would have heard the soft heartsick keening of Allison working through the stations of her grief. The sound was low and intermittent, a stunted release of air followed by a sodden gargling that might have been the wheeze and rattle of the sprinklers starting up, and it took me a minute to realize what it was and that it was coming from the adjoining yard. In the instant, I forgot all about what had just transpired in my own kitchen and thought of Allison, struck all over again by the intensity of her emotion.

We'd managed to get the dog off the carcass, all three of us shouting at once while the girl grabbed for the leash and I delivered two or three sharp kicks to the animal's hindquarters, but Allison's dead pig was none the better for it. The girl, red-faced and embarrassed despite her IQ and whatever other attributes she might have possessed, slouched across the lawn and down the street, the dog mincing beside her, and we both watched till she was gone, at which point I offered to do the only sensible thing and bury what was left of the remains. I dug a hole out back of Allison's potting shed, Allison read a passage I vaguely remembered from school ("The stars are not wanted now: put out every one; / Pack up the moon and dismantle the sun"), I held her in my arms for the second time that day, then filled the hole and went home to make my drink and have Connie slam the front door and lay her demands on me.

Now, as if I were being tugged on invisible wires, I moved toward the low hedge that separated our properties and stepped across it. The first thing I saw was Allison, hunched over the picnic table on her patio. She was still dressed in the taupe blouse and black skirt she'd worn to work, and she had her head down, her scarf bunched under one cheek. When I got closer I saw she was crying, and that got to me in a way I can't explain, so that before I knew what I was doing I'd fallen down a long dark tunnel and found myself consoling her in a way that seemed—how can I put this?—so very *natural* at the time.

It was dark when I got home. Connie was sitting on the couch in the living room, watching TV with the sound muted. "Hi," I said, feeling sheepish, feeling guilty (I'd never strayed before and didn't know why I'd done it now, except that I'd been so furious with my wife and so strangely moved by Allison in her grief, as if that's an excuse, and I know it isn't), but trying, like all amateurs, to act as if nothing were out of the ordinary. Connie looked up. I couldn't read her face, but I thought, at least by the flickering light of the TV, that she looked softer, contrite even, as if she'd reconsidered her position, or at least the way she'd laid it on me. She didn't ask where I'd been. Instead, she said, "Where's the glass?"

"What glass?"

"Your cocktail? The one you mixed before you stormed out the back door?"

"I don't know—outside, I guess." I shrugged, though most likely I'd left it next door, at Allison's, the MacGuffin that would give me away and bring our marriage crashing to the ground. "I'm sorry," I said, "but I was upset, okay? I just went for a walk. To clear my head."

She had nothing to say to this.

"You eat yet?" I asked, to change the subject.

She shook her head.

"Me either," I said, feeling the weight lift, as if ritual could get us through this. "You want to go out?"

"No, I don't want to go out," she said. "I want a baby."

And what did I say, from the shallow grave of my guilt that

was no deeper than the layer of earth I'd flung over the shrunken and lacerated corpse of Allison's pet? I said, "Okay, we'll talk about it."

"Talk about it? The appointment is Thursday, ten a.m. That's non-negotiable."

She was right—it *was* time to start a family—and she was right too about cosmetology and auto mechanics. What responsible parent wouldn't want the best for his child, whether that meant a stable home, top-flight nutrition and the best private-school education money could buy—or tweaking the chromosomes in a test tube in a lab somewhere? Understand me: I was under duress. I could smell Allison on me still. I could smell my own fear. I didn't want to lose my wife—I loved her. I was used to her. She was the only woman I'd known these past twelve years and more, a known quantity, my *familiar*. And there she was, poised on the edge of the couch, watching me, her will like some miasma seeping in under the door and through the cracks around the windows until the room was choked with it. It was like the moment in a wrestling match where the whistle blows and the grip gives way and nobody gets pinned to the mat. "Okay," I said.

Which is not to say I gave in without a fight. The next day—Wednesday—I had to go into the office and endure the usual banalities of my coworkers till I wanted to beat the walls of my cubicle in frustration, but on the way home I stopped at a pet store and picked up an eight-week-old dogcat. (By the way, people still aren't quite sure what to call the young, even now, fifteen years after they were first created. They're not kittens and they're not puppies, but something in between, as the name of the new species implies. Kitpups? Pupkits?) The sign in the window read simply *Baby Dogcats On Special*, and so I picked out a squirming little furball with a doggish face and tabby stripes and brought it home as a surprise for Connie, hoping it would distract her long enough to reevaluate the decision she was committing us to.

I'd tucked the thing inside my shirt for the drive home, since from the minute the girl behind the counter had put it in its cardboard carrying container it had begun alternately mewing and yipping in a tragic way, and it nestled there against my chest, warm and content, until I'd parked the car and gone up the steps and into the house. Connie was already home, moving briskly about the kitchen. There were flowers on the table next to an ice bucket with the neck of a bottle of Veuve Clicquot protruding from it and the room was redolent with the scent of my favorite meal—pipérade, Basque-style, topped with poached eggs—which, I realized, she must have made a special stop for at Maison Claude on her way home. This was a celebration and no two ways about it. In the morning, we would procreate—or take our first steps in that direction, which on my part would involve producing a sperm sample under duress (unlike, I couldn't help thinking, the way it had been with Allison).

We didn't hug. We didn't kiss. I just said, "Hey," and she said "Hey" back. "Smells great," I said, trying to gauge her expression as we both hovered over the table.

"Perfect timing," she said, leaning in to adjust the napkin beside her plate, though it was already precisely aligned. "I got there the minute they took it out of the oven. Claude himself brought it out to me—along with a fresh loaf of that crusty sourdough you like. Just baked this morning."

I was grinning at her. "Great," I said. "Really great."

Into the silence that followed—neither of us was ready yet to address the issue hanging over us—I said, "I've got a surprise for you."

"How sweet. What is it?"

With a magician's flourish, I whipped the new pet from the folds of my shirt and held it out triumphantly for her. Unfortunately, I seemed to have startled the thing in the process, and it reacted by digging its claws into my wrist, letting out a string of rapid-fire barks and dropping a glistening turd on the tiles of the kitchen floor. "For you," I said.

Her face fell. "You've got to be kidding me. You really think I'm that easy to buy off—or what, distract?" She made no effort to take the thing from me—in fact, she clenched her hands behind her. "Take it back where you got it."

The pupkit had softened now, retracting its claws and settling into the crook of my arm as if it recognized me, as if in the process of selecting it and secreting it in my shirt I'd imparted something essential to it—love, that is—and it was content to exist in a new world on a new basis altogether. "It's purring," I said.

"What do you want me to say—hallelujah? The thing's a freak, you're always saying so yourself every time one of those stupid commercials comes on—"

Suddenly the jingle was playing in my head, a snatch of the last lulling measures of Pachelbel's Canon, over which the announcer croons, *Dog person? Cat person? It's all moot now.* "No more a freak than that girl with the dog," I said.

"What girl? What are you talking about?"

"The one with the dog that bit me. She must have been six-four. She had an IQ of 162. And still she let the dog out and still it bit me."

"What are you saying? You're not trying to back out on me, are you? We had a *deal,* Roy, and you know how I feel about people that renege on a deal—"

"Okay, okay, calm down. All I'm saying is maybe we ought to have a kind of trial or something before we—I mean, we've never even had a *pet.*"

"A pet is not a child, Roy."

"No," I said, "that's not what I meant. It was just, I'm just—" The crowparrots started up then with one of their raucous dinnertime chants, squawking so piercingly you could hear them even with the windows shut—*Big Mac, Big Mac*, they crowed, *Fries!*—and I lost my train of thought.

"Are we going to eat?" Connie said in a fragile voice, and we both looked first to the microwave and then to the animal excreta on the kitchen floor. "Because I went out of my way," she said, tearing up. "Because I wanted this night to be special, okay?"

So now we did hug, though the pupkit got between us, and, coward that I am, I told her everything was going to be all right. Later, after she'd gone to bed, I took the pupkit in my arms, went next door and rang the bell. Allison answered in her nightgown, a smile creeping across her lips. "Here," I said, handing her the animal, "I got this for you."

Fast-forward seven and a half months. I am living in a house with a pregnant woman next door to a house in which there is another pregnant woman. Connie seems to find this amusing, never suspecting the truth of the matter. We'll glance up from the porch and see Allison emerging heavily from her car with an armload of groceries and Connie will say things like "I don't envy her," and "I hope she doesn't have to pee every five minutes the way I do" and "She won't say who the father is—I just hope it's not that A-hole from Animal Control, what was his name?"

This is problematic on a number of levels. I play dumb, of course—what else can I do? "Maybe she went to GenLab," I say.

"Her? You're kidding me, right? I mean, look at that string of jerks she keeps dating. If you want to know the truth, she's lower class, Roy, and I'm sorry to have to say it—"

"I don't see her dating anybody."

"You know what I mean."

I'm not about to argue the point. The fact is, I tried everything I could to talk Allison out of going through with this—

finally, to my shame, falling back on the same argument about the whole Übermensch/Untermensch dynamic Connie used on me, trade school, cosmetology, self-denigration, back-of-the-classroom, the works, but Allison merely gave me a bitter smile and said, "I trust your genes, Roy. You don't have to be involved. I just want to do this, that's all. For myself. And for nature. You believe in nature, don't you?"

You don't have to be involved. But I *was* involved, though we'd had sex only the one time (or two, actually, counting the night I brought her the pupkit), and if she had a boy and he looked like me and grew up right next door playing with our daughter, how involved would that be?

So there comes a day, sometime during that eighth month, a Tuesday when I'm working at home and Connie's at the office, and I'm so focused on the problem at hand I keep putting off my bathroom break until the morning's nearly gone. It's the way it always is when I'm deeply engaged with a problem, a kind of mind-body separation, but finally the body's needs prevail and I push myself up from my desk to go down the hall to the bathroom. I'm standing there, in mid-flow, when I become aware of the sound of a dog barking on the front lawn, and I shift my torso ever so slightly so that I can glance out the window and see what the ruckus is all about. It's the red dog, the Cherry Pit that set all this in motion, and he's tearing around on my hybrid lawn, chasing something. My first reaction is anger—anger at the tall girl and her fixer father and all the other idiots of the world—but by the time I get down the stairs and out the front door and into the sunlight, it dissipates, because I see that the dog isn't there to kill anything but to play. And that what it's chasing is being chased willingly (Allison's dogcat, now a rangy adolescent and perhaps a third the size of the dog).

For all my fretting over the lawn, I have to say that in that moment, with the light making a cathedral of the street trees and the neighborhood suspended in the grip of a lazy warm autumn afternoon, I find something wonderfully liberating in the play of those two animals, the dogcat especially. Allison named him Tiger in respect to his coloration—dark feral stripes against a kind of Pomeranian orange—and he lives up to his name, absolutely fearless and with an athleticism and elasticity that combines the best of both the species that went into making him. He runs rings around the pit bull, actually, feinting one way, dodging the next, racing up the trunk of a tree and out onto a branch before leaping to the next tree and springing back down to charge, dog-like, across the yard. "Go, Tiger!" I call out. "Good boy. Go get him!"

That's when I become aware of Allison, in a pair of maternity shorts and an enormous top, crossing from her front lawn to ours. She's put on a lot of weight (but not as much as Connie, because we opted for a big baby, in the eleven-pound range, wanting it— her—to have that advantage right from the start). I haven't spoken with Allison much these past months, once it became clear that whatever we once felt for each other was over—or to put it more bluntly, whatever business we'd conducted—but I still have feelings for her, of course, beyond resentment, that is. So I lift a hand and wave and she waves back and I watch her come barefooted through the glowing grass while the sun sits in the trees and the animals frolic around her.

I'm down off the porch now and I can't help but smile at the sight of her. She comes up to me, moving with a kind of clumsy grace, if that makes any sense, and I want to take her in my arms but can't really do that, not under these conditions, so I take both her hands and pull her to me to peck a neighborly kiss to her cheek. For a minute, neither of us says anything, then, shading her eyes with the flat of one hand to better see the animals at play, she says, "Pretty cute, huh?"

I nod.

"You see how Tiger's grown?"

"Yes, of course, I've been watching him all along . . . Is that as big as he's going to get?"

The sun catches her eyes, which are a shade of plain everyday brown. "Nobody's sure, but the vet thinks he won't get much bigger. Maybe a pound or two."

"And you?" I venture. "How are you feeling?"

"Never better. You're going to be seeing more of me—don't look scared, that's not what I mean, just I'm taking my maternity leave though I'm not due for, like, six weeks." Both her hands, pretty hands, shapely, come to rest on the bulge beneath her oversized blouse. "They're really being nice about it at work."

Connie's not planning on taking off till the minute her water breaks because that's the way Connie is and I want to tell her that by way of contrast, just to say something, but I notice that she's looking over my shoulder and I turn my head to see the tall girl coming up the walk, leash in hand. "Sorry," the girl calls out, "—she got loose again. Sorry, sorry."

I don't know what it is, but I'm feeling generous, expansive. "No problem," I call out. "She's just having a little fun."

That's when Connie's car slashes into the driveway, going too fast, and all I can think is she's going to hit one of the animals, but she brakes at the last minute and they flow like water round the tires to chase back across the lawn again. It's hard to gauge the look on my wife's face as she swings open the car door, pushes herself laboriously from behind the wheel and sets first one foot, then the other, on the pavement (I really should go help her, but it's as if I'm frozen in place), then starts up the walk as if she hasn't seen us. Just as she reaches the front steps, Connie swivels round. I can see she's considering whether it's worth the effort to come greet our neighbor and get a closer look at the tall girl who hovers behind us like the avatar she is, but she decides against it. She just stops a moment, staring, and though she's thirty feet away I can see a kind of recognition settle into her features, and it has to do with the way Allison is standing there beside me as if for a portrait or an illustration in a book on family planning, male and female, the *xy* chromosome and the *xx*. It's just a moment, and I can't say for certain, but her face goes rigid and she turns her back on us, mounts the steps and slams the door behind her.

When the CRISPR technology first came to light, governments and scientists everywhere assured the public that it would only be employed selectively, to fight disease and rectify congenital deformities, editing out the mutated BRCA1 gene that predisposes women to breast cancer, for instance, or eliminating the ability of the *Anopheles* mosquito to carry the parasite that transmits malaria. Who could argue with that? Genome editing kits (Knock Out Any Gene!) were sold to home hobbyists, who could create their own anomalous forms of yeast and bacteria in their kitchens, and it was revolutionary—and beyond that, fun. Fun to tinker. Fun to create. The pet and meat industries gave us rainbow-colored aquarium fish, sea horses that incorporated gold dust in their cells, rabbits that glowed green under a black light, the beefed-up supercow, the micropig, the dogcat and all the rest. The Chinese were the first to renounce any sort of regulatory control and upgrade the human genome, and as if they weren't brilliant enough already, they became still more brilliant as the first edited children began to appear, and, of course, we had to keep up ...

In a room at GenLab, Connie and I were presented with an exhaustive menu of just how our chromosomes could be made to match up. We chose to have a daughter. We selected emerald eyes for her—not iridescent, not freakishly bright, but enhanced for color so that she could grow up wearing mint, olive, Kelly green, and let her eyes talk for her. We chose height too, as just about everybody did. And musical ability—we both loved music. Intellect, of course. And finer features too, like a subtly cleft chin and breasts that would be optimal, not too big but not as small as Connie's either. It *was* a menu, and we placed an order.

The tall girl is right there with us now, smiling like the heroine of a Norse saga, her eyes sweeping over us like searchlights. She looks to Allison, takes in her condition. "Boy or girl?" she asks.

The softest smile plays over Allison's lips. She ducks her head, shrugs.

The girl—the genius—looks confused for a moment. "But, but," she stammers, "how can that be? You don't mean you—?"

But before Allison can answer, a crowparrot sweeps out of the nearest tree, winging low to screech *Fuck You!* in our faces, and the smallest miracle occurs. Tiger, as casual in his own skin as anything there is or ever was, erupts from the ground in a rocketing whirl of fur to catch the thing in his jaws. As quick as that, it's over, and the feathers, the prettiest feathers you'll ever see, lift and dance and float away on the breeze.

THE FIVE-POUND BURRITO

He lived in a world of grease, and no matter how often he bathed, which was once a day, rigorously—and no shower but a drawn bath—he smelled of *carnitas, machaca* and the chopped white onion and soapy cilantro he folded each morning into his *pico de gallo*. The grease itself was worked up under his nails and into the folds of his skin, folds that hung looser and penetrated deeper now that he was no longer young. This was a condition of his life and his livelihood, and if it had its drawbacks—he was sixty-two and never married because what woman would want a man who smelled so inveterately of fried pork?—it had its rewards too. For one thing, he was his own boss, the little hole-in-the-wall café he'd opened back in the sixties still doing business when so many showier places had come and gone. For another, he was content, his world restricted to what he knew, the sink, the dishwasher, the griddle and the grill, and he saw his customers, the regulars and one-timers alike, as a kind of flock that had to be fed like the chickens his mother had kept when he was a boy. What did he do with himself? He scraped his griddle, took his aprons, shirts and underwear to the Chinese laundry that had been in operation nearly as long as he had and went home each evening to put his feet up and sit in front of the TV.

His only employee was a sour woman named Sepideh, an Iranian (or, as she preferred it, Persian) immigrant who had escaped her native country after the regime change and was between forty-five and sixty, depending on what time of day you asked her. In the mornings she was unconquerably old, but by closing time her age had dropped, though she dragged her feet, her shoulders slumped and her makeup grew increasingly tragic. She was dark-skinned and dark-eyed and she dyed her once-black hair black all over again. People took her for a Mexican, which was really a matter of indifference to him—he didn't care whether his waitress was from Chapultepec or Hokkaido, as long as she did her job and took some of the pressure off him. And she did. And had for some twenty years now and counting.

On this particular day, mid-week, dreary, the downtown skyline obliterated by fog or smog or whatever they wanted to call it, Sepideh was late because the bus she took from the section of town known as Little Persia, where she lived with her mother and an equally sour-faced brother he'd met once or twice, had broken down. As luck would have it, there was a line outside the door when at eleven o'clock on the dot he shuffled across the floor and flipped the sign from *Closed* to *Open*. In came the customers, most of them wearing familiar faces, and as they crowded in at the counter and unfolded their newspapers and propped up their tablets and laptops on the six tables arranged in a narrow line along the far wall that featured the framed black-and-white photo of a dead president, he began taking orders.

First in line was Scott, a student from the university who had the same thing five days a week, black coffee and the chorizo and scrambled egg burrito he lathered with jalapeños, *Just to wake up,* as he put it on the mornings when he was capable of speech.

Next to him were Humberto and Baltasar, two baggy-pants old men from the neighborhood who would slurp heavily sugared coffee for the next three hours and try to talk him to death as he hustled from grill to griddle to the refrigerator and back, and here were two others easing onto the stools beside them, new faces, more students—but big, all head and neck, shoulder and belly, footballers, no doubt, who would devour everything in a two-foot radius, complain that the portions were too small and the burritos like prisoners' rations, and try to suck the glaze off the plates in the process. Of course, he should be happy because the students had discovered him yet again—and how many generations had made the same discovery only to fade away in the lean months when he could have used their business?

He dealt out a stack of plastic menus as if he were flipping cards like the dealer at the blackjack table at Caesars, where he liked to spend his two weeks off every February, bathed in the little spotlight that illuminated the table, a gratis rum and coke sizzling at his elbow. Then he leaned over the counter and announced in the voice that was dying in his throat a little more each day as he groped toward old age and infirmity, "No table service today. You people back there got to come up to the counter if you want to get fed." That was it. He didn't need to give an explanation—if they wanted Michelin stars, let them line up over in Beverly Hills or Pacific Palisades—but he couldn't help adding, "She's late today, Sepideh."

And so it began: breakfast, then the lunch rush, furious work in a hot cramped kitchen, and all he could see was people's mouths opening and closing and the great wads of beans and rice and marinated pork, chicken and beef swelling their throats. It was past noon before he could catch his breath—he didn't even have time for a cigarette, and that put him in a foul mood, the lack of nicotine—and when he saw the face in the tortilla that provided the foundation for the burrito he was just then constructing, he ignored it. It was nobody's face, eyes, nose, cheekbones, brow, and it meant nothing except that he was exhausted, already exhausted, and he still had six and a half hours to go. And sure, he'd seen faces before—Mohammed, the Buddha, Sandy Koufax once, but Jesus? Never. The woman over on Broadway had seen Jesus, exactly as He was in the Shroud of Turin, only the shroud in this case was made of unleavened flour, lard and water. He could have used Jesus himself, because that woman got rich and the lines for her place went around a whole city block. If he only had Jesus, he could hire somebody more competent—and dependable—than Sepideh and sit back and take a load off. That was what he was thinking as he smeared *refritos* over the face of the tortilla and piled up rice and meat and guacamole and *crema,* cheese, shredded lettuce, *pico de gallo,* the works—and why not?—for yet another pair of footballers who were sitting there at the back table like statues come to life. Call it whimsy, or maybe revenge, but he mounded the ingredients up till the burrito was as big as a stuffed pillowcase. Let them complain about this one.

That was when he had his moment of inspiration, divine or otherwise. He would weigh it. Actually weigh it, and that would be his ammunition and his pride too, the biggest burrito in town. If he didn't have Jesus, at least he would have that.

We each live through our time on earth in an accumulation of milliseconds, seconds, minutes, hours, days, months and years, and life is a path we must follow, invariably, until the end. Is there change—or the hope of it? Yes, but change is wearing and bad for the nerves and almost always for the worse. So it was with Sal, the American-born son of Mexican immigrants who'd opened Salvador's Café with a loan from his uncle James when he was still in his twenties, and now, nearly forty years later, saw his business take off like a rocket on the fuel of the five-pound burrito. Suddenly his homely café was a destination not only for his regulars and the famished and greedy of the neighborhood, but for the educated classes from the West Side who pulled up out front in their shining new German automobiles and stepped through the door as if they expected the floor to fall away beneath the soles of their running shoes and suck them down to some deeper, darker place.

This was change, positive change, at least at first. He hired a man to help with the dishes and the sweeping up and a second waitress, a young girl studying for her nursing degree who gave everybody in the place something to look at. And on the counter, raised at eye level on a cloth-covered pedestal, was the big butcher's scale on which he ceremoniously weighed each dripping pork, chicken or beef burrito before Sepideh—or the new girl, Marta—made a show of hefting the supersized plate and setting it down laboriously in front of the customer who had ordered it. A man from the newspaper came. And then another. The line went around the block, and never mind Jesus.

Sal was there one early morning—typically he arose at five and was in the kitchen by six, preparing things ahead of time, and, of course, with success came the need for yet more preparation— when he felt a numinous shift in the atmosphere, as if those timid first-timers from the West Side had been right after all. The floor didn't open up beneath him, of course, but as he cut meat from the bone and shucked avocados for guacamole, he felt the atmosphere permeated by a new presence, and no ordinary presence but the kind that makes a dog's hackles rise when it sniffs at the shadows. For a moment he felt dizzy and wondered if he was having some sort of attack, the inevitable myocardial infarction or stroke that would bring him down for good, but the dizziness passed and he found himself in the kitchen still, the knife clenched in his hand and the cubes of pork gently oozing on the chopping block before him. He shook his head to clear it. Something was different, but he couldn't say what.

The morning wore on in a fugue of chopping, dicing and tearing up over the emanations of habaneros and jalapeños, his back aching and his hands dripping with the juice of the hundred-millionth tomato of his resuscitated life, and he forgot all about it till the knock came at the alley door. This was the knock of Stanford Wong, who delivered produce to the restaurants of the neighborhood and was as punctual as the great clock in Greenwich, England, that kept time for the world. Sal wiped his hands on his apron and hurried to the door because Stanford, understandably, didn't like to be delayed. There might have been a noise outside the door, a furtive scratching as of some animal trying to get in, but it didn't register until he pulled back the door and saw that it wasn't Stanford stationed there at all but an erect five-and-a-half-foot rooster dressed in Stanford Wong's khaki shorts and khaki shirt with the black plastic nameplate—*Stanford*—fixed over the breast.

Was he taken aback? Was he seeing things? He'd had his breakfast, hadn't he? Yes, yes, of course: eggs. Chicken embryos. Fried in butter, topped with a sprinkle of Cotija cheese and served up on toast. He just stood there, blinking, but the bird, which somehow seemed to have hands as well as wings, was impatient and brushed by him with a crate of lettuce and half a dozen clear plastic bags of tomatillos, peppers and the like balanced against his—its?—chest, setting the load down on the counter and swinging round abruptly with Stanford's receipt book in hand. But there were words now, the bird saying something out of a beak that snapped and glistened to show off a pink wedge of tongue, and yet the words made no sense unless you were to interpret them in the usual way, as in, *Same order tomorrow?* and *You take care now.*

The door swung shut. The crate sat astride the counter, just as it had yesterday and the day before and the day before that. It took him a moment—and maybe he'd better have another cup of coffee—before he went to the crate and began shoving heads of lettuce into the refrigerator, all the while thinking that there were two possibilities here. The first and most obvious was that he was hallucinating. The second and more disturbing was that Stanford Wong had been transformed into a giant rooster. Either way, the prospects could hardly be called favorable, and if he was losing his mind in the uproar over the five-pound burrito, who could blame him?

Next it was Sepideh, dressed in black skirt and white blouse, but with her head covered in feathers and her nose replaced by a dull puce beak and no shoes on her feet because her legs, her scaly yellow legs, supported not phalanges and painted toenails but the splayed naked claws of an antediluvian hen. She was never talk-ative, especially in the morning, but whatever she had to say to him came in a series of irritable clucks and gabbles, and he just— well, he just blew her off. Then came Marta and she was a hen too and by the time Oscar Martí, the cleanup man, showed his face, it was no surprise at all that he should be a rooster just like Stanford Wong—and, for that matter, once the door opened for business, that all the male customers should be crowing and flapping their wings, while their female counterparts clucked and brooded and held their own counsel over pocketbooks stuffed with eyeliner, compacts and lipstick that had no discernible purpose. Some-thing was wrong here, desperately wrong, but work was work and whether he could understand what anybody was saying, custom-ers or staff, really didn't seem to matter, as everything by this junc-ture had been reduced to routine: spread the tortilla, crown it with toppings, fold it, dip the ladle in the salsa verde and serve it up on the big white scale.

That was Monday. Mondays were always a trial, what with forcing yourself back into the routine after the day of rest, the Lord's day, when people went to church to wet their fingers with holy water and count their blessings. Sal locked up after work that night and if he noticed that everyone, every living man, woman and child on the streets and sealed behind the windows of their cars, was a member of a different species—poultry, that is—he didn't let it affect him. Even so, the minute he came in the door of his apartment he went straight to the mirror in the bathroom and was relieved to see his own human face staring back at him out of drooping eyes. He poured himself a drink that night, a practice he found himself engaging in less and less as he got older, heated up a burrito (regular size) in the microwave, and watched reality TV till he couldn't hold his eyes open anymore. It would be one thing to say that his dreams were populated with hens, roosters and bobbing chicks, but the fact was that he dreamed of nothing—or nothing he could remember on wakening. He was a blank canvas, tabula rasa. Mechanically, he shaved. Mechanically, he broke two eggs in a pan and laid three strips of bacon beside them, and he drove mechanically to work. In the dark.

When Stanford Wong's knock came precisely at eight, Sal moved briskly to the door, his mood soaring on his second cup of coffee—with a shot of espresso to top it off—and the prospect of yet another record-setting day. If things kept up like this, he'd soon be sitting in a chair all day long watching the world come and go while the new grillman he'd hire and train himself did the dirty work. And it was all due to the inspiration of that day six months back when he'd brought out the scale and piled up the burrito and made his statement to the world. The five-pound burrito. It was a concept, an innovation unmatched by anybody in the city, whether they had a sit-down place or a lunch cart or even one of those eateries with the white tablecloths and the waiters who looked at you as if you belonged on the plate instead of sitting upright in a chair and putting in an order. People just couldn't understand what it took to consume a burrito of that caliber—no individual, not even the greediest, most swollen footballer, could ever hope to get it all down in a single sitting. Though people placed bets and Sal had agreed to advertise that if you could manage to eat the whole thing, it was on the house. Very few could. In fact, only one man—skinny, Asian, the size of a child—was able to accomplish the feat incontrovertibly, and it turned out later that he was world famous as a competitive eater who'd won the Nathan's hot dog–eating contest three years running.

But here was Stanford Wong's knock, and as he opened the door, he didn't know what to expect, least of all what he saw standing there before him on its hind legs—*his* hind legs. This wasn't Stanford Wong and it wasn't a chicken either—no, this was a hog, with pinched little hog's eyes and a bristling inflamed snout, but it was dressed in Stanford Wong's khaki shorts and khaki shirt with the black plastic nameplate fixed over the breast. It—he—trotted brusquely into the kitchen and set the crate of lettuce and plastic bags of vegetables on the counter, then swung round with Stanford Wong's accounts ledger clutched under one arm and grunted and snuffled out a sentence or two that could only have meant, *How they hangin'?* and *See you tomorrow, same order, right?*

Right. So he chopped peppers and grilled pork and made a pot of *albondigas* soup, shredded lettuce and stirred up yesterday's steam trays of rice and *refritos* and thought nothing of it when Sepideh appeared as a grunting old sow in her black skirt and white blouse and then Marta, resplendent in red shorts and a clinging top, in her guise as a smooth pink young shoat who nonetheless stood five feet seven inches tall on her cloven hoofs and managed to wield her tray and heft the big burritos as if she'd been born to it. As on the previous day, work consumed him, and if his customers vocalized in a cascade of snorts and aspirated grunts, it was all the same to him. Back at home that night he passed on the burrito left over from work, though he hated waste, and instead slipped a package of frozen meatless lasagna into the oven and poured himself not one but two drinks before he let the TV lull him into a dreamless sleep.

He found himself on edge the next morning and drank a cup of tea instead of coffee and had toast only instead of his usual fried eggs with bacon, ham or chorizo. It was dark as he drove to work and if his headlights happened to catch a figure walking along a shadowy street or spot a face behind an oncoming windshield, he made himself look away. What next? That was all he could think. Cattle, no doubt. Huge stinking lowing steers speaking their own arcane language and demanding big burritos, the biggest in town. When Stanford Wong's knock came this time, he was prepared, or thought he was, but oh, how mistaken he turned out to be. This wasn't Stanford Wong and it wasn't a rooster or a hog or a steer either—it was an alien, and not one of the *indocumentados* of which his late sainted parents were representatives, but one of the true aliens, with their lizard skin, razor teeth and eyeballs like ashtrays. Of course, this one was wearing Stanford Wong's clothing and was carrying his crate of lettuce, but its claws were wicked and long and scraped mercilessly at the linoleum, and when it spoke—*How's business?* and *That five-pounder's going to make you rich*—it could only hiss.

All day, as the aliens crowded the café and his own aliens, Sepideh and Marta, served them their big dripping chile verde-drenched burritos, he kept wondering about their spaceship and if it was like the ones in the movies, all silver and gleaming and silent, and, more to the point, where they'd parked it. No matter. The aliens lashed at their food with a snap of their gleaming teeth and a quick release of their forked tongues and the cash register rang and the line went round the block.

It was around then, on that day, the third day, almost at closing time, that Sal saw a new face in the tortilla he laid on the grill for the burrito he was preparing for a big square-shouldered footballer alien. This face—the brow, the blind eyes and moving lips that swelled against the pressure of his tongs—was one that leapt out at him in its familiarity. And who was it? Not Jesus, no, but someone . . . someone more important even, if only to him. It was his father, the man who'd held him in his arms and pushed him on the swing and showed him how to grip a baseball and figure his equations in algebra—his father, dead these thirty years and more. The lips moved—and here Sal felt himself lifted into the arena of the fantastic—moved and spoke.

"You're over-reaching, Salvador. Pushing your luck. Flirting with excess and exception, when the truth is you're not exceptional at all but just a mule like me, made to work and live an honest proportionate life. Go back to two pounds, Salvador. Two maximum. And please, for the love of God and His angels too, dump some aromatic salts in that bathtub . . ." And then the lips stopped moving in that impress of dough and the voice faded out.

But there it was, revelation from the mouth of a flour tortilla, and the next day, despite the complaints of his customers—human beings, just like him—he went back to the standard-sized burrito. Trade fell off. He had to let Marta go and then Oscar too. The chickens went back to their henhouses and the hogs to their pens and the aliens trooped out across the lot to wherever they'd parked their spaceship and whirred off into the sky in a blaze of light, still traveling as day turned to night and the stars came out to welcome them home.

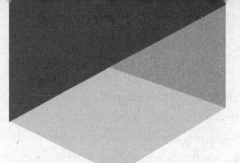

THE ARGENTINE ANT

(PACE CALVINO)

The baby had been ill, we'd exhausted our savings and our patience too, equally weary of the specialists who seemed to specialize only in uncertainty and of the cramped noisy conditions of our apartment in student housing, so when the chance came to rent the place in Il Nido we jumped at it. We'd never been that far south, but my uncle Augusto had lived in this particular village during the happiest period of his life and had never stopped rhapsodizing it—and since the rent was a fraction of what we were paying for our apartment and my fellowship would provide us with a small but steady income for the coming year, there was nothing to stop us. Provided that the baby stayed healthy, that is. At sixteen months, he was a fine, sturdy-looking child, whose problem—a super-sensitivity to touch, which might have been dermatological in origin or perhaps neurological, depending on which specialist you talked to—seemed to be improving as he grew into the squat stance of his chubby legs. Would there be specialists in this flyspeck of a fishing village on the tip of the southern peninsula? Pediatricians? Neurologists? Dermatologists? Not likely. But in a way, that would be a relief, since his condition was hardly life-threatening and the various diagnoses and explanations for it were more worrisome than the condition itself. No, what our son needed was to get out from under the impress of our dreary northern clime, with its incessantly dripping gutters, and into the sunshine where he could bask and thrive—and, no small consideration, so could we.

A Signora Mauro was the landlady, and our connection with her was through my uncle, who'd rented the house from her twenty years back when he was between marriages and working on a novel that was never published. I don't remember anything of the novel, portions of which he'd read aloud to me and my sister when I was a boy and he was occupying the guest room over the garage, but I recall vividly his portrait of the village and the tranquillity he'd found there, though, in retrospect—in light of what fell out, that is—I suppose this was fiction too.

My wife and I questioned nothing. This was an adventure, pure and simple. Or more than an adventure: an escape. We took the train and then a succession of buses, the last of which deposited us in front of Signora Mauro's rambling house in the village, and all the time the baby was well-behaved and my wife, Anina, and I stared out the jolting windows and dreamed of a long period of respite in our lives, she no longer trapped in a minimum-wage job as a temporary secretary and I free to work on solving the projective algebraic problem known as the Hodge Conjecture and thereby winning the one-million-dollar Millennium Prize, a sum that would set us up handily for some time to come. Did I have unrealistic expectations? Perhaps. But I was twenty-eight years old and terminally exhausted with the classroom and academic life, and it is a truism that mathematicians, like poets, do their best work before thirty. So we packed our things, boarded the express and found ourselves on Signora Mauro's doorstep in the sun-kissed embrace of Il Nido.

The house we were to rent was on a bluff overlooking the sea and it was crowded between two others—both, like ours, modest single-story structures of two or three rooms. Signora Mauro, exhibiting traces of a former beauty that was now for the most part extinct but for the low-level radiation of her eyes, found two men to help carry our things up the parabolic hill to the house on the bluff and spent the next quarter hour showing us the essentials—how to light the gas stove and regulate the temperature of the refrigerator and such—before nudging me to hand over a few crumpled bills to each of the workmen and then vanishing down the hill, looking satisfied with herself.

It took no more than half an hour to put away our things—clothes, books, baby paraphernalia, a box of kitchen items Anina had insisted on bringing along though the house had come furnished and the essentials were all in place—and get a quick impression of the living space. There were three rooms—kitchen, bedroom, sitting room—as well as an indoor bathroom featuring a grand old claw-foot tub big enough to bathe armies, and the casement windows in back gave onto a narrow elongated garden (or former garden: it was dried up and skeletal now) that ended in a low hedge and another fifty feet or so of scrub that fell away to the ocean below. "Look, Anina," I called, pushing through the back door and out into the yard, "there's space for a garden! We can grow tomatoes, squash, cucumbers. Beans, beans too."

My wife, so reticent in public, so proper (humorless, was how my mother put it), was anything but in private. She took a critical view and always seemed to see things for what they were while I tended to romanticize and hope for the best. I watched her come out the door to me, after having set the baby down in his carrier at the foot of our new bed, where he'd promptly fallen asleep. She was grace incarnate, the wafting streamers of her hair caught up in the breeze she generated, her hips rotating in the earthy way that defined her and her lips parted as if in passion, but what she said wasn't at all graceful or passionate. "You call this a garden? It's nothing but stones and leached-out soil."

"The house has been sitting empty—what do you expect? Some seeds, a little water, manure—"

"Where's the water? I don't see any water."

I snatched a look round me. There was a birdbath—or former birdbath—set beside the central path that bisected the yard, the blistered remnants of a wheelless bicycle that looked as if it had been there since Uncle Augusto's time and a rusted watering can snarled in a tangle of yellowed vines, evidence that the garden had once been provided with water. "But there"—I just now looked behind me to the whitewashed wall of the house to discover the faucet and a length of ancient hose coiled beneath it. I pointed. "What do you call that?"

She didn't say a word but just walked back up the path to the house, bending to the hose bib as if to twist open the valve and prove me wrong, when she pulled up short and let out a low exclamation. "My god," she said, the voice dwindling in her throat. "What is *that*?"

What it was—and I hurried across the yard to see for myself—was a black sinuous ribbon of ants emerging from the ground beneath the hose bib to flow up the wall of the house and vanish into a crevice where the stucco met the overhang of the roof. I didn't react at first, rooted in fascination over this glistening display of coordination and purpose, a living banner composed of thousands, hundreds of thousands of individuals in permutations unfathomable (though already I was thinking in terms of algorithms). "Ants," I heard my wife declare. "I hate ants."

Without going into detail about her unhappy undergraduate

romance with a biologist at the university who happened to be ten years her senior, married and a myrmecologist to boot, I'll just say that when she snatched up the hose and leveled it on that column of ants she saw nothing fascinating about the creatures—quite the opposite. The hose flared, a stream of water jetted out and the ants fell away, only to mass at the base of the wall, realign themselves and start climbing again, this time in two separate ribbons that converged just above the locus of the spray.

"That won't help," I said. "It's only temporary."

My wife abruptly shut off the faucet. "You'll have to go into the village for poison then. Some sort of powder, what is it? My father used to use it. You sprinkle it along the base of the walls—"

"We can't use poison here, are you crazy?" I said, thinking of the baby, and in that very moment a high sputtering scream echoed from the depths of the house. We stared at each other in horror, then my wife dropped the hose and we both bolted for the bedroom only to discover that the floor had been transformed into a sea of ants—dislocated ants, angry ants, ants that had fled the wet and come to the dry—and that the baby, all considerations of skin tone aside, was black with them.

The irony wasn't lost on me. Here was a child whose condition one specialist likened to the feeling of having phantom ants crawling all over him, and now the sensation was real and the ants no phantoms. He threw back his head in his extremity, screeching till we thought his lungs would burst while I lifted him out of the cradle and my wife tore off his terrycloth pajamas, balled them up and employed them in frantic quick jerks to swipe the ants from his torso and limbs. They were everywhere, these ants, foaming in miniature waves over our sandals to work their way between our toes even as they scurried up our fingers and arms where we came into contact with our son. When finally we'd succeeded in brushing him clean, I went for the broom and attacked that roiling black horde with a pestilential fervor until many thousands of them, crushed and exuding their peculiar acidic odor, were swept out the door and into the courtyard. The baby, whimpering still, was in my wife's arms as she rocked with him, cooing little nonsense syllables to soothe him, and the remaining ants retreated into one of the crevices where the tile of the floor joined the wall. "This is intolerable," my wife spat, spinning and rocking, but with her eyes fixed on me like a pair of tongs. "We can't live here. *I* can't live here—not like this."

I told her, in a quiet voice, though I was seething too, that we really had no choice in the matter, as we'd already put down a deposit and first and last months' rent and that I had my desk to set up and my work on the prize to do if we ever hoped to rise to the next level.

"The prize?" She threw it back at me. "Don't make me laugh. You're going to become a millionaire by solving an all but impossible problem that every other mathematician in the world is probably working on right this minute—without ants? In real houses, in university offices, with air-conditioning, polished floors and *no insects* at all!"

This stung. Of course it did. Here we hadn't been in our new home—in our new life—for more than an hour and already she was questioning the whole proposition, and worse, my abilities, my intellect, my faith in the exceptionalism that set me apart from all the others. I'd been close to a solution—it had floated there, just out of reach, for months now, a matter of discovering and applying the right topology—and I knew that if I could just have these months of tranquillity here by the sea to focus my mind, I could do it. I dropped my voice still lower. "I'm going to try."

A long moment transpired, I standing there in the doorway to the bedroom, she bouncing the baby, before she turned to me again, conceding the point but obstinate still, upset, her nerves frayed by the move and the baby's fragility and everything given figurative expression in these swarming insects that didn't even belong here, migrants from across the sea in South America. "All right," she said, biting her lower lip and swinging round on me with the baby as if she'd taken him hostage, "but you'd better find a solution to *this* problem, to these, these *pests,* before you even think about sitting down at that desk."

We hadn't eaten, either of us, and as it was now late in the afternoon, I thought I'd walk down to the village to pick up a few things for a quick meal—bread, cheese, salami, a fiasco of wine, milk for the baby—and take the opportunity to inquire about whatever non-toxic powders and sprays might be available for application, anything to discourage the ants—especially after dark. I had a grim vision of tossing all night in a strange bed as the ants boiled up from a crack in the floor and made a playing field of the expanse of my flesh. And my wife's. I could already foresee hanging the baby's cradle from a hook in the ceiling like a potted plant—ants couldn't fly, could they? Or not this species, anyway. In any case, I'd just started down the flagstone path for the front gate when I heard music (jazz violin, sensuous and heartrending over the rhythmic rasp of the bow) drifting across the yard from the house next door and a low murmur of voices punctuated by laughter. On an impulse—and out of a feeling of neighborliness, that too—I changed direction and made my way to the low hedge that separated our property from that of the house next door and peered over.

I was immediately embarrassed. Here were my neighbors, a man and woman in their forties and dressed in swimsuits—he in trunks and she in a two-piece that left little to speculation—staring up at me in surprise. They were seated at a glass-topped table, sipping Campari and soda, and they both had their bare feet propped up on the two unused chairs in the set of four. She was dark, he was fair, and they both looked harmless enough—in fact, once over their initial surprise they both broke out in broad smiles and the woman, whose name, I was soon to learn, was Sylvana, cried out, "Hello, there! You must be the new neighbor." And the husband: "Come join us. You must. I insist." And then the wife: "No need for formality—just hop over the hedge. Here, come on."

I was dressed in khaki trousers and a rayon shirt with sleeves I'd rolled up to the elbows, nothing formal, certainly, but here they were all but naked, so I put away my scruples and vaulted the hedge, and if I came away with a handful of ants where I braced myself atop the vegetation to swing my legs and hips over, it was nothing to eliminate them with a covert clap of my hands. Neither husband nor wife rose, though the wife shifted her (very shapely) legs to prop her feet on the same chair as her husband's, making room for me. I sat and we made our introductions—he was Signor Reginaudo ("Call me Ugo")—and soon I was enjoying a cool Campari with ice and a slice of lemon.

How long was it before I began itching? Minutes? Perhaps even seconds? Both the Reginaudos let out a little laugh. "Here," Sylvana said, a flirtatious lilt to her voice, "put your feet up beside mine—"

It was then that I noticed that the legs of the chairs—and the table as well—were anchored in old pomodoro cans filled with what I presumed to be water, and it was my turn to laugh. "The ants," I said, and suddenly we were all laughing, a long riotous laugh shot through with strains of relief, frustration and commonality, a laugh of friendship and maybe desperation too. Nodding his head and giggling till he had to steady himself with a deep draught of his Campari and a hyperactive pounding of his breastbone, Ugo repeated the noun, the plural noun, as if it were the most hilarious term in the language.

This was succeeded by an awkward pause, during which I

became aware of the violin again and we simultaneously sipped our drinks, trying not to look too closely at the stems, leaves, fronds and petals that surrounded us as if in some miniature Eden for fear of spoiling the illusion. Every blade of grass, every stone, every object in that yard was animated by a dark roiling presence as if the earth itself had come to life. Sylvana gave me a look caught midway between mortification and merriment and I heard myself say, "We have ants next door too," and then the three of us were howling with laughter all over again.

"This is a fact of life here in Il Nido," Ugo began, once he'd recovered himself (again, with a gulp from his glass and a rapid thrust of one fist to his breastbone), "but we've devised ways of dealing with it."

I lifted my eyebrows even as Sylvana shifted her feet so that her sun-warmed toes came into contact with mine and rested languidly there.

"Hydramethylnon," he pronounced, giving me a tight grin. "That's the ticket."

A frown of irritation settled between his wife's eyebrows. "Nonsense. Sulfluramid's the only way to go."

Ugo shrugged, as if to concede the point. "Azadirachtin, pyrethrum, spinosad, methoprene, take your pick. They're all effective—"

"At first," Sylvana corrected.

Another shrug. He held out his palms in a gesture of helplessness. "They adapt," he said.

"But we stay one step ahead of them," Sylvana said. "Isn't that right, darling?" Her tone was bitter, accusatory. "One step ahead?"

Ugo pushed himself impatiently up out of the chair, his fair skin showing a pink effusion of sunburn across the shoulders and into the meat of his arms. "What is this, a debating society?" he demanded. "Come, friend, follow me out to the shed and I'll give you a good healthy sample of them all—and you can decide for yourself which is best."

I was on my feet now too, gazing down on the gap between Sylvana's breasts and the long naked flow of her abdomen, which, I have to admit, stirred me in spite of myself.

"Come," Ugo repeated. "I'll show you what I've got."

"But what about the baby?" I gazed from him to Sylvana and back again even as I felt the itch start up in my feet and ankles. "He gets into everything. Worse: everything goes in his mouth."

"That's a baby for you," Ugo said. "But this stuff's harmless, really. Even if he—is it a he or she?"

"He."

"Even if he somehow gets into it, it won't do him any harm—"

"Ha!" the wife exclaimed, stretching her legs so that I could see the muscles of her inner thighs flex all the way up to the tiny patch of cloth that covered the mound where they intersected. "And it won't harm the ants either. Least of all the ants."

Though I felt a bit tipsy from the effects of the alcohol on an empty stomach, I had no problem vaulting the hedge with two large shopping bags full of various cans of insect powder Ugo had insisted I take, including one labeled "Ant-Away" and another called "Anti-Ant." When I entered the house to tell my wife what I'd discovered, I saw that both she and the baby were asleep, Anina stretched out diagonally across the bed and the baby tucked in beside her, and perhaps because I wasn't exercising the soberest of judgment, I spread a healthy dose of Anti-Ant along the base of the outside walls, and, for good measure, dumped a can of Ant-Away (active ingredient malathion, whatever that was) atop it. I didn't see any ants in the house and I suppose I didn't really look all that hard for fear of what I'd uncover, but instead made my way back down the hill to the grocery.

This was an old-fashioned grocery, dimly lit, kept cool by the thickness of its ancient walls and smelling strongly of the meats and cheeses in the refrigerated cases—provolone, with its potent smoky aroma, above all else. It was a pleasant smell, and as I carried my basket through the deserted aisles and made my selections, I began to feel at home, as if everything were going to work out as planned and the solution to all our problems was at hand. I selected the wine, found milk and butter in the cooler and a dry salami hanging from its string in the front window, added bread, cheese, olives, artichoke hearts. Once I'd concluded my business, I carried my basket up to the checkout counter, behind which waited a solitary woman in a stained white apron. We exchanged greetings, and as the woman rang up my purchases I couldn't help inquiring if she knew of a reliable product for ant control. At first I thought she hadn't heard me, but then she lifted her eyes to mine before dropping them again. "Signore," she said, her voice no more than a whisper, "here we don't talk of such things."

"Don't talk of such things?" I repeated incredulously. "What do you mean? I see that you carry several ant powders, including Anti-Ant, and I just wanted to ask if you find it effective. If it's the best product, that is. And safe. Is it safe?"

She just shook her head, refusing to look up from the counter as she wrapped my things, then shifted her eyes furtively to my left and I saw that we were not alone. A man stood there beside me, not young, not old, wearing some sort of official uniform—matching trousers and shirt, which bore an insignia patch on one shoulder. He wore his hair long and slicked it back beneath an undersized cap in the same hue as his clothing and he was giving me a quizzical smile. "And you are——?" he asked, his voice a kind of rumble that rose on the interrogative.

I introduced myself and we shook hands.

"Ah, of course," he said. "I should have known—you're the new tenant of the Mauro place, am I correct?"

"Yes," I said, "we just moved in—today, in fact. And I was just, well"—I shrugged by way of adducing the age-old relation between the sexes—"my wife sent me down here to the grocery to pick up a few things. For our first meal in the new house." I shrugged again, as if to say, *You know how it is.*

"I'll be there first thing in the morning," he said. "Would six be too early?"

I gave him a look of bewilderment. "I'm sorry," I said. "And who are you, exactly?"

He straightened up then and perhaps I was imagining it but his heels seemed to click as if ready for action. "Forgive me," he said, digging a card out of his shirt pocket and handing it to me. "Aldo Baudino," he said with a bow. "Of the Argentine Ant Control Corporation."

I wanted to question him further—*Ant Control? Six a.m.?*— but the woman behind the counter was shaking her head and jerking her eyes toward the door, trying to warn me off, trying to tell me something, but what? I thanked her, paid, bade them both farewell and went out the door sans further comment.

Arriving at home, just as I swung open the gate and started up the path, I was startled by a shriek that all but stopped my heart. I dropped my packages and broke into a run. At that moment the door flung back and Anina came down the steps with the baby clutched to her and I saw in an instant what had happened: the baby was dusted all over with the ant powder and there was a greenish crust of it round his mouth where he must have crawled across the floor to ingest it. "The doctor!" Anina cried. "We have to get him to the doctor!"

My heart was pounding and I felt nothing but guilt and horror: How could I have been so stupid? What were ants, a plague of ants, every ant in the world, compared to this? But where was the doctor and how would we find him? We didn't have a phone—or we did, but it hadn't been connected yet—and the only thing I could think of was the Reginaudos. They would know. Without a word—and here Anina must have thought I'd lost my mind—I veered right and sprang over the hedge into their yard, expecting to find them still seated at the table with their feet up, sipping Campari. They weren't there. Ants boiled up around my feet and I saw then that a whole swift roiling river of them was heading for our house, as if the powder had attracted rather than repelled them. Anina shrieked again. And then I was pounding on the Reginaudos' door, peering through the glass and shouting for help.

A moment later, Ugo appeared, looking annoyed—or perplexed, perhaps that's a better word. "Yes?" he said, pulling back the upper half of the Dutch door to his kitchen. "What is it, what's all the commotion?"

"The baby!" I could barely get the words out—and now, even as I noticed that Ugo was wearing a pair of rubber galoshes and that the concrete floor of the kitchen seemed to be glazed with half an inch or more of water, Anina was there beside me, jabbering excitedly and holding the baby out in evidence.

That was the tableau we presented, the four of us—and the ants, of course. The baby, for his part, seemed calm enough, grinning a broad greenish grin and clinging to his agitated mother as if nothing were amiss, as if ant poison were no more a concern than lime Jell-O and every bit as irresistible. Ugo waved a dismissive hand. "I see he's been into the Ant-Away," he said. "But not to worry, it's nothing. No more harmful than sugar and water."

My wife just stared at him, her eyes—her beautiful olive eyes—so swollen they looked as if they would burst. "What do you mean, it's nothing? Can't you see? He's eaten ant poison!"

And here came Sylvana, still in her skimpy two-piece, sloshing barefoot across the floor. "I told you," she called out, "—it's harmless."

But my wife wouldn't be assuaged—and nor would I, though I was trying to make sense of this. Why would anyone market an ant powder that was harmless, unless it was harmless only to humans and fatal to the insects? But if that was the case, then why were there so many of them?

Finally, leaning over the frame of the door even as a single column of ants worked its way down along the wall to join the phalanx heading for our house, Sylvana said she'd call the doctor if we really insisted. "But he'll do nothing, believe me. He's seen it before, a hundred times. You want my advice? Give the kid a tablespoon or two of olive oil and let him bring it up."

"No," my wife said, shaking her head emphatically, and I realized, absurdly, that she hadn't even been introduced yet. "The doctor."

Both the Reginaudos exchanged a look and shrugged, and then Ugo sloshed across the kitchen to where the phone hung from the wall. I turned to my wife, ignoring the boots and the soaked floor and what they implied. "Anina," I said, "this is our neighbor, Sylvana. Sylvana, my wife, Anina."

The baby grinned and stuck a green finger in his mouth.

"Pleased to meet you," Sylvana said, extending her hand.

The doctor came on foot, toting his bag up from the village below. He was a jaunty, bowlegged man of indeterminate age, though I figured him to be twice as old as I, if not more. "Ah, you must be the new people," he exclaimed, pushing through the front gate as I came up the path to meet him, followed by an anxious Anina clutching the baby in her arms. "And this," he said, slipping a pair of reading glasses over the bridge of his nose and bending to the baby, "must be the patient." He held out his arms and Anina handed the baby over. The doctor hefted him, then clucked his tongue in the way of doctors everywhere—even specialists—and stated the obvious: "I see he's been into the Ant-Away, eh?"

This was the signal for Anina to pour out her concerns to him, beginning with the story of awakening to find that the baby had crawled down from the bed and somehow managed to push open the screen door that someone had carelessly left ajar (and here she shot me a look), then segueing into the medical issues we'd had with the child over the past six months and ending with a long unnecessary coda about our trip down from the north and our surprise—shock, really—over finding the house infested with ants.

The doctor wasn't really listening. He was shuffling his feet and whirling about with the baby thrust high in his arms, cooing baby talk, as our son, giddy with the attention, peeled back his lips in a wide green smile and cried out his joy. It was then that I realized that all three of us were unconsciously shuffling about—motion the only thing to discourage the ants underfoot—and I found myself giving in to impatience. "But the baby," I said, trying to get the doctor's attention as he cooed and spun, "—is he all right?"

"Oh, he's fine," the doctor assured me, handing the baby back to Anina. "A little malathion never hurt anybody." The birds were settling into the trees by this time and the sun sat low in the sky. My stomach rumbled. It had been a long day and still we hadn't eaten. "And you, little mother," the doctor said, focusing on Anina now, "feed him nothing but pastina for a day or two and examine his diaper carefully. If the result is in any way greenish, you must bring him to my offices; if not, forget the whole business and feel blessed because there isn't a thing in the world wrong with this little fellow." And here he leaned in to mug for the baby. "Isn't that right, Tiger?"

"But aren't you going to examine him?" My wife, usually so reserved with strangers, was in a state, I could see that. She'd practically attacked the Reginaudos and now here she was making demands of the doctor—and this was only our first day in town.

Shifting from foot to foot in a kind of autonomous tarantella, the doctor just grinned. "No need," he assured her, "no need at all," and already he was swinging round to go. "Just remember," he called over his shoulder, "pastina and a close scrutiny of the diapers."

Furious and muttering to herself—I distinctly heard her spit out the term *quack*—Anina spun round and stamped back up the path and into the house, murdering ants all the way, while I followed the doctor to the gate to see him out. "What about your fee?" I asked, pulling open the gate for him.

He seemed to shiver all over and he brusquely swiped one pantleg against the other. "No need to worry about it now," he said, grinning and twitching as the sinking sun made a lantern of his deeply fissured face, "I'll send a bill tomorrow." He held out his hand and I took it. "*Specialists,*" he pronounced, and for an instant I thought he was going to spit in the dirt, but he merely squeezed my hand, swung his bony shoulders round, and headed back down the track to the village below.

It was then, just as I plucked the paper bags of groceries up off the ground, almost idly brushing the ants from them and thinking of dinner and a glass of wine—some surcease to all the turmoil of the day—that I heard a "Pssst-pssst" from the hedgerow that divided our southerly neighbor's property from ours and turned to see a man beckoning to me from the shadows there. He was squat, big-bellied, with an enormous head and eyes that seemed to absorb all the remaining light till they glowed like headlamps.

He was known only as "the Captain," he was a foreigner, from Mexico, and he'd formerly been enforcer for one of the narcotics gangs until he was shot three times in the abdomen and his wife, who'd been sitting beside him in their convertible where they were stopped at a red light, was killed by yet another bullet meant for him. Now he was retired and—according to the Reginaudos, who'd filled me in on the details and warned me against him (they called him an extremist)—he didn't get out much. Which, I suppose, was only understandable.

I crossed to the hedge and offered him a *"Buona sera,"* but he didn't return the greeting or bother with introductions. He merely said, "The Reginaudos? Don't trust them. She's a slut—and come to think of it, so is he. All they do is throw down their powders and lie around screwing all day."

I lifted my eyebrows, though I wasn't sure if he could read my expression in the fading light. I wasn't especially happy—I didn't want to hear criticism of my neighbors or get caught up in pitting one against the other, and the ants, naturally, had begun to discover me standing there with the bags of groceries in hand—but I was polite, polite to a fault. Or so Anina claimed.

"You want to know how to deal with this scourge? Huh? I mean, *really* deal with it, the final solution and none of this pussy-footing? Here, step over the hedge and I'll show you."

The Captain didn't use powders or sprays. He used traps of his own devising. Baited wires suspended over coffee cans filled with gasoline, into which the ants, in their frenzy, would drop singly and sometimes by the dozen, as well as electrical connections timed to give a fierce jolt to a rotting fish head or scrap of stinking meat every thirty seconds. For the next half hour, though I wanted only to go home, sit down to dinner and devise some sort of plan to keep my own ants out of the bedroom for the course of a single night, this night when I was so exhausted I could barely make sense of what the Captain was saying in his vertiginous accent, I patiently followed him around and forced myself to make little noises of approbation over one device or another.

"This is the Argentine ant," he said at one point, "and I

don't know if you quite comprehend what that means. They are invaders"—and here he paused to give me a sharkish grin—"like me. But they're from the true south, in the Americas, in the jungle where you have to fight without quarter every minute of every day even to have a prayer of staying alive. They've out-competed the native ants everywhere they wash up, destroyed them, devoured them. You know what these ants are like?"

I shook my head.

"Like the cells of your body, each ant a single cell and all working in concert, one thing, one living organism, and the queen is the brain. My plan is to starve her by taking her workers away from her in the way you cut up a corpse, piece by piece." There was a silence broken only by the snap of electricity and the faint hiss of ants dropping into cans of gasoline. "Here," he said, and he gestured toward one of his suspension traps, "take as many of these as you like—it's your only hope."

In the morning, at first light, after having spent an all-but-sleepless night at war with the ants (resorting finally to encircling the bed with a frangible wall of green powder, despite any fears for the baby), I was awakened by a noise in the garden. I arose, pulled on my slippers and went to investigate, crushing ants underfoot all the way across the bedroom, through the kitchen and out the back door. I saw a figure there, bent to the wall of the house, and though my mind wasn't as clear as I would have liked, it took only a moment to identify him—the undersized cap, the slicked-back hair, the shoulder patch—as the Ant Man, come as promised. Or threatened, if you prefer. "Good morning," I said, irritated and relieved at the same time—here was intrusion, here was hope.

He didn't look up. "You have a problem," he said. His voice rumbled like a tremor in the earth.

"A problem?" I said, throwing it back at him. "Isn't that stating the obvious? Don't we all, as you say, *have a problem*? My question is, what are you going to do about it?"

Down on one knee now, working the dirt with a trowel, he glanced over his shoulder and gave me a sardonic smile, as if to concede the point. "My intention," he said, speaking slowly, his voice a rolling fervent peal, "is to eliminate that problem. Come. Look here."

I bent closer.

"You see this?" I saw now that he had set a clay saucer in the depression he'd made in the soil where it came into contact with the wall of the house. There was something in the depths of the saucer, a thick amber substance that glistened in the early-morning light as if it were a precious gift. "This is my special formula—honey, yes, but laced with an insecticide so fast-acting and fatal that you'll be ant-free here within the week. I guarantee it."

"But what of the baby?" I said. "Won't the baby—?"

He made a small noise in the back of his throat. "This is for ants, not babies," he said. "If you're so anxious, why not keep the infant inside—you can do that, can't you? Don't you think it's worth the effort, considering the alternative? Wake up. This is the planet Earth we live on—and it has its terms and conditions like anything else."

"Yes, but—"

"Yes, *nothing*. Just do as I say. And these traps the Captain has given you"—he made a rude gesture toward the traps I'd set up in the garden the night before—"don't you think gasoline is fatal to babies too? Eh? Or don't you think at all?" And now he rose, giving me a hostile look. "Amateurs," he said, jerking his chin first toward the Captain's house, then the Reginaudos'. "Do you really suppose that eliminating a few thousand workers will have any effect at all? No, you have to get the queen, you have to entice the workers to bring her this incomparable bait, to feed it to her and worry over her as she withers and desiccates and the whole stinking horde goes caput. You're a mathematician, aren't you? Or so I've heard—"

I nodded.

He held me with his acerbic eyes, then nodded back, as if we were in agreement. "Do the math," he said, and then he bent to set the next saucer in the ground.

A week went by. Several times during that week, and at the oddest hours—dawn, midnight—Signor Baudino appeared to refill his saucers, a secretive figure who became almost as much of an annoyance as the ants themselves, which, despite his promise, seemed even more abundant than ever. We slept little, though I finally resorted to setting the four posts of the bed in their own pomodoro cans of water, and that gave us a measure of relief, though Anina and I tossed and turned, dreaming inevitably that the swarms had overtaken us and gnawed us right down to our meatless bones. For the baby, even his waking hours were a kind of nightmare, the ants attacking him the moment we released him from his cradle, and when I look back on that period I have a vision of him itching himself, his former condition complicated now by a melding of the imaginary and the actual so that he could never be sure what he was feeling, just that it was a perpetual harrying of the flesh, and I felt powerless to console him. I see Anina too, growing more sullen and combative by the day and blaming me for all our problems, as if I had any control over this plague in our midst. The Reginaudos stopped by to offer advice and yet more powders and sprays, and the Captain, unbidden, twice slipped into the yard to set up his gasoline traps. For my part, I felt as harried as my wife and infant, trying gamely to pursue my work at a desk set in cans of water and scratching my equations across a page only to see them devolve into streams of ants that were as insubstantial as the ones crawling through my dreams.

On the seventh day, a Monday, Anina came to me at my desk, the baby clasped in her arms. "This is fraud," she informed me, her voice rigidly controlled but right at the breaking point.

I glanced up, noticing a thoroughfare of ants descending the wall before me—or no, they were ascending. Or no, descending. Descending and ascending both. I'd been lost in concentration, in another world altogether, and now I was back in the world of existence. "What is?"

"The contract. The old lady." And here she spat out Signora Mauro's name as if it were a ball of phlegm. "She never once mentioned the ants—and the ants negate that contract, which was made under false pretenses, fraudulent pretenses. This isn't paradise, it's hell, and you know it!"

I was being berated and I hardly deserved it or needed it either. I was going to throw it back at her, going to say *Can't you see I'm working?* but in that moment the truth of it hit me. She was right. We'd come to the end of pretense. "Get your handbag," I said.

She just glared at me. The baby twisted his mouth and began to cry.

"We're going down to the village to see Signora Mauro. And demand an explanation."

The landlady's house, which we'd scarcely noticed the day we stepped off the bus, was a long low meandering structure with an intricate web of iron grillwork out front that must have dated from the Renaissance. It was situated in the better part of town, surrounded by imposing villas, the vegetation lush, the air so fresh it might have been newly created. My wife threw back the gate and marched up the walk to the front door, where she jabbed at the bell with a vengeful thrust of her finger. A moment passed, the two of us framed there beneath a trellis shaped like an ascending angel, the baby for once quiet in my wife's arms. Anina drew in an angry breath, then depressed the doorbell again, this time leaving her finger in place so that the bell buzzed continuously. Finally, the heavy oaken door eased open just a crack and a maid the size of a schoolgirl stood just behind it, gaping up at us. "We've come to see the signora," I said.

The maid's face was like a wedge cut from a wheel of fontina. Her eyes were two fermented holes. "The signora is not at home to visitors today," she said.

"Oh, but she *is*," my wife countered, forcing the door open and striding into the foyer as I followed in her wake.

We found ourselves in a dark echoing space, the only light a series of faint rectangles that represented the margins of the drawn shades. Furniture loomed in the darkness. There was a smell of dust and disuse. To this point, I'd been swept up in my wife's fervor, but now, standing there in the gloom of a stranger's house—a house we'd forced ourselves into, uninvited—I began to have second thoughts. But not Anina. She raised her voice and called out, "Signora! Signora Mauro! We've come to see you—we *demand* to see you. Right this moment!"

There was a stirring at the far corner of the room, as if the shadows were reconstituting themselves, and then a match flared, a candle was lit, and Signora Mauro, in a widow's colorless dress, was standing before us. "Who are you?" she demanded, squinting through the glare of the candle.

"We've come about the lease," I said.

"It's a fraud," Anina added, her voice rising. "The conditions," she began, and couldn't go on.

"Vermin," I said. "It's infested with vermin and you never said a word about it."

Signora Mauro's voice was the voice of a liar and it came to us in a frequency that wasn't much more than a liar's rasp: "I know nothing about it."

"Ants," my wife put in. "The ants." At the mention of his

nemesis, though he could hardly have been expected to know the term, the baby began to squirm and gargle.

"You've got to keep things clean," Signora Mauro said. "What do you expect, with your filthy ways? I've got a mind to double your rent for abusing my property. And don't think I haven't had reports—" Even as she spoke I could see that she was twitching in some way, furtively scratching, rubbing one leg against the other, flicking a hand across her hips and abdomen.

I threw it back at her. "What about you? What makes you impervious?"

"Me? I don't have pests here. I keep a clean house. Scrupulously clean." Again she twitched, though she tried to suppress it.

"But you do," I said. "I know you do."

"I don't."

"We want out of this contract," Anina said. "We demand it."

The signora was silent a moment. I could hear her drawing and releasing her harsh ragged breath. "Demand all you like, but I'll take you to court—and you'll never see a penny of your deposit, I guarantee it."

"No, we'll take *you* to court," I said, surprising myself by taking a step forward—what was I going to do, attack her? Even as I said it, I knew I was bluffing. She had the power, she had the position, she had our first and last months' rent and absent the house on the bluff we wouldn't even have a roof over our heads.

"Go ahead," she said, her voice jumping an octave as she squirmed in her clothes and stamped her feet on the carpet that must suddenly have come alive there in the dark. "I'd like to see that. I really would."

In the next moment, Anina, my sweet Anina, transformed now in her rage and grief beyond all recognition, shoved me roughly aside, stormed out the door and slammed the iron gate behind her so furiously the entire house seemed to shake. I was left there in the gloom to make an awkward bow and bid the old woman a good afternoon before awkwardly hurrying after my wife. When I reached the street, I jerked my head right and left, in a panic over what she might do next—I'd never seen her like this, violence erupting from her like a lava flow, and I was afraid for her and the baby too. The street was busy enough, pedestrians and vehicles alike making their way from one end to the other, and at first I couldn't find her in that shifting chaotic scene, but finally I made out the unmistakable rotating motion of her hips as she veered left down a side street at the end of the block. I ran to catch up.

By the time I turned into that block, she was already at the next, swinging right now, descending toward the section of town where the fishermen lived in their ancient stone houses amidst a petrol station and a few tumbledown canneries that once pro-cessed the sardines that had become rarer and rarer over the course of the years. "Anina, what are you doing?" I called, but she ignored me, her shoulders dipping over the burden of the baby in her arms, her legs in their faded blue jeans beat-ing double-time along the walk. Then I was beside her, plead-ing with her—"Let's go home and talk this over, there's got to be a solution, calm yourself, please, if not for me, then for the baby"—but she just kept on going, her mouth a tight unyielding slash in a jaw clenched with rage.

We went down another street, then another, until finally I saw where she was headed—a warehouse just a block from the sea, a place of concrete block and corrugated iron that had seen better days. As I followed her up the walk to the front door, still pleading, I spotted the hand-lettered sign over the lintel—*The Argentine Ant Control Corporation*—and at the same time became aware of the smell. And the ants. The smell was of rot, of the spoiled fish heads and lumps of offal the Captain might have used for bait, and the ants were swarming over the walls in such legions they must have been six inches deep. Anina tried the front door—locked—and then began pounding on the metal panels, dislodging ants in great peeling strips like skin. "Come out of there, you son of a bitch!" she shouted. "I know you're in there!"

I snatched at her arm, shook her, and now the baby had gotten into the act, bellowing till he was red in the face. "What are you doing?" I demanded.

There were tears in her eyes. The baby howled. "It's true what they say, don't you see? He claims to be doing a governmental service, this Ant Man, but in fact he's breeding them. Don't you get it?"

"No," I said, "frankly, I don't. Why would he do a thing like that?"

She gave me a look of contempt and pity, a look for the fool blind to the realities of life. "If the ants are eliminated, so is his job. It's as clear as day. He's not baiting the insects, he's *feeding* them!"

Of course, that couldn't be. I saw that distinctly. And I saw that through no fault of our own we'd been distracted from our path in life, that we'd become disoriented and at odds with each other. And all for what? For *ants*? I still held on to her, my grip firm at her elbow, and even as the idea came into my head I swung her around, the baby still mewling, and began guiding her down the street to where the sea crashed rhythmically against the shore. We made our way amongst the rocks to the pale bleached sand of the beach and I just held her for a long moment, the baby calming around the deceleration of his miniature heartbeat, the sun a blessing on our upturned faces.

In that moment, the solution to Hodge's conjecture came to me, or the hint of a solution that would require pencil and paper, of course, but the intuition was there, a sudden flashing spark in my brain that made everything come clear. It was an abstraction, yes, but math was the purest thing I knew, a matter of logic, of progression, of control. The ants were nothing in the face of this. We could learn to live with them. We *would*. I took a deep breath and looked out to sea, Anina and the baby pressed to me as the surf broke and receded and broke again. Here was a gathering force that predated everything that moved on this earth, the waves beating at the shore until even the solidest stone was reduced to grains, each a fraction of the size of an ant and each lying there inert on the seabed, stretching on, clean and austere, to infinity.

SURTSEY

All he could think about was bailing, one bucket after the other, as if the house he'd lived in all his life was a boat out on the open sea. The front door was sandbagged, inside and out, but the waves kept rolling across the yard, already as high as the seat on the swingset he used to play on as a kid, and there was no stopping them. The ridiculous thing was, where was he supposed to put the water? He just opened the window and flung it out, but since the whole yard was the lagoon now it would have taken the sorcerer's apprentice—or no, the sorcerer himself—to put an end to it. Every bucket he tossed was one more bucket leaking in around the doorframe. His father had the mop, really going crazy with it, and his sister, Corinne, was bailing too, but they had the same problem he did, just dumping the water out the window as if the window was on top of a mountain somewhere, and the wind blowing half of it back in again anyway. As for his mother, she did what she did anytime they had a crisis, like when the stovepipe overheated and burned a hole in the roof so for two weeks it was as cold inside as it was outdoors or when his father had an accident on his ATV and broke his collarbone in two places: she just got in bed with one of her books and started reading.

That was where she was when the storm surge hit, and though the house was four feet up off the ground on pilings, that wasn't really going to help all that much because this was a storm surge riding in on a supertide, the sun and moon in alignment on the autumn equinox and the bad luck of a major storm on top of it. A.J. didn't like seeing her there in the bed with the water already rippling across the floorboards in little wavelets and the bedposts dark with wet, but that was her way—what was going to happen was going to happen and there wasn't anything anybody could do about it. Try arguing with her. Try telling her they needed to bail and mop and save what they could, stack the best things on top of the not-so-good things and the not-so-good things on top of the throwaway things, make do until they had no choice but to go over to the school, which sat on the highest ground of the island—all of eight feet above sea level, but that was better than where they were—and she would just say, We'll go when we go, and, What do I look like, Noah?

He tried hard, he did. Everybody knew what was coming because this wasn't the first time and the science teacher at school, Mr. Adams, took them through the global warming thing like it was the Bible or something, nobody arguing about it now, the shore ice that used to protect the island forming later in the season and melting earlier, ocean levels rising all around the world, carbon dioxide building up in the atmosphere, the loss of the albedo effect with the loss of the ice and all the rest. When they'd seen the eclipse the night before, that was the giveaway, the sun and moon on the same line and pulling together, tug of war against the earth, and he put his best clothes in a knapsack along with his video games and his basketball trophy and got ready to evacuate to the school. His father—he was a genius, he really was—got the idea of anchoring hooks in the ceiling beams so they could pulley his and Corinne's beds up off the floor by a couple of feet and so they did that, but their parents' bed was too heavy so they just put cement blocks under the bedposts and hoped for the best. And yes, he was hopeful, of course he was, sixteen years old and full of his own strength, thinking if they just kept at it everything would be all right—they could live with an inch or two in the house, no problem, and the storm would stop and the water recede, like always—but this was different, this was the supertide, and there was his mother, wrapped up in bed, her eyes tracking across the page while the edge of the one blanket, the one that was slipping off the end and she didn't even seem to notice, was turning dark where it was soaking up water like a sponge, and he didn't know what to do except keep on bailing.

By the time they finally gave up and made for the school, most people were already there, and the only way they could get to it at that point was in the boat, which wouldn't start, so his father had to row and his mother sat in back, in the stern, but she was so heavy it was like a seesaw up front, where he and Corinne were trying to balance out the weight. His mother was the heaviest woman on the island, fat actually, obese, though he didn't like to think of her like that or use that term either. She always said she was big-boned, that was all, and laughed when she said it. Still, no matter what you wanted to call her—and the kids at school never stopped ragging him about it, as if any of them were any better or their mothers either—just getting her into the boat was a trick, the water at the level of the front porch now and bubbling up through the floorboards and the waves beating at the windows and sending jets of foam right up to the roof, but Corinne helped her put on her boots and her rain slicker and the two of them got her down the hallway to the porch while his father held the boat as steady as he could. Himself, he could

have walked, the water up to his waist and the wind screaming and flapping the hood of his parka, no problem, the school
only five blocks away at the end of town, but his father needed
him there in the boat to help balance out the weight. They didn't
bring much with them because they didn't think they'd be gone
more than maybe overnight, just a couple black garbage bags of
emergency things, flashlights, sleeping bags, cereal, underwear
and socks, his mother's nightgowns that were like army tents in
the movies and an armload of her books too. The house, if it
didn't get wrecked, would stink till summer with that rot smell,
and the thought of that depressed him—he really didn't want to
go anywhere, least of all back to school, but when they finally did
make it up the flooded steps and through the front door, everybody was there and it felt like a holiday.

The first thing, the first order of business, as Mr. Adams would
say after he got done checking the roll each morning, was to get
his mother out of her wet clothes and into something warm, blankets, spare blankets, and did anybody have any spare blankets?
The problem was, just when they'd got the boat there on the beach
that just yesterday afternoon was the playground, and his mother,
with him on one side and Corinne on the other, stepped out of
the boat, a wave came shooting in and the thing surged forward
and took her legs out from under her and she went down hard.
It wasn't that cold, low forties maybe, but the water was always
freezing and even if you were used to it (and she wasn't) you didn't
want to be sitting in it up to your neck. In a storm. With sixty mph
gusts riding in across the Chukchi probably all the way from Si-
beria. That wasn't fun for anybody, and he was shivering himself,
pretty much wet to the crotch, and so once they got inside he'd
had to go around to everybody and see if they could borrow a
couple of blankets because theirs were wet, or damp anyway, and
the sleeping bags wouldn't fit her. And no, he wasn't one of these
kids who's ashamed of his parents, he was bigger than that, but still

people were making jokes and that would have got to him except the whole situation was so weird, like Christmas and a basketball game and the community monthly movie all rolled in one.

Corinne took their mother into the girls' room to help her out of the wet clothes and he and his father went down to the gymnasium, where people had already staked out the best spots and had their sleeping bags laid out and all their stuff scattered around them as if it had crashed through the ceiling, radios tuned to a whisper, a rustle of potato chip bags, crackers, whatever, and the men were all squatting in little groups, talking in low voices and drinking coffee out of stained mugs. And smoking. Everybody was smoking so it was like they were drying sheefish inside except the smell was totally different, not appetizing, not at all.

He didn't feel hungry, or not yet, though he must've burned through ten thousand calories with all that bailing and the rest of the frantic activity around the house, so he just made the rounds, not only in the gymnasium but the classrooms too, looking for his friends and wondering where Cherry was, if her family had even come here or if they were waiting it out at home—they had a two-story house, which meant they could all just go upstairs. Her father, Mr. Pollard, was one of the four white teachers at school, along with Mrs. Cato, Mr. Nordstrom and Miss Rumery, who taught the elementary school classes, and if he was pretty clueless about hunting and even fishing he was all science and math and maybe the single smartest person on the island, which meant that he was ahead of everybody else when it came to emergency preparation because everybody else was like his mother with all those generations of wait-and-see in their blood. So maybe Cherry wasn't there, that was what he was thinking, and he was depressed all over again. But then a wave came up and slapped the window of Mrs. Koonook's classroom, which was impossible, and the wind raised its voice till it was the only thing he could hear, and he knew she had to be there somewhere.

When he found her—Jimmy Norton said he thought he'd seen
her go into the library, and that was where she was, way in back,
though he'd already looked twice—she was sitting with his cousin
Charlotte Swan and the other A.J., the one that made his stomach
turn. The other A.J., first of all, didn't have a name that stood for
anything—it was just initials (he himself was Arthur James, after
his father). The second thing was that this A.J., who'd only been at
McQueen for six months, was black, African American, whatever
you wanted to call it, and not only did that make him special right
off as the only one in the whole Northwest Arctic Borough School
District, but it gave him instant basketball cred even though he
couldn't hit a three-pointer to save his life and his father was a
crazy man who'd come to the island to go native and kill beluga
and bowfin and caribou and live off the fat of the land, none of
which he did at all—he just lived off his army pension and drank
alcohol in his shack all day even though alcohol was banned in the
village. The third thing, the worst thing, was that this A.J. had a
crush on Cherry, or he was coming on to her anyway, and Cherry
was *his* girl. Period. And nobody was going to tell him different.

So he came up to them and made as if it was no big thing,
them sitting there together like that, and said Hi at just the very
instant the lights began to flicker. The other A.J. rolled his eyes
and waved a hand at the lights and said, All we need, and Cherry
said Hi and scooted over one chair and then, in a lower voice, We
saved a place for you.

Pretty crazy, huh? he said. I mean, last year was bad—but
you weren't here, were you? he said, looking the other A.J. dead
in the eye. Remember? They thought those HESCOs were going to hold and they wound up all smashed and scattered in like
the first hour?

This is worse, Cherry said.

Yeah, Charlotte put in, and was she wearing eye makeup?
She never wore eye makeup because her mother wouldn't let her,

and here she was wearing eye makeup on a night they might all
have to evacuate the island? They say it's a supertide, she said.

What's a hesco? the other A.J. asked, but everybody just ignored him.

They were a stupid idea in the first place, HESCOs, these
wire mesh things like supersized crab traps with a white fabric
lining and filled with dirt, as if that was going to withstand a sea
as angry as this. Now, at a cost, his father said, of over a million
dollars, they had a rock revetment built by the Army Corps of
Engineers, which the other A.J.'s father used to be a part of.

The lights went out then, a sudden switch from seeing to not
seeing, from three dimensions to none, and all they could hear
was the wind and the barking of the dogs, all the island's dogs,
out there cold and wet and mean-tempered, going at one another
in the black void beneath the building. He didn't say anything
more, though Charlotte let out a little scream and the other A.J.
said, Motherfucker, and then repeated himself, All we need, shit!
No, he just took Cherry's hand there in the dark, her hand he
knew as well as his own—better—from holding it through all
the never-ending days of sun and on into the dark tunnel of the
winter that was coming on day by darkening day, and then he
pulled her to him and put his lips to hers and felt her tongue in his
mouth and just stayed there like that, hard as a rock, till somebody started up the generator and the lights came back on and he
saw that Charlotte and the other A.J. were doing it too.

Food was not going to be a problem, even if they had to stay
longer than just the one night, and with a storm like this—a bliz-
zacane, Mr. Adams was calling it now, the rain predicted to turn
to sleet by midnight and then snow after that—it could be two
or three days, maybe even more. By the time people began to
realize it was too late to evacuate because the airstrip was un-

derwater and there was no way to get a boat across the mouth of the lagoon with waves cresting at twenty feet, the most amazing smell began seeping through the whole building from the direction of the cafeteria. The lights had come back on and Cherry had just pushed him away—you didn't make out with people watching, and especially not in school—when the smell hit him and he realized he was ravenous.

Smell that? He looked at Cherry and the other A.J. looked at him. You know what that is?

Stew? Cherry guessed, and she guessed right, because what else would it be?

My uncle Melvin, he said.

What, the other A.J. said, your uncle smells like stew now? Should be sweat. That's what he smells like to me.

Charlotte said, Hey, that's my dad you're talking about, but she said it with a laugh and he couldn't help wondering if she was going to start going around with the other A.J. now, the black A.J., and how his aunt was going to feel about that. Or Melvin. Though Melvin, as one of the village's best hunters, was out on the ice or away inland most of the time, getting meat, which he shared in the way of the old times and which was how he got the things he needed in return. Mr. Adams talked about that a lot, how the people were balanced on a razor's edge between the old ways and the consumer society of all the vast country strung out below them, the place where there were palm trees and Hollywood and New York City and alligators, which they only knew from satellite TV and the books and magazines in the library.

My uncle got a caribou yesterday morning—before the storm hit? There was a rumbling beneath the building, as if the whole thing was shifting under their feet. Nobody said anything for a long moment, the four of them just listening. Then he reached over and gave Charlotte a nudge. Isn't that right, Charlotte?

Charlotte nodded.

Okay, he said. Okay, right? That means caribou stew, and I don't know about you, but I'm going to go down there and get me some of it, like right now?

So they pushed themselves up from the library table with its scatter of books and the computer screens that were like poked-out eyes and went out the door, down the hall past the gymnasium and on into the cafeteria, where the bubbled-up smell of caribou stew was a hundred times stronger and made him feel almost dizzy with hunger. Everybody was there already, lined up outside the kitchen with bowls in their hands, and a couple of the women stood at the stove by the big shining pots of stew, ladling it out one person at a time. He picked up a tray and bowl and utensils and tried to ignore the screech of the wind and the way the waves shook the building—and the dogs, the dogs that were howling now, just howling, and he wondered whether they were all going to drown or get washed out to sea because the school barely had room for the people, and the dogs were going to have to fend for themselves.

What about your dogs? he said to Cherry, and they were like anybody else's dogs, sled dogs, though she only had three and nobody's dogs pulled sleds anymore, not when they all had snow machines and ATVs. Which were all going to be ruined if the water got any higher.

My mom put them in the house, like, upstairs in the hall?

Cherry's mother was blond, like her daughter, and she had a face like a three-quarters moon shining out over the ice, but she was all right really, and she fit in as well as anybody, even people who'd lived here their whole lives (which was about ninety-eight percent of everybody he knew).

The smell of the food was overpowering. He said, I hate this. You know what I'm going to do, like, when this is over?

Hate what?

I don't know, like, this, this storm. It used to be we would just stay inside till it blew itself out, but now we have to worry if the island's even going to be here when it's over. Plus the house stinks. Everybody's house stinks.

So what're you going to do about it? You heard Mr. Adams—this whole place'll be underwater in ten years. Cherry was wearing the white sweater her mother had knitted her, the one that clung to her across the chest and showed the outline of her bra straps in back. He could still taste her on his tongue.

I'm going to go to California, he said, and, I don't know, go surfing, pick coconuts all day.

Right, she said. And I'm going to Washington. I'm going to be president, didn't I tell you?

No, he said, really. I am. I am so out of here. This was a theme he'd been developing lately, trying it on for size, though they both knew he wasn't going anywhere. Her father had met her mother at college and they expected Cherry to go to college too and the whole idea of that—of her going away—just froze his heart like the ninth circle of hell Mr. Nordstrom told them about in English class, no devil breathing fire but a big frozen-over place just like this would be if the skies never grew light again and the ducks never came back and the winter went on forever.

He was going to say more, puff himself up, show her how cool he was, how dedicated to her, how worthy and true and not really desperate, not desperate at all, when Corinne came up to him, took hold of his arm and hissed, Mom needs you. Like, right *now*?

His father had found a place for them in the gym, but not up against the wall where you could at least have a little privacy—all those spots were gone—but out in the middle of the room, right where the key of one of the baskets was painted on the floor. The *Go, Qavviks!* banner from last weekend's three-day tournament with Kotzebue, in which they'd got killed and his

legs had felt so heavy he might as well have been playing underwater, was peeling away from the wall behind the backboard,
one long fold of brown construction paper drooping to the floor
like the tongue in the dead head of a whale. Everybody who
wasn't in the cafeteria was here except for some of the kids who
were out there in the halls doing whatever, and whether they'd
eaten yet or not he didn't know, not that it mattered—the stew
would last for days, just like the loaves and fishes in the Bible
story, plenty for everybody even if the storm went on for a week.

The thing that surprised him was seeing his mother lying
there on her back in a pile of blankets and black garbage bags of
clothes instead of sitting up cross-legged, which was her usual
pose. Was she going to bed already? It was only eight-fifteen.
And she was a book addict who'd stay up all night sometimes
when she really loved a story, so this wasn't what he'd expected.
That was when he saw the look on her face, all the color gone out
of her till she was as white as Cherry's mother, and that brought
him right to attention. What? he said. What is it, Ma—you sick?

She forgot her medicine, Corinne said, and she didn't look
scared the way she had the last time their mother'd had an attack
and went all pale like this—just pissed. Or exasperated, that was
a better word.

Where's Dad? He found himself staring into the face of Joe
Sage's mother, who was perched on her bear rug not three feet
away, but then Mrs. Sage, who never missed a thing, turned her
face away and pretended to watch somebody else.

He says he's not going back out there. Nobody is.

You mean for her medicine?

He says she's just going to have to tough it out.

That was when his mother's eyes opened up like two breathing holes in the ice and she whispered his name and he went down
on one knee and bent close to her. You all right, Ma? he asked.

Nothing. All he could hear was the soft murmur of the hundred conversations sifting round him—that and the wind. And the howling of the dogs down there beneath the floor that was just like the wind, only angrier.

Ma?

Her voice was weak and fluttery, caught deep in her throat. I need my medicine. The heart medicine?

What about your insulin? You have your insulin?

She shook her head against the bag she was using as a pillow. The black plastic rippled and glittered dully under the overhead lights. Go get it for me. You know where it is.

Corinne was hanging over his shoulder now with her big face and crooked teeth and her breath that smelled like seal oil. She said, You heard Dad. He says it's too dangerous.

He wants me to die, I guess. Is that what that means? And you—you want me to die too?

His sister said, No, no, Ma, it's not that, but he was already on his feet and picking his way across the gymnasium floor, dodging little kids and stepping over people's things. He didn't care what his father said or anybody else either—he was going out there and he was going to get in that boat or do anything, swim, whatever, because he wasn't going to let his mother suffer like that, not for one minute more.

The dogs were right there, right at the door, a whole pack of them fighting for purchase on the two wooden staircases that sloped down into the rising water. He pushed his way through the door and the wind snatched the breath out of his lungs. The rain was a presence, all-enveloping, and it wasn't rain anymore but ice, windborne pellets rattling against the side of the building like bird shot. Get down! he shouted at the dogs. Get! And they all nosed up to him, whirling and fighting and scratching at the door, and when he kicked them they snarled at him and that just set him off so he kicked harder until he was down the stairs and into the icy water that was up to his knees and rolling in with that crashing surf—the whole island, as far as he could see, just rolling and rolling. That scared him. If it was up to his knees here, what was it like at the house?

The school loomed above him, a big dark box with the waves disappearing under it. He saw right away the boat was no use. It was straining at its tether, pushed deep under the building along with everybody else's boats, and it was a miracle the rope hadn't snapped. He tried to pull it to him but it felt like it weighed a hundred tons and he realized the boat was tangled up with the other boats and maybe wrapped around one of the pilings, and even if he could get it out there would have been no way to row into this wind anyhow. What he did, and he was already wet through and shivering, was double-tie the knot, to make sure it was secure, then he hunched into the wind and started wading.

The buildings across the street helped because they broke the wind and the surge of the water and it came to him that the best thing to do was pull himself along the side of the near building and then the next one and the one after that. By the time he got to the Native Store, which was only halfway, the water was up to his chest, running at his face, and basically he was swimming now, but that wasn't any good because his parka was dragging him down and he took a lungful of water and before long he was just hanging there, clinging to the rail out front and coughing till he thought he was going to black out. And the cold—he was numb with it. Outsiders, like the other A.J., were always saying how his people didn't even seem to notice the cold because they were born to it, they were used to it, it was in their blood (*You got ice in your veins, man, but me, I'm African and I tell you I can't take this shit*), but that was only partly true. You get wet, you die, like Ray Kinik, who'd fallen through rotten ice last spring and never came back again.

So what was this? Hypothermia, that was what it was. And

if the water was rolling in here and the wind whipping it up, his own house must have been flooded right up to the top of the door frames and all their clothes and all their things and his mother's medicine flooded along with it. He was sixteen years old. He had a thing for Cherry—he loved Cherry, *loved* her—and Cherry was going away to college and he wasn't because he couldn't fool himself and he knew damn well he was going to end up working the Red Dog Mine digging zinc out of the ground like everybody else, and what was the sense of that? The cold gripped him. It lulled him. That was the way you died on the ice when a floe took you out to sea: you went to sleep. He was sixteen years old. He had a thing for Cherry. And he loved his mother and his father and Corinne too, and he wasn't going to be able to get back to the house and he wasn't going to die here on the washed-out steps of the Native Store either—he was going to turn around and go back to the school and get warm and drink black coffee and eat caribou stew, bowl after bowl of it, steaming hot, hot as the shower at the Washeteria when you turn it up full and don't use any cold, so what was he waiting for?

He pulled himself along, everything black-dark and the wind slapping his face the way women slap men in the old movies when the men get out of line and try to kiss them, and why he was thinking of movies when all the blood was going to his core and he couldn't feel his feet or his hands either he couldn't say. Maybe he was hallucinating like that time when Lucy Kiliguk had a marijuana blunt and shared it with him. He concentrated on keeping the water out of his mouth—and his legs, his legs that had to keep going, just like in the basketball tournament, only he was drowsy now and he was freezing and he couldn't have held on to a basketball if it was made out of solid gold. Then he came around the corner of Leonard Killbear's house and saw the lights of the school and the water let him go. All at once he was wading again, the wind shoving him forward like a pair of hands pressed to his shoulder blades, and when he reached the stairs and the dogs clawed at him and snarled and barked he just hoisted himself up by the railing and jerked open the door and went inside, back inside, and if one of the dogs bit the hell out of his numb right hand—a cross-eyed bitch that belonged to the Adamses—he didn't hardly even notice.

Long night, long, long night. Everybody made a fuss over him, people called him crazy for going out there, but they knew he had heart and they knew he'd done it for his mother, to try and help, to save her. His father chafed his limbs and helped him into dry clothes and he sat right by the furnace for the longest time and Mrs. Nashookluk, the school nurse, bandaged his hand. His mother was asleep on her back on the floor of the gymnasium, snoring the way she did, and when he looked down on her he had to smile because under any other conditions he would have been embarrassed for her, but not now. She's going to be okay, his father said. Just let her sleep. And his father chewed him out in front of everybody, but you could see it was just for show. Cherry came and sat with him for a while, but then it was one o'clock in the morning and her mother came to get her because it was time for everybody to settle down to bed and listen to the wind scream and the dogs howl and the waves crash against the windows of Mrs. Koonook's classroom until the next day broke and they could see if there was anything left out there except water.

He closed his eyes for a while, trying to sink down into sleep, but it was too strange with the whole village sprawled all around him and everybody snoring in their own key till it was like one of the atonal compositions Mrs. Cato made them listen to in Music Appreciation. It was hot, too hot, and if there was irony in that, he was way beyond it. His father was asleep beside his mother, spooning into her, their faces gone slack, and Corinne lay just beyond them, her cheek pressed to her pillow and her mouth squeezed like a fish's, softly snoring to her own rhythm. In the morning, first thing, no matter what, he was going to go get his mother her medicine because she would need it then more than ever and he was thinking about the times when she overslept and her blood sugar plummeted and she was like a crazy woman, fighting everybody with her eyes dilated and the veins standing up in her neck till they got some juice in her and she balanced out. The wind blew—kept on blowing. Somebody moaned in their sleep.

The gymnasium was the biggest room in the school, and most people had set up in here, but they were scattered around in the classrooms, the library and the cafeteria too. Cherry's family was camped in the library with maybe six or seven other families, including—and this got him—the other A.J. and his father. That was nothing intentional, just luck of the draw, but it rankled him anyway and that was another reason he couldn't sleep. Not that he was worried. The last thing she'd said to him, just as her mother came picking her way across the room to come fetch her, was, Two o'clock, okay? If you can stay awake that long. Think you can? For me?

He'd kissed her then, a public kiss, just a quick brushing of the lips, but he had an instant hard-on and he lifted his head to watch her all the way across the floor and out the door before he bent to set the alarm on his watch, because here was the deal: she was going to get up to go to the bathroom at two and so was he. Except they weren't going to go to the bathroom at all but cruise right past the doors marked "Girls" and "Boys" and on down to the end of the hall, where the janitor's closet was. If nobody was looking—and why would they be at two o'clock in the morning?—they were going to go in there and be together for as long as they could. The promise of that, of what she might let him do, kept everything else at a distance, because the house was wrecked, he knew that in his heart, and the island was doomed and Cherry was going away, but not now, not tonight, not when they had the janitor's closet all to themselves and nobody the wiser.

In his dream, the whole school and everybody in it was lifted off the pilings and swept up into the sky on the tractor beam of an alien spacecraft that hovered over him like a bird beating against the sun, and whether the aliens were going to put them down in Hawaii or Tahiti or even California, he never knew because his alarm was going with a soft *ping, ping, ping,* and his eyes flashed open on the darkened room and the shadows humped there like seals pulled out on the ice in the twilight. Cherry, he thought, and he was already pushing himself stealthily up, thinking of the last time—at her house—when they had half an hour before her mother came home from her card game and how they'd both got naked and she'd let him touch her everywhere.

The only illumination was from the emergency lights glowing red at both ends of the room, but it was enough to see by so he could avoid stepping on anybody, though that was a trick in itself because people slept in all sorts of bizarre positions and they moved in their sleep too. He was almost at the door when he lost his balance and came down square on somebody's stretched-out arm—one of the men, he couldn't see who it was—and there was a curse in the dark and he froze and whispered Sorry, and was going to add, Just going to the bathroom, but then there came a quick sharp snort of air that was like a gunshot and whoever it was was asleep again.

The hallway was as strange at this hour as if he was still in his dream, time frozen, nobody there, no kids, no teachers, no shouts and taunts and girls giggling and lockers slamming, but then the door to the boys' room opened and out came Jimmy Norton rubbing his eyes. A.J. murmured Hi, but Jimmy didn't say anything, dead on his feet. He waited till Jimmy brushed by him before he pulled open the door to the bathroom, but that was just for show, and he stood there, his heart beating fast, watching Jimmy out of sight, then eased the door shut and tiptoed the length of the hall to the janitor's closet.

She was already there. He opened the door and the faint light of the hall seeped in and there she was, in her white flannel nightgown that was like the ones his mother wore, only smaller, a whole lot smaller, and she said, Shhhhh. Come on. Come in. Shut the door.

He was confused—electrified, yes, so excited he was trembling, but there was no light in the closet and he'd forgotten to bring a flashlight or even matches. Or no, he hadn't forgotten—he'd never even thought of it.

But there's no light in there.

Shhhhh! Just shut the door!

Her eyes were red flecks that gave back the glow of the emergency light at the end of the hall. He couldn't see her face or her hair or anything else but her voice was right there front and center, impatient now—exasperated—and he realized she was as excited as he was. Which excited him all the more.

He did as he was told, the door pulling shut behind him with an audible click that was like a thunderclap, and then he had hold of her and they were kissing and he could feel her breasts flattening against his chest. Usually, when they were kissing, he had his eyes closed and it was like when he sang along with a song he liked, just feeling it, but now his eyes were open wide and he couldn't see a thing and it made him feel strange, as if he wasn't anyplace at all.

I want to see you, he said.

No.

Come on, just let me open the door a crack, I mean, an inch, just an inch, and he reached back for the knob but she took hold of his wrist and her grip was like iron because she was strong and beautiful and like nobody else on the island and he loved her, he really loved her more than anything. He could have thought of all the things they'd done together, a whole DVD of their life, of wrestling on the shore when they were kids, hiking to the end of the island and back, playing board games, video games, racing their ATVs on the airstrip, of their first kiss and the first time he told her he loved her, could have reminded her, but all he could say, there in the blackness, were two words he thought he'd never utter: I'm scared.

Scared? Of what—the dark?

No, he said, and faintly, beneath the floorboards, he could feel the slap and slash of the waves. Not the dark. Just, I don't know, *scared*.

Of me? She let out a laugh and now it was his turn to shush her. You didn't seem so scared at my house the other day.

He could feel her breath on his face. Don't be scared, she said, liking the word, liking the notion of it, and she moved into him and they kissed again, the deepest kiss, the warmth of her all there was in the world, but he broke away and said, Please? Just a crack?

In answer, she pulled the nightgown over her head—he could hear the soft whisper of the material letting go of her skin—and pressed herself to him. Feel me, she said, feel me here.

There was a smell of the janitor's things—bleach, floor wax—and when they went to lie down, using her nightgown and his shirt as protection against the cold of the floor, their limbs kept banging into things in the dark—brooms, he guessed. Mops, buckets. She had never let him go all the way with her and she wasn't going to do it this time, he knew it, and he didn't have a condom anyway, but her skin was on fire and so was his and he kissed her all over. He kept closing his eyes and opening them again, the whole universe spinning there in the dark with him, the flecks of light Mr. Adams called floaters strung out like constellations in a depthless black void. He came twice, both times on her belly, and she squeezed him so hard it was like he was back out there again in the crush of the water gasping for air.

He lay there awake after she fell asleep with her head pressed to his chest and her nightgown wrapped around them like a sheet. It took him the longest while to make out the faint sliver of light at the bottom of the door, which must have been there all along because it couldn't be morning yet, could it? Soon he would have to wake her so they could both sneak back before they were missed. But not yet. For now he just lay there, letting the night spin round him, his mother drifting there in his consciousness and the dogs too, the dogs that were quiet now so that the only sound was the keening of the wind and the hiss of the water running on and on, unstoppable, in the darkness beneath them.

He felt her breathe, in and out, rhythmically, and tried to time his own breathing to hers and that made him feel strong again, in control, no matter how dark it was or what came next. His mother was going to die and his house and the village and the school were all going to die too and Cherry was going away. The whole thing was too depressing and it would have brought him back down again, except that just then the image of Surtsey came into his head, Surtsey, the island that had risen up out of the sea fifty years ago off the coast of Iceland, in the other ocean, the Atlantic. He had to smile at the thought. Mr. Adams had done an entire lesson on it, on how the underwater volcano erupted and made this new place high above the waves, and how things had blown across the water—seed pods, insects, pollen—to make it alive, a whole new island, a whole new world. That was something, Surtsey, and maybe he would go there one day, he thought, maybe he would.

He shifted his arm ever so slightly and Cherry snuggled in closer. He listened to the wind, listened to the waves, and then he was asleep.

THEFT AND OTHER ISSUES

THE DOG

The dog was old, arthritic and fat, and she belonged to my live-in girlfriend, Leah, who'd had her for eight years before we met. The dog's name was Bidderbells (don't ask) and you couldn't really leave her at home for long stretches because of her tendency to chew up the cushions on the couch, or at least gum them, and then take a dump on the kitchen floor. So I had her with me the day I brought my laptop to the library to work in peace (they're renovating the building across the street from the apartment and the noise is multidimensional) and, of course, I couldn't park on the street because the sun would make a furnace of the car. I got lucky at the parking garage. Just as I took my ticket and the gate lifted I spotted an SUV backing out of a prime space on the left-hand side and I eased right in, feeling good about myself and the little unexpected rewards of life. I cracked the windows, gave the dog a rawhide bone to gum and walked down the ramp and out into the sunshine.

The library is one of my favorite buildings in town, a sandstone monument to culture and learning built in a time when people cared about such things. Of course, it's principally a repository of bums these days, men mostly, who crowd the armchairs and big oak tables with their oozing bags of possessions and idle away the hours bringing up porn sites on the computers, scribbling in their journals or snoozing with their heads thrown back and their mouths hanging open. Not that I'm complaining. They've got a right to live too and we've got a lot of bleeding hearts in this town (read: bum advocates) and though I'm not really one of them I guess you'd have to say I'm tolerant, at least.

At any rate, I worked for maybe an hour and a half, then packed up and headed back out into the sun for the stroll across the street to the parking structure. Was I thinking I was about to be violated? No. I was thinking nothing—or just, I suppose, that it was a nice day, it was time for lunch and the world was an equable place.

THE ABSENCE

The car wasn't there. I walked directly to the spot where I'd left it and found a motorcycle parked there instead. The motorcycle was a handsome thing, a chopper actually, with high handlebars and a dragon decal on the fuel tank, but it wasn't my car and I was at least ninety-nine percent sure that this was where I'd parked. Now I began to exercise my neck, looking up and down the row of parked vehicles, wondering if I was somehow mistaken, if my internal compass had confused this trip to the library with the last and that it was on the last visit I'd parked here and today elsewhere. Like up there at the top of the ramp. I started walking up the gradual incline, scanning the vehicles on both sides, and when I got to the point where the ramp gave on to the second floor of the garage, I went back down again, rechecking every spot. Still no car. So back up the ramp I went, turning the corner to Level 2, and I checked every space there as well before continuing on to ascend all the levels, including the sixth and top floor, which was outside in the glare of the sun and no possibility at all because I was certain I would never have parked there with the dog in the car, not on this day or any other.

I didn't really know how much time dribbled away in this wasted effort, this idiotic obsessive-compulsive tramping through the entire parking structure checking and rechecking the same cars over and over as if one of them would magically morph into mine. Half an hour? More? And wasn't this the definition of true idiocy, repeating the same behavior and expecting a different result? It was at this point that I realized the car must have been towed—and yet why I couldn't imagine, since this wasn't metered parking and the gate wouldn't have admitted me in the first place if I hadn't taken a ticket. Suddenly I was in a hurry, thinking of what this was going to cost me—and of the dog, of course, who at the very least would have been confused if not disturbed or even frightened by the clanking of the tow truck and the unnatural elevation of the car—and I was practically jogging as I descended through the levels and made my way back down to the exit. Here was a sharp curve and a narrow lane that led from the mouth of the parking structure to a kiosk and gate, and I found myself squeezed between the unforgiving concrete pillars on the one side and the autos backed up at the ticket kiosk, feeling awkward and vulnerable on foot in the domain of big-grid tires and steel.

The ticket taker was a high school kid in a hoodie who looked startled when I popped my head in the door. In his idle moments he'd been underlining passages in a creased paperback of *Crime and Punishment*, which lay on the scratched aluminum counter before him. I was beginning, deep in that place of flap and panic in the center of my chest, to see a theme revealed here. "Did you guys tow any cars today?" I asked him, hopefully, and I must have looked confused or disoriented, like one of the bums he no doubt had to negotiate at regular intervals.

There was the screech of tires somewhere above and behind us. A sweetish smell of exhaust hung in the air. He gave me a wary look. "We don't tow cars out of here," he said. "Unless they're like left for a week or something . . ."

"No, no," I said. "I just parked two hours ago"—I flipped my wrist to consult my watch—"at ten past ten or so."

He was shaking his head so that the flaps of the hoodie generated their own little breeze. "I've been on since eight and I definitely haven't seen any tow trucks."

That gave me pause. I looked off across the street to the courthouse and saw the way the sun drew radiant lines across the sandstone blocks a previous generation had stacked up there in defiance of time, temblors and the depredations of weather. Then I brought my gaze back to the kiosk, to which a shining white Lexus was just pulling up. The driver of the Lexus, a faux blonde with a reconstructed face, gave me a look, then handed the ticket to the kid in the hoodie, and I stood there observing the gate rise and listening to their parting remarks ("Have a nice day now"; "You too"), feeling helpless and embarrassed.

"That's a camera there, right?" I said, after the Lexus had wheeled off down the street.

The kid looked to where I was pointing, just to his right and above his head. "Yeah, I guess," he said.

"So if anybody"—and here the word caught in my throat for just a moment—"*stole* my car, you'd have it on film, right?"

UNRAVELING THE MYSTERY

The kid called his supervisor, a lean, gum-chewing athlete in his forties with a little pencil mustache and a name tag affixed to his sportcoat that read GREG. Greg shook my hand and asked, "What seems to be the problem?"

"I think somebody stole my car."

"You parked it here?"

I said yes.

"You're sure? Absolutely sure?" Greg had been through this before, you could see that. And you could see that in ninety percent of the cases it turned out that people had parked on the street or in another lot or had simply walked right by their own vehicle without recognizing it because people got confused, especially if they'd been in the library focused on a page or computer screen and not on the real and actual.

I nodded. A slow pounding had started up in my chest and quickly migrated to my head, where it began to beat like a big bass drum. "And my dog was in the car," I said. "My girlfriend's dog, I mean." Here a vision of Leah rose before me, Leah when she was perplexed by the spill of coffee grounds leading across the kitchen floor from the counter to the trash or upset over something she'd heard on the radio, her brow contorted and her eyes coiled, ready to strike. How was I going to break the news to *her*?

"Make and year?" Greg's gaze never left my face. He was trying to get a read on me and I didn't blame him for that. I could only imagine the sort of nut cases he had to deal with on a daily basis.

"Crown Victoria, 2003. Blue. Dark blue, that is. Almost looks black, depending on the light?" The car had belonged to my mother and it had come my way when she passed on last year. It was a bit of a gas hog, but it was in prime condition because she'd hardly ever driven it and it had less than thirty thousand miles on it. When we went on trips—up to Oregon to visit Leah's sister or to Vegas for R&R—we took Leah's Honda to save on gas.

Greg gave me a smile that stretched his mustache to the breaking point. "Let's go have a look," he said.

So I spent the next half hour tramping back through the parking structure, this time with Greg at my side. "I'll be your point man," he said, and we started off up the ramp on the first level, Greg keeping up a stream of chatter the whole time though the drum was beating ever louder in my brain. I heard him as if at a great distance, the ramp swaying under us as cars labored on by. He filled me in on the problems of running a public parking structure, the fistfights over spots when there was a big event going on, the graffiti, the vomit, the sex in the stairwells and the bums making their nests in cars people had foolishly left unlocked. Anytime we came to a car of any make that happened to be blue or black, he pulled up short and asked, "This it?"

But of course it never was.

"All right," he said finally, "let's have a look at that tape and see if we can find out what happened to your vehicle."

THE PERPETRATOR'S SLEEVE

I don't have any tattoos, though Leah has a blue and gold butterfly just under the crease of her right buttock so that it seems to flutter when she's walking ahead of you on the beach in her bikini. I mention it because the perpetrator—the thief—was a tattoo junkie and it was his sleeve that gave him away.

Greg and I went back to his office, which turned out to be a room not much bigger than the ticket kiosk located on the lower level of the parking structure, and waited for his "tech person" to come across town from one of the other garages to extract the feed from the camera and play it for us. "Fifteen minutes," Greg said. "Twenty at most." Then he looked into his computer and I pulled out my laptop, though I couldn't concentrate and wound up staring at the wall above Greg's desk for the hour and a quarter it took the tech person, another high-schooler, to arrive (and that was frustrating because the thief had obviously stolen the car in a narrow window of time and the sooner we got the cops on it the sooner the situation would be resolved, the car restored and Bidderbells returned to me. And Leah. Who was at work and as yet didn't know a thing about it.).

The high-schooler, who actually turned out to be a university student, played the feed for us on Greg's monitor, all three of us leaning in to watch the kid in the hoodie jump and dance and sit and spring up again as we fast-forwarded through the morning's transactions till finally I shouted out, "There! There it is!"

My car had entered the scene, a grainy presence, sleek and substantial, and here was the window rolling down and the shadow of the dog in the backseat, pressing her nose to the glass there. The kid in the hoodie extended his hand and the thief handed him my ticket, his arm casually resting there on the window frame until the amount showed on the kiosk's display—$1.50, first seventy-five minutes free, $1.50 for each hour after that. Which meant that the car had been broken into, hot-wired and driven to the exit just minutes before I emerged from the library, *minutes*! What was I feeling? Anger and regret in equal parts. If only I'd been there I could have stopped him before he'd even got started, the son of a bitch, but the problem was he was a son of a bitch without a face—or at least we couldn't see his face given the perspective of the camera and the shadows inside the car resulting from the angle of the sun at that hour. All we could see was his sleeve—the tattoos he wore on his left arm, dark solid blocks of color like a grid of railroad ties running from his wrist to his bicep. Then the money was exchanged, the gate rose and my car was gone.

OFFICER MORTENSON

Two hours later Officer Mortenson pulled up in front of the parking structure in a Crown Victoria very much like the one that had been stolen from me, with the exception that hers—a newer model—carried a roof rack of flashing lights and bore the San Roque city logo on both front doors, with POLICE emblazoned beneath it in block letters. I was sitting on the low concrete wall outside the library in the company of half a dozen bums and watched her pull up opposite the kiosk and park along the curb in the No Parking Anytime zone, at which point I rose and hurried across the pavement to where she was just emerging from the car. "Hi," I said, tense still but feeling just the smallest relief of the pressure that had been building in me over the course of the past two hours. Here she was, the servant of the law, ready to put things to rights.

Unfortunately, I seemed to have taken her by surprise, approaching the car too eagerly, I suppose, so that as the greeting emerged from my mouth she was in the act of squaring her shoulders and adjusting her duty belt, her fingers running familiarly over the service revolver, the nightstick, mace and handcuffs, and she swung round on me so precipitously you would have thought I was the perpetrator. Or *a* perpetrator. A perpetrator in potentia.

So there we were. The sun beat at the back of my head. I tried for a smile but couldn't quite manage it—I was that wrought up. Nor did it help that I towered over her, my six-three to her five-five or -six. Add to that that she looked too young to be a cop and maybe a bit heavier than the ideal, which made me think of the junk food she must have been forced to bolt down during her busy rounds taking statements from agitated citizens whose safe, secure little worlds had just been cracked open like so many walnuts.

She surprised me then by coming up with the smile I couldn't manage and a soft sympathetic gaze out of eyes the color of the caramel chews Leah likes in lieu of dessert every once in a while. "You're the one whose car's missing?" she asked.

"Yes," I said, and in the next moment it was all pouring out of me in a rush of verbiage, every detail I could think of, from the car's description and license plate number to where I'd parked and how I'd spent my morning and the salient—and most corrosive—fact that Bidderbells was in the backseat and for all I knew being held hostage.

She heard me out, but she wasn't writing anything on her pad beyond the make, model and plate number. When I'd run out of breath, she said, "Let's back up a minute here. Name?" she asked. "And I'm going to need an address and a number where you can be reached."

Once she'd recorded the information, she straightened up and swept a look round the area, scanning the faces of the bums, to whom this was all in a morning's entertainment, and then she turned back to me. "Well," she said, "let's have a look at that video feed, shall we?"

We were in stride now, heading into the shadow of the parking structure, when another thought came to me. "It's not just the car. And the dog. I just remembered my golf clubs are in the trunk. And my fishing equipment. Which includes my fly rod? That my grandfather gave me? I mean, it's handmade split bamboo and pretty much irreplaceable."

She gave me a sidelong glance and I shortened my stride to stay even with her. "You say he has tattoos?"

In the agitation of the moment I thought she was talking about my grandfather, but then I saw my mistake and nodded.

"Don't you worry," she said, "we'll get your car back and

your dog and your golf clubs too. My bet? He's got a rap sheet, which means those tats are going to give him away."

I wanted to thank her, wanted to thank her extravagantly and tell her I was feeling much better and that I appreciated her help in resolving this matter as expeditiously as possible, but all I could think of was Leah and the dog and what would happen if Officer Mortenson was wrong. Or maybe overconfident. Maybe that was a better word.

THE BLAME GAME

One thing I like to do in the late afternoon once I'm done with work (I consult for a couple of the big wine-growing operations on the Central Coast) is pour a glass of wine, put on some music and wait for Leah to get home so we can decide what to do about dinner. Half the time we wind up going out. We're not foodies per se, but there are a whole lot of fine restaurants in this little tourist enclave by the sea, and our choices are virtually limitless. Plus, our two favorite places are an easy walk from the apartment. On this particular afternoon, the afternoon of the theft of the car and abduction of the dog (whether planned or incidental), I got back late, having declined an offer of a lift from Officer Mortenson only to wind up walking the twenty blocks home. Every step of the way I'd been thinking about Leah—her look of shattered disbelief when she found out, the tragic extenuation in the way she would freeze her lips and pinball her eyes, her uncanny ability to hurtle from shock to sorrow to accusation and play the blame game—and if I'd already put away half a bottle of an ambrosial Santa Rita Hills pinot by the time she came in the door, who could blame me? It had been a day. And it was far from over.

About Leah: she's thirty-seven, a year older than I, and she works for a sometimes intemperate older woman named Marjorie Biletnikoff, who has her own interior design business here in town. Most days are placid, meeting with clients, choosing fabrics, carpets, antiques, that sort of thing, but every once in a while—once a week, it seems—things can get inordinately stressful because Marjorie Biletnikoff goes off the wagon in a major way (if she ever even bothered to climb up on it in the first place) and tends to take her frustrations in life out on Leah. Maybe I'm imagining things, but from the moment I heard Leah's key turn in the lock I thought I could detect the sort of forward thrust and abrupt wrist action that would indicate that today was one of those days.

The door yawned open, slammed shut, and here came Leah down the entrance hall and straight into the kitchen, where I was standing at the counter, cradling my wineglass. She didn't say hi and I didn't either and there was no pecking of kisses or embraces or anything usual because as soon as she came through the door I said, "Something happened," and she said, "You're drunk," and I was on the defensive.

Finally, when I got the news out that the car had been stolen from the parking structure at the library, she softened and murmured, "Oh, James, that's awful," even as she went to the cabinet to reach down a wineglass for herself. "You must feel terrible."

"Yeah," I said, shifting my gaze, "but that's not all."

She'd swung round, glass in hand, and had lifted the bottle by its neck before she paused, her eyes boring into me.

"They got Bidderbells," I said. "I mean, she was in the car. They probably didn't even know. And the police, I went to the police, and they said they—"

"What are you telling me? You took my dog? To the library? Left her in the *car*? And you, you—you lost her?" Implicit in this, which rode in on an accusatory tone I didn't particularly need or like, was her history with Bidderbells, a rescue dog she'd got after her divorce, the dog who had *literally saved her life* when she was so depressed all she could think about was killing herself every minute of every day and nothing on this earth seemed worth living for. Until she went to the shelter and saw that sweet thing with the big-eyed gaze and her furry front paws scrabbling there on the wire mesh till it was like to break her heart, etc.

"It's not my fault. How was I to know? And I'm just as upset as you are."

Very slowly, she set the bottle back on the counter and put the empty glass beside it. I watched her face, the interplay of emotions there, as if something caught under her skin was trying to fight its way out.

I gave her a pleading look. "You know we can't leave her alone in the apartment."

"But why? Why did you even go out? I thought you were supposed to be *working*—?"

I pinched my lips together and pointed out the window to the construction site. "The noise," I said. "I couldn't concentrate."

I thought she was going to say something more then, something with a barb in it, overgenerous with blame, as if I was the criminal and not the loser with the tats who'd started all this in the first place, but she just looked past me and murmured a soft exclamation. "Jesus," she said, and then she did fill her glass.

THE PHONE CALL IN THE NIGHT

Dinner was sandwiches washed down with wine and tap water, Leah far too agitated even to think about going out. We tried to watch an old movie on TV, one of those screwball comedies that feature people running in and out of rooms while mistaking each other for somebody else and hiding Jean Arthur in one closet or another, but neither of us could really get into it. For one thing, Leah kept pacing and fretting, the wineglass held out before her like a mood sensor. For another, without even realizing it, we both drank more than was good for us—three bottles, in all. She kept saying, over and over, "The cop did say he'd call, right, if they heard anything?" and I kept correcting her with regard to the pronoun. "*She*," I said. "I told you, it was a woman cop. Officer Mortenson."

"Not *Julie* Mortenson?"

I was on the couch. Jean Arthur flickered by on the screen. "I don't know. She didn't give me a first name. Officer Mortenson, that was all."

"Christ," she said, flinging back the dregs of her wine. "That's all I need. Of all people, *Julie Mortenson*—"

"What, you know her?"

Furious now, every twitch of her brain focused in her eyes, which were focused on me: "Know her? She's a backstabber and a slut, is all. She bullied me on the volleyball team in high school till I had to quit and then turned around and stole my boyfriend senior year, who I'd been going with, like, from my sophomore year, Richie, Richie Lopez? If it's the same Julie Mortenson, and how many could there be in a town this size?"

That was when the phone rang.

I won't say it was like a bomb going off, because that's a cliché, but it did stop the conversation dead in its tracks. I got up and answered it.

"Mr. Mackey?"

"Yes?"

"This is Officer Mortenson. We haven't yet located your vehicle but we did find your dog."

I said something like "Wow, great," while mouthing the information to Leah, whose face froze in expectation.

"Apparently the suspect let her out on the off-ramp at Glen Annie Road and a witness saw what was happening and stopped for the dog, otherwise things could have been a lot worse."

I was trying to process this information, picturing the dog mangled on the freeway but for the intercession of some dog-loving Good Samaritan, when Officer Mortenson added, "The dog—Bidderbells, is that right, a basset mix?—she's at the animal shelter on Turnpike and all you have to do is present ID to reclaim her."

"But I can't—I mean, I've had maybe a glass of wine with dinner? And I wouldn't want to, you know, get behind the wheel—"

Officer Mortenson—she had a voice like honey heated on low in the microwave—just laughed. "I meant, in the *morning*. They close at five weekdays. Open at eight, I think—you can check it out online."

I would have felt relief, but for the fact that Leah was glaring at me, all the tension and blame-assigning of the past few hours livid in her face. I looked down at the rug. Cupped the phone to my mouth. "Okay," I said. "Thank you so much. This is huge." The conversation should have ended there, but the wine sat thick on my tongue and thicker in my brain. "Could I ask you something?" I said, lulled by the patient rhythm of her respiration on the other end of the line. "Is your first name Julie, by any chance?"

There was a pause that allowed me to feel just how far I'd stepped over the line here, attempting to personalize what was a purely formal, bureaucratic transaction, but then her voice came back to me, soft and almost sugared. "It's Sarah," she said, and broke the connection.

THE THIEF REVEALED

Leah was still furious with me in the morning. She'd hardly slept at all, she claimed, thinking of Bidderbells locked up in that cell with strays and pit bulls and she didn't know what else. Did I realize that since Bidderbells had come into her life, they'd never spent a night apart. Never?

I hadn't realized it and I was sad to know it now. I kept my counsel, leery of provoking her, though my own sorrow was a new and festering thing that the loss of a car to a car thief couldn't even begin to contain. Breakfast was a cold and hurried meal. We were out of the apartment by seven-thirty because I had to drive Leah to work so I could use her car to go rescue the dog. Which I did. Promptly at eight. Here came the dog scrabbling down the linoleum hall on a leash gripped by a humorless woman who made me sign a form and pay a fine because Bidderbells' license had lapsed, and then I was in the Honda and heading home to sit at my desk and work as best I could through the noise of the construction across the street. The dog ate lustily and looked no worse for wear, though one account had the thief flinging her out the door while the car was still moving.

The next call from Officer Mortenson came at half-past two, when I was deep into my work—a proposal for expanding the acreage of the Escalera Vineyards on the south slope of the foothill property they were thinking of acquiring from the rancher next door—and didn't at first hear the phone ringing. There was a distant sound, and it finally woke me from my trance on what might have been the fifth or sixth ring for all I knew. No matter. There was Sarah Mortenson's soft, soft voice on the other end of the line, betraying not the least hint of impatience.

"Mr. Mackey, good news. We've located your golf clubs, or what we think are your clubs, which you'll have to come down and identify, and we have the suspect in custody."

I was still in the vineyards. I murmured something incoherent.

"Actually, he was already in custody, arrested early this morning on a drunk and disorderly, and the tats we ran yesterday came up bingo."

I felt my mood elevate. "So you have my car?"

There was a pause. "Unfortunately, no. The suspect—he's known to us, minor perp, long rap sheet—admits taking the car but claims he doesn't remember what he did with it. The golf clubs he sold to two other suspects, who tried to fence them at Herlihy's, out by the public course?"

I tend to get wrapped up in things, I admit it. Someone else might have taken this little violation, this theft of his late mother's and grandfather's property, in stride, but in that moment I couldn't let it go. I wanted my car back. My fly rod. And I wanted to see some punishment meted out too. "What's his name?" I asked. "The car thief? Mr. Tattoo?"

"We don't disclose that information. Not at this stage of the investigation."

"Come on," I said. "Sarah. Look, I'm the victim here."

Another pause, longer this time. I listened to her breathe, pictured her caramel eyes and the eyeliner she wore on duty to emphasize the depth of them. "Reginald Peter Skloot," she said. "A.k.a. the Reg-Dog."

COUNTY

"County" was the diminutive people intimate with the San Roque County Jail used in a familiar way, be they inmates, gang members, jailers or attorneys, and it was the temporary residence of the man who'd stolen my car and my girlfriend's dog and was the only link to the whereabouts of the car and the things contained in its trunk. I'd been to County once previously, in the bad old drinking days before I met Leah, to bail out a buddy who'd spent the night there on a DUI after he'd dropped me off at the apartment because I'd had my own DUI in the past and wouldn't get behind the wheel if I'd had more than three or four drinks. And I had. And did.

At any rate, Officer Mortenson—Sarah—had warned me to stay away from the suspect, the Reg-Dog, because my talking to him would only complicate things, might endanger me in the future and would serve no good purpose. So, naturally, and without even thinking twice about it, I dropped Leah off at work two days later and drove out to County for visiting hours, thinking maybe the Reg-Dog would take pity on me and tell me what he'd done with the car, especially since I'd discovered through a lawyer friend that the Reg-Dog had some money in the bank from his insurance settlement (motorcycle, gravel) and once he was convicted—and he would be, no question there—I could put a claim in and take that money away from him. Tit for tat. Of course, there was a second reason for my driving out there—to get a look at him, at this dirtbag who'd unthinkingly reached out and inflicted damage on a total stranger, me, who'd been put through the wringer and whose live-in girlfriend had stopped speaking to him. Period. Because she couldn't trust him anymore. And why not? Because he had bad judgment. Fatally bad. As it was, she was reconsidering their whole relationship vis-à-vis what she was giving and what she was getting back and he—I—could only thank his lucky stars that Bidderbells hadn't been physically abused, though she saw signs, painful signs, of what the mental toll had been. The dog was eating compulsively, she was skittish, peed secretly in the closet and had gummed Leah's best pair of Liz Claiborne pumps till they were fit for nothing but the garbage.

That was what the Reg-Dog had inflicted on me and I wanted some of my own back—or if not that, just to look at him, to see the sleaze of him and the shame in his eyes.

I wasn't nervous, or not particularly, but as I showed my ID at the desk and stepped through the metal detector, I was afraid that maybe someone had bailed him out or that he wouldn't bother with seeing me, because what was in it for him, but my fears were misplaced. A guard showed me to a chair set before a window in a whole line of them, and there he was, the Reg-Dog, the thief, sitting right in front of me. He was about my age or maybe a couple years younger, with the kind of electric-blue eyes that can be so arresting on people with dark hair. He was in an orange prison jumpsuit, which covered up his tattoos and somehow even managed to seem elegant on him, and he wore his hair short but with long pointed sideburns like daggers.

It took him a minute, assessing me with those jumped-up eyes, then he leaned into the speaking grate in the window that separated us and said, "Don't tell me *you're* my lawyer?"

"No," I said, and I tried to hold steady, but had to look down finally. "I'm the victim."

"Victim? What are you talking about? Victim of what?"

I raised my eyes, fastened on that magnetic blue gaze that must have let him get away with a whole lifetime of petty and not-so-petty crime, and said, "Of you." I gave it a beat to let that sink in. "That was my car you stole. With my girlfriend's dog in it?"

He just blinked at me, no apology, no shame, no recognition even. I was wound up, and I couldn't help delivering a little lecture about what he'd cost me, emotionally and financially too, and if I went into detail about Leah and Bidderbells and my grandfather's fly rod, I'm sorry, but in a society like ours where everything is instant gratification and nobody even knows their neighbors, somebody's got to take responsibility for their own actions. I didn't like what he'd done to me and I let him know it.

And here was where he surprised me. He heard me out, even nodding in agreement at one point. I'd expected he'd throw it right back at me, maybe threaten me, but he didn't. He just bowed his head and murmured, "I'm sorry, man. I wasn't thinking, you know?"

THE CONFESSION

"Look, since my accident? It's like I'm just not right in the head. And tell me that doesn't sound lame because I know it does, but it's the truth. You want to know something? I wasn't even stoned or boozed up or anything when I saw your car there—and I swear I didn't know the dog was in the backseat, or not at first anyway. My father, before he killed himself, used to have a car like that, or maybe not exactly, but you know what I mean. Boom, goes my brain. Time for a *ride*. And you're right, man, I wasn't thinking about you or whoever or what kind of damage I was doing because I just kind of *went off*—"

"So where's the car?"

"Truthfully? I can't remember."

"What if I told you I have a lawyer friend who says I can take your bank account for damages—would that help you remember?"

"Oh, man, don't do that to me. I got my own troubles. As you can imagine. But hey, I'm straight up with you here—I just don't have any recollection because, well, you know, *forgive me*, but that change and dollar bills and all you had in the glove box? I started boozing it, I'm sorry. And then somebody had some oxy—"

"So you're really not going to tell me?"

"Uh-uh. But I'll tell you something else—that lady cop's really got it for you."

MISSING LEAH

I do miss Leah, with that empty bottomless-pit kind of feeling that hits you first thing in the morning, the minute you open your eyes, and I miss Bidderbells too, because you'd have to be one cold individual to live with a dog for a whole year and not feel affection for her, even if she was the kind of animal who would gum the pillows and make her deposits on the kitchen floor so that you were all but compelled to take her to the library with you. In your car. Which just sits there in the shade waiting for somebody like Reginald Peter Skloot to come along and covet it with his burning blue-eyed gaze. But then, if it weren't for that particular chain of events—and their aftermath—I might not have discovered just how intolerant, unfair and vindictive my live-in girlfriend really was. This is what's called experience.

Did I ever get the car back? No. Will I ever see restitution from the Reg-Dog? That's a question of time. Geologic time. I picture the glaciers rolling in again and my friend the lawyer (I'll name him, Len Humphries) pulling a check out of the inner pocket of his zipped-up parka and the three of us, Len, the Reg-Dog and I, retiring to the nearest pub to tip back a celebratory glass.

The car I have now is a newer model, harder to steal, and pretty much unremarkable, the kind of thing nobody would really notice even if it did have its windows cracked and a dog in the backseat. I'd just parked it the other night in front of the apartment after a trip into the Santa Ynez Valley to meet with the Escalera people when a police cruiser pulled up at the curb behind me and Officer Mortenson swung open the door and stepped out onto the sidewalk, adjusting her duty belt as if she were wriggling into a girdle. I saw that her eyes were done up and that she'd changed her hair and maybe even lost a bit of weight, I couldn't say. She said hi and then told me she was sorry to say there was nothing new to report about my car. "My guess?" she said. "They took it straight down to Tijuana. Or somebody chopped it."

"Chopped it?"

"You know, for parts? Like auto body shops. It's a scam. And a shame too, a real shame."

"I see you've still got *your* vehicle," I said, nodding at the cruiser where it sat sleek at the curb. "Crown Victoria, isn't it?"

She gave a laugh. "Yup. All mine. Except I have to share it with about six other officers."

There was a silence, during which the little sounds of the street came percolating up, the buzz of a distant radio, a window slamming shut, snatches of conversation drifting by like aural smoke.

"You know, did I ever tell you what I do for a living?" I asked, following her gaze down the block to where a small cadre of bums was just settling down for the night in the alcove out front of the auto parts store. I waited till she came back to me and shook her head no.

It was a golden evening, the sun just cresting the line of buildings above us to illuminate the windows up and down the far side of the street. There was a faint breeze wafting up from the sea. Birds flared in the palms like copper ingots. "Here," I said, digging a card out of my wallet and handing it to her. "That's me. I'm in the wine business. And you know, I wouldn't call myself a connoisseur, or maybe I would, but I was just thinking—"

I watched her turn the card over in her hand as if it were a piece of evidence, then smile up at me.

"What I mean is, I was just wondering, do you like wine?"

SUBTRACT ONE DEATH

Riley didn't like dogs, or not particularly. They were like children (of which he had none, thankfully), bringing dirt, confusion and unlooked-for expense into your life. But here was a dog, a darting elaborately whiskered thing in the seventy- to eighty-pound range with a walleye and one collapsed ear, barking inquisitively at him from the terminus of its chain. Behind him, in the drive, Caroline stuck her head out the car window, her face leached of color. "Don't tell me *this* is the place?"

"Wait'll you see inside," he called over his shoulder, the dog's explosive barks underscoring the dreariness of the day, which was gray and coldish for mid-May.

He'd rented the house for a week because the few local hotels had been booked for graduation across the river at West Point and he most emphatically did not want to go down into the city, which was what Caroline most emphatically did want but wasn't going to get. He hated cities. Hated the seethe of people, the noise, the crush of everybody wanting everything at the same time. What he liked was this, simplicity, nature, the river spread out at his feet and his gaze carrying all the way across to the wooded mountains on the other side, which, apart from the rail line—and what was that, an oil tank?—couldn't have looked all that much different when Henry Hudson first laid eyes on them. He felt his heart lift. All was right with the world. Except for the dog. And Caroline.

But Caroline liked dogs, and she was out of the car now, striding across the wet lawn in her heels, calling to the dog in a clucking high childish voice. "Oh, that's a good boy, he's a good boy, isn't he? What a good *boy*," she called until she was right there and the dog was fawning at her feet, rolling over on its back so she could apply her two-hundred-dollar manicure to its underbelly. After a minute of this—and Riley was just standing there watching, not with the proprietary pride he'd felt after their marriage four years ago but with a vague kind of quotidian interest, the same interest, dulled and flattened, that just barely got him out of bed in the mornings—she turned round to him and said girlishly, sweetly, "This must be Meg and Brian's new dog. I wonder why they didn't say anything? I mean, I remember the old one, when they came to visit that time? The one that died—I'm picturing German shepherd, right? Wasn't it a German shepherd?"

He just shrugged. One dog was the same as another as far as he was concerned. Meg had said she'd be home from work by four to give him the keys to the rental, which belonged to her next-door neighbors, an older couple who were away in Tuscany for the month on some sort of culinary tour. But it was already half-past four, there were no cars in Meg's driveway, and her house—a modest one-story place shingled in gray that had had its basement flooded twice in the past year after storms upriver—looked abandoned. Except for the dog, that is, which was clearly Meg's, since its chain was affixed to a stake on her side of the rolling expanse of lawn the two properties shared. If Meg was home—or Brian—the dog would have been in the house.

"Give her a call, why don't you?" he said, and watched Caroline straighten up and dig in her purse for her phone. He didn't carry a cell phone himself—one, because he despised technology and the grip it had on the jugular of America, and two, because he didn't want the federal stooges mapping his every move. Might as well have them attach one of those tracking devices. Like with wolves—or parolees. Or better yet, just tattoo your social security number across your forehead.

Caroline, slim still, with gym-toned legs tapering down to those glistening black patent-leather heels, had turned her back to him, as if for privacy, the phone pressed to her ear. It was a picture, her standing there framed against the river like that, and he would have snapped a photo too—if he had a cell phone. But then what was the use of pictures anyway? Nobody would ever see them. It wasn't like the old days, when he was a kid and Polaroid was king. Then you could snap a picture, hold it in your hand, put it in a photo album. Today? All the photos were in the Cloud, ready for the NSA to download at their leisure. And pleasure.

Leisure and pleasure. He liked the sound of that and made a little chant of it while he waited for Caroline to turn round and tell him Meg wasn't answering, or Brian either.

It began to drizzle. This had the effect of intensifying the otherworldly greenness of the place, and he liked that, liked the weather, liked the *scene,* but the shoulders of his new sportcoat seemed strangely sponge-like and his coiffure—the modified pompadour he still affected—was threatening to collapse across his forehead. He let out a curse. "What now?" he said. "Jesus. She *did* say four, didn't she?"

There was something in his tone that got the dog barking again, which drove a fresh stake through his mood. He was about to swing round, get back in the car and go look for a bar somewhere when Meg's generic little silver car swished into the drive next door and he moved toward her, foolishly, because that put him in range of the dog, which reared up on its hind legs to rapturously smear mud all over his white linen pants and attempt to trip him in the process. "Shit," he cursed, shoving the dog down and trying vainly to wipe away the mud, a good portion of which transferred itself to his hands. But was it mud—or the very element he'd just named?

No matter. So what if his jacket was soaked, his pants ruined and dirt of whatever denomination worked up under his finger-nails? He wasn't here to show off his fashion sense or dine out with celebrities or sit for press interviews. No, Lester was dead. And he was here for the funeral.

One thing, among many, that Caroline didn't know was that he'd been involved with Meg all those years ago, long before he met her—or either of his first two wives, for that matter—but if she did he suspected she wouldn't have cared much one way or the other, except to drop the knowledge like a fragmentation de-vice into the middle of one of their increasingly bitter squabbles, squabbles over nothing. Like whose turn it was to empty the litter box and why they needed a litter box in the first place when the cats could just shit outside, but no, she insisted, that was the kind of thinking that was driving birds to extinction and how could he be so short-sighted, and he, in his shortsightedness, countering with *What birds? There's nothing but crows out there. Crows and more crows.* And she: *My point exactly.* Or who'd conveniently forgotten to fill up the car or buy cheese at the market, and not blue cheese, which tasted like hand soap, but a nice Gruyère or Emmentaler? Or how you pronounced her brother Cary's name, which he rendered as "Carry" and she as "Kierie" in her Buffalese.

And what was that all about? Boredom, he supposed, the two of them locked away in their restored eighteenth-century farmhouse in the midst of a peace so unshakable it was like living in a tomb. Which was all right with him—he was a novelist, "high midlist," as he liked to say, bitterly, and he'd chosen to isolate himself for the sake of his writing—but after the remodel was done and she'd selected the antiques and the rugs and the fire irons and dug her flowerbeds and landscaped the front portion of their six-point-five acres, what was left for her? You choose rural, you choose isolation. And Caroline didn't especially like isolation.

But none of that mattered now because Lester was dead and Meg was crossing the lawn to him, her eyes already full. Before he could think he was wrapping her in a full-body embrace that rocked them in each other's orbit far too long while Caroline stood there watching and the mud staining his trousers imperceptibly worked itself into Meg's jeans. He was feeling sorrow, a sorrow so fluent it swept him in over his head, Lester gone and Meg pressed tight to him, and it really hadn't come home to him till now because now he was here, now it was real. He'd always suppressed his emotions in the service of cool, of being cool and detached and untouchable, but suddenly there were tears in his eyes. He might have stood there forever, clutching Meg to him, so far gone he couldn't think beyond the three questions he and Lester used to put to each other when they were stoned (*Who are we? Where are we? Why are we?*), but for the fact that Brian's car had somehow appeared in the drive, right behind Meg's. If Caroline didn't know how he'd once felt about Meg, Brian certainly did, and the knowledge of that—and of some of the extracurricular things Brian had said to him at a party a few years ago— made him come back to himself.

He became aware of the rain, which was more persistent now. Lester's face rose up suddenly in his consciousness, then melted away, as if he'd taken a match to a photograph. He let go of Meg, dropped his arms to his sides, took a step back. "Hi, Brian," he called, lifting one hand in a crippled, fluttering wave though Brian couldn't have heard him since the window was rolled up and the motor running. Still, he couldn't help adding, "Great to see you!"

The house was one of twelve set on a slim strip of land between the river and the train tracks, a smallish 1940s bungalow that had been recast as a two-story contemporary, with fireplace, boat mooring and panoptic views of the river. It was nothing like the farmhouse, of course, but once you stepped inside it gave a good first impression: rustic furniture, framed photos of Hudson scenes on the walls, a brass telescope for stargazing or catching the eye-gleam of the tugboat captains who pushed barges up and down the river all day long. The second impression was maybe a hair less favorable (cramped kitchen, a smell of what, bilge?) but he was gratified—and relieved—to see that Caroline was going to be all right with it. "I love the view," she said, striding across the parquet floor to pull the curtains open wide. "It's"— she searched for the word, turning to him and holding out her hands. If he thought she was going to say "inspiring" or "sublime" or even "awesome," he was disappointed. "It's nice," she said, and then clarified—"I mean, it works, right?"

They were just mixing their inaugural cocktail—vodka gimlet, Lester's touchstone—when the first train entered the scene. On a theoretical level, Riley had understood that the proximity of the tracks might give rise to a certain degree of noise now and again, but this was something else altogether. There was a sudden shattering blast, as of a jet fighter obliterating the sound barrier, then the roar of the wheels, the insult of the horn and the chattered-teeth rattle of every glass, cup, dish and saucer in the cupboard. The whole thing, beginning to end, couldn't have lasted more than ten seconds, but it managed to spike his blood pressure and induce him to slosh Rose's lime juice all over the granite countertop the older couple had installed to fortify their barely adequate kitchen. "Jesus," he said, "what was that?"

Caroline, deadpan: "The train."

"How're we supposed to sleep? I mean, what's the schedule? Are there night trains—or no, there wouldn't be, right?"

"Ask Meg and Brian."

"You get used to it, is that what you're saying?"

She shrugged. Implicit in that shrug and the tight smile that accompanied it was the reminder that they wouldn't have been having this discussion if they were on the twelfth floor of the Algonquin or even the Royalton or Sofitel and that any train they might have run across would have been a conveyance, only that, a means of getting them from the city to this benighted place and back again.

"Jesus," he repeated, looking round for the paper towels, and he was just sopping up the mess—sticky, redolent, probably ninety percent sugar—when there was a tap at the sliding door and Meg was there, framed in the glass panel as in a Renaissance painting, *Our Lady of the River*. She'd changed out of her jeans and into a skirt and she'd done something with her hair. He waved, enjoying the moment, till Brian's head and shoulders entered the frame, and then, at hip level, the dog. She tapped again, grinning, and held up a handle of vodka.

They had a round of gimlets in memory of Lester, then another, after which they switched to wine, a Bordeaux from the case Riley had brought down from Buffalo to help ease Lester's passage, or at least his own immersion in it. He'd written about death to the point of obsession, but he'd been spared the experience of it, if you except the death of his parents, which had happened so long ago he couldn't even remember what they looked like, and he was finding the process of mourning in someone else's living room increasingly disorienting. He tried to make small talk, but small talk wasn't going to work, not with Lester hanging over them like some great-winged bird. The shadows deepened. The river went the color of steel. Everything he said seemed to begin with "You remember when?" And here were Meg's eyes, inviting him right in, the most patient, salvatory eyes he'd ever seen. He was drunk, of course, that was it, and if Caroline and Brian were forced to hover on the fringes of the conversation, that was something they'd just have to get used to because they hadn't been there with Lester right from the beginning and he had. And Meg had too.

"You're slurring your words," Caroline said at one point, and he looked up, wondering how it had gotten dark so quickly—and without his noticing.

"Maybe we should eat something?" he heard himself say, even as the lights of a barge drifted by on the dark shoulders of the river and the dog, agitated by something beyond the range of human senses, began to whine.

Brian pushed himself up from the easy chair in the corner, an empty wineglass in one hand. He was big-headed, white-haired, and, Riley noted with a certain degree of satisfaction, he'd begun to develop a pot belly. He looked old, tired, bored. "I'm ready for bed."

"Pizza?" Meg made a question of it. "They'll deliver."

"Count me out," Brian said, and gave a little laugh that was meant to be self-deprecating but to Riley's ears sounded just this side of rude. He was a killjoy, Brian. A nonentity. And Meg was wasted on him. "But if you three want"—Brian waved at the air—"I mean, go ahead."

"I don't eat pizza," Caroline put in, her voice light and incisive, no slurring for her though she'd had as much to drink as anybody. She let out a laugh. "It's not Paleo."

"You're telling me they didn't have pizza delivery in the Stone Age?" Riley had used the joke before, somewhere, sometime, and nobody responded to it now. He was sunk deep in the easy chair beside Brian's, feeling as if he'd never summon the volition to move again. Somehow he found the dog's head in his lap, and he began idly stroking its collapsed ear.

"We could go out," Meg offered, but Caroline just shook her head and he sank deeper into the chair, wondering how he was even going to get up the stairs to bed, let alone negotiate the car and deal with lights, people, waiters, menus.

Just then there was a tap at the glass, which sent the dog into a frenzy, its head rocketing up out of Riley's lap, paws scrabbling on the floor, the barking rising in pitch till it was nearly a scream, and Riley looked up to see a ghostly face illuminated there at the door, a woman's face, nobody he knew, but it made his heart seize all the same.

As it turned out, she was Meg's neighbor from the next house up and she had some bad news to impart, some very bad news, in fact. Meg slid the door back and the funk of the river rushed in to overwhelm him. "Turn on the TV!" the woman shouted, thumping into the room and going directly to the television—a wall-mounted thing Riley hadn't to this point even noticed—and clicked it on. "I can't believe it," she sang out as images of wreckage, flames, emergency flares and stunned onlookers played across the screen in a way that had become the nightly reality and every bit as believable as anything else out there in the world. The feed at the foot of the screen read *Florence, Italy*, and gave the time there, *5:30 a.m.* "They got Ted," she said.

Meg gave her a look of disbelief. "What are you talking about? *Who?*"

"The *terrorists*. I just had a call from Nadine." And here her voice broke. "It was, I don't know, wrong place, wrong time." She was fiftyish, this woman, bottom heavy, her hair cut short but for a spray of pink-dyed strands sprouting like feathers at the back of her neck. "She's going to be okay, but Ted—he didn't make it."

Loudly, in a rising wail, Meg denied it.

"Who's Ted?" he asked, puzzled, even as the tension began to sink its claws in his stomach, deep down, where he was most vulnerable.

"Ted Marchant," Meg said without turning her head. "I can't believe it," she echoed, her eyes jumping from the screen to the woman who'd come to destroy their evening. Or night. It was night now. Definitely. "When?" she demanded. "Are you sure?"

"Who's Ted Marchant?"

Brian loomed over him with his big white head, the empty glass arrested in mid-air. "The guy," he said flatly, "whose chair you're sitting in."

So there were two deaths. First Lester, and now this. Ted Marchant. Whose name Riley must have written across the face of a check, though he had no recollection of it, who'd sat in this very chair and trained his telescope on the stars or maybe a girl going topless in a speedboat on the far side of the river, who, as it would turn out, had been unlucky enough to be sitting at a corner table in a Florentine café, sipping his espresso, at the very moment the black-clad gunmen had rumbled up on their stolen Ducatis and begun shooting. He'd never met Ted Marchant or his wife of forty-five years either—Nadine—but here he was in possession of the dead man's home and all the dead man's things, drinking out of the dead man's wineglasses. It made him queasy to know it.

The television talked to them and they leaned forward in their chairs and watched the images play across the dead man's screen, listened to the voices of the reporters, the same old thing, the tiredest thing, except that one of the seventeen dead had plodded across these floors and breathed this same dank river air that smelled of a whole array of deaths, from fish to worms to clams and the algae that bloomed on a bounty of phosphates and died back to nothing again. It was staggering. He almost wanted to protest—this wasn't about Ted Marchant, whom he didn't even know, it was about Lester—but instead, into the void, he said, "Maybe we should leave?"

Meg turned away from the screen, her features saturated with the garish light, and looked him full in the face. "No," she said, fierce suddenly, as if the killers were in the room with them, "no way. You're going to stay."

He glanced at Caroline for support, but Caroline's eyes never left the screen. "But won't the wife—? She'll be coming back now, she'll have to, the widow, I mean—"

"Are you serious? Something like this—it could be weeks, months, who knows." Meg's voice caught in her throat. "Poor Nadine—can you imagine?"

"The weirdest thing"—and here the woman who'd brought the news gave him a long look—"is that you're here . . . for a funeral, right?" A glance for Meg. "Or that's what Meg said. And that makes this whole thing so, I don't know, *spooky,* I guess you'd have to say—"

He didn't deny it. In fact, he was spooked right down to the superstitious God-denying soles of his feet. It was like that time in Alaska when the surviving pilot of a two-man air service told him his partner had crashed while delivering a family of Inuit to the next village for the funeral of a family of Inuit killed in an air crash the previous day. Was that how the fates were aligned? Did death come in pairs, like twins? Lester had died of melanoma, a cruel, preposterous thing that had begun as a blister on the little toe of his right foot and spread to his brain and killed him so fast Riley hadn't even known he was sick, let alone dying. It wasn't cool to die, wasn't hip, that was how Lester felt—he had an image to maintain—and so he'd done it alone. That was what hurt. He hadn't called, e-mailed, written, hadn't breathed a word. He'd just crawled off to some hospice in California and spared them the pain.

Later, after Caroline had gone up to bed and Brian took the

dog back across the lawn to his own house and shut out the lights one by one till the fading image of it vanished into the night, there were just the three of them left there in the dead man's living room. Everything was quiet, the lights muted, the TV screen gone blank now. He was the one who'd finally got up and shut it off, Meg whispering "Thank you" and the other woman (her name was Anna or Anne or maybe Joanne, he never quite caught it, not that it mattered—she was the Messenger of Death and that was all he needed to know) seconded her. "These media hyenas," she said, waving her hand in dismissal. "Really, it's just disgusting." For a long while no one said anything, the only sounds the tap of bottle on glass and the consolatory splash of the wine, but then the house began to quail and rattle and here came the blast again, that violent rending of the air, and a train hurtled past with a last fading shriek.

"Oh, my god, I didn't realize it was so late," the woman said, rising from her chair and setting her glass down on the nearest horizontal surface—an inlaid end table, already blemished with a dozen fading circular scars, not that Ted Marchant was going to care. In the next moment she was embracing Meg, the two of them tearful, exuberant in their grief, and then the woman was gone and he was alone with Meg. She looked at him and shook her head. "It's terrible, isn't it?"

He didn't know what to say. It was. Of course it was. Everything was terrible—and getting worse.

He watched her as she bent for her glass, stood up and drained it, one hand on her hip. She looked dazed, uncertain on her feet, and she set the glass down carefully beside the one her neighbor had left, then sank heavily into the couch. "Here," she said, giving him a tired smile, "sit here beside me. Take a load off. It's been a day."

So he sat beside her and felt the warmth of her there in the house that had taken on a chill with the lateness of the hour, and then he put his arm around her and pulled her to him and they kissed and though he felt the tug of her like some elemental force of reconciliation and surcease, he didn't give in to it. What he did do, with the smallest adjustment, was stretch out his legs and lay his head in her lap so that the warmth became a heat and his eyes fell shut, and the death, the two deaths, faded into oblivion.

The next morning, Caroline, declaring the situation "too weird for words," took a train into the city to lunch with her roommate from college and engage in a little resuscitative shopping, and by the time he extracted himself from the bed he'd somehow managed to find his way to at some unfathomable hour of the night, he was just in time to see Meg pulling out of the driveway on her way to work. Brian's car was gone too, as was his own—Caroline had taken it up to the Garrison station and left it there because he was too enfeebled by the night's reversals to get up and drop her off. So he was alone there in the dead man's house (the *murdered* man's house) poking through the cupboards with the idea of coffee in mind—and maybe something to ease his stomach, like dry toast. Or . . . the zwieback he somehow found in his hand, the pastel rendering of a baby grinning up at him from the front of the cardboard box. But why would the old couple stock baby crackers? Grandchildren? Dental issues? He put a zwieback in his mouth, experimentally, then spat it back out in the palm of his hand. Milk. Maybe milk would settle his stomach. He poured out a clean white glass of it, set it on the counter, and stared at it a long moment before trying, with mixed success, to pour it back into the carton. In his distraction, it must have taken him five entire minutes before he remembered that Lester was dead. And that the funeral, at which he'd be expected to get himself together long enough to deliver a eulogy, was tomorrow.

He looked up at a sudden noise—a thump—and there was the dog, pressing its nose to the glass of the sliding door, a ruptured length of chain trailing away from its throat like essential jewelry. The day was bright, he noticed now, yesterday's clouds and drizzle driven back over the hills and the sun dividing the lawn like a chessboard into patches of shadow and light, and the irritation he would normally have felt at the intrusion gave way to something lighter, more tenable, something almost like acceptance. He was glad Caroline had gone into the city and Meg to work, glad to be alone here so he could slow things down, take a walk, sit by the river, commune with Lester on his own terms, and never mind Ted Marchant—Ted Marchant was another issue altogether and he wasn't going to go there.

The thump came again. The dog was pawing the glass as if it wanted something, as if it had a message to convey, some extrasensory glimpse into the process that had claimed Lester and Ted Marchant and would repurpose itself, in good time, to claim the survivors too. Or maybe it was just hungry, maybe that was it. Or, more likely, it wanted in so it could go take a crap on the carpet—wasn't that what dogs were famous for? But then it occurred to him that the dog shouldn't be there at all, that it had, in fact, broken free of its chain, which meant that it was in danger, or potential danger—hadn't Meg complained about how vigilant you had to be or it would bolt out the door and make straight for the train tracks? He got up from where he was sitting at the kitchen table, thinking to let the dog in—to trap it in the house—and then see if he could do something about reinforcing the chain.

But what was the thing's name? Something with a *T*—Tuffy? Terry? Or no, Taffy, that was it, because of its coloration, as Meg had explained shortly after it had annihilated his pants. Anyway, he got up from the kitchen table, went to the door and slid it open, which, far from having the desired effect, caused the dog to back away from him so precipitately it fell from the porch in an awkward scramble of limbs. For the briefest moment it lay there on its back, its legs kicking in the air, and then it sprang up and bolted headlong away from him, straight in the direction of the tracks. "Taffy!" he called, feeling ridiculous, but nonetheless coming down off the porch and hustling across the lawn after him (or her; he wasn't even sure what sex the thing was). "Taffy! No!"

It was at that moment the train appeared, the 9:50 or 10:10 or whatever it was, the air shrieking, the wheels thundering, a great onrushing force that eclipsed the animal as if it had never been there at all. Running now, his heart slamming at his ribs, Riley reached the tracks just as the last car—*the caboose*, a term that came to him out of a buried past, childhood, Lionel, mittens pressed to ears, *Take Daddy's hand now*—raged on by and the tracks stood vacant, shining malevolently in the hard gleam of the sun. What he expected was death, another death, the dog's remains dribbled like ragout up and down the line—and what was he going to tell Meg?—but that wasn't what he found. The dog was there, intact, remnant chain and all, sitting on its rump on the far side of the tracks and staring at him stupidly across the void.

"Taffy," he called, trying to control his voice, the edge of hysteria there, of fury. "Come!"

But Taffy didn't come. Taffy never budged, except to contort himself (he was a male, Riley saw now, the sheath of the organ, the tight dark balls like damson plums) so he could reach up and scratch his chin with one back paw. Riley looked up and down the tracks, a long tapering *V* to the vanishing point in either direction, then called again, again without response. *Maybe if I turn my back on him*, he thought. Or maybe—and here he felt embarrassed with himself, because what was he now, a dog whisperer?—maybe he should just say fuck the whole business. Let the dog take his chances. Right. Fine. He swung abruptly round and made his way through the damp grass to mount the porch of the dead man's house and see if he could find the means to make himself a cup of coffee.

He wasn't really tracking the time, but it must have been

around noon or so, the sun high overhead and the dog frisking back and forth across the lawn, chain in tow, when he looked up from his coffee and toast and his eyes came to rest on the canoe where it lay overturned on the dock. He'd been reading a very dull book, trying not to think beyond the next dull paragraph, wondering how he was going to get through the rest of the day, and there it was, this vision: the canoe. It was just the thing he needed—to get out on the river, clear his head, let nature be his guide. What could be better? The sun-spanked waves, the breeze fresh out of the north, a little exercise—he could always use the exercise, and really, how often did he have the opportunity to get out here on the Hudson, the river of his boyhood, of his connections, of his past, of *Lester*? All right. A plan. A definite plan.

It took him a while to find the paddles, secreted as they were in the back of the garage behind a six-foot-tall rusting metal cabinet that contained the other boating things: blue flotation cushion, orange life vest, various fishing rods, crab traps, gigs and landing nets. He took the cushion, a spinning rod and a tackle box stocked with Ted Marchant's lures—why not?—balanced a paddle over one shoulder and crossed the lawn to the dock. If he didn't bother with the life vest it was because he never bothered with life vests—he knew what he was doing, and even at his age (he would be fifty-six in December, though officially he admitted only to fifty) he was a strong swimmer, had always been, and for a moment he saw himself in his twenties, racing Lester out to the raft on Kitchawank Lake over and over again, one sprint after the other, the loser having to swig a shot of the tequila their girlfriends, leaning over the edge of the raft, held out for them even as they laughed and cheered and kicked up a froth with their pretty, tanned feet.

The canoe—aluminum, indestructible—was surprisingly heavy, but he managed to flip it over, stow his gear and slide it into the water before lowering himself into it and equalizing his weight. In the next moment he was stroking hard against the tug of the current, the first strokes the best, always the best, all the power gone to your shoulders and upper arms in a flush of resurgent joy. It was sensational. Transformative. Dip, rise, dip again. He must have been a hundred feet from shore when he realized he'd forgotten a hat, which would have been nice to have to keep the sun out of his face, and his water bottle too, but that wasn't a problem because he wasn't going to stay out that long. Cruise up the river and back again, forty-five minutes, an hour. Max. Though, admittedly, he did feel a bit dehydrated and maybe hungover into the bargain, and the thought flickered in and out of his mind that he might paddle up the river to Garrison, to the bar there, and then drift back down when the tide reversed, but that was too ambitious . . . no, better to keep it simple.

Ahead of him on the right, just past the promontory where the last of the twelve houses sat, was a low trestle that gave onto the marsh on the far side, and he paddled for the entrance, thinking he'd do a little exploring. Meg had taken him back there the last time he'd visited and he remembered it as a magical place, alive with birds of every description, turtles stacked up like dinner plates on the butts of half-submerged trees—and better yet, the sense of enclosure and privacy it held, as if you were miles away from anyone. The point, he realized, as he dug the paddle in and flew across the gray froth of the river, was that Lester was dead and he wasn't. He was alive, never more alive. The burden of grief was a burden we all carried—*Lester! Lester!*—but there was this too, this living in the moment, the sunstruck chop, the breeze, the scent of the wildflowers clustered round the mouth of the trestle till it could have been a bower in a Rossetti poem. He flew for it. But then, drawing closer, he saw that the tide was up higher than he'd realized—the space seemed barely adequate for the canoe itself to pass under, no more than three feet of vertical clearance, if that.

Riley, for better or worse—worse, actually—never backed

down from a challenge, and once he'd made up his mind to shoot the entrance, he just kept going. At the last moment, he slid down supine on the floor of the canoe and let the inrushing current carry him, which wouldn't have been a problem if he'd arrived fifteen minutes earlier, when he would have had another two or three inches between him and the concrete belly of the trestle. As it was, he could have glided right through if he'd been in a kayak or riding a surfboard, but unfortunately the twin high points of the canoe, at bow and stern, struck the ceiling with a sound like grinding molars, the current dragging the canoe forward till finally, a dozen feet from the far side, it stuck fast.

He saw his predicament and experienced a moment of regret, but regret wasn't going to get him out of this, was it? The water was streaming in and soon it would engulf the entire space, right to the ceiling, or at least that had to be a possibility, didn't it? All right. No need to panic. He raised his arms and pushed hard against the concrete above him and the boat edged forward, scraping in protest. What he hadn't counted on—but he hadn't counted on anything, just acted, and acted stupidly, suicidally, really—was the unevenness of the structure, which, as it turned out, had subsided ever so imperceptibly on the far side, not that it was any of his business, but what, exactly, was wrong with the maintenance people on the New York Central Line? Didn't they inspect these things?

Whether they did or not, the fact remained that he was stuck. On his back. In a space that was like a coffin, with the tide rushing in and no more than a few spare inches of clearance between him and the cold gray lid above him that might or might not have been home to various spiders and biting insects and water snakes too, an example of which had just whipped past him in a display of muscular urgency. What else? The cold. The smell of mud, muck, the decay the river fostered and throve on, and all at once he was remembering the story his father had told him of the drowned woman in Annsville Creek whose corpse had floated to the surface in a twitching scrum of blue-claw crabs. This was serious. He was in trouble. He was going to drown, that was what was going to happen, and he could already see the headlines—*Author Drowns in Boating Accident*—and the pre-packaged rudiments of his obituary: his books, his wives, the early promise, the bloated middle years, the prizes, the checks, survived by his loving wife. Minutes, that was all he had till the water started pouring in over the gunwales, but in that moment he could picture the newspaper account as clearly as if he were sitting at the big oak table in the kitchen at the farmhouse, the overhead lamp bright and his reading glasses clamped over the bridge of his nose.

He'd often wondered how he'd respond in a crisis, at the same time praying he'd never be obligated to find out (and how was it for Ted Marchant, protecting Nadine with the shield of his own body in the millisecond before the AK rounds split him open?). To this point, the closest he'd come was some thirty years ago in the company of Lester, both of them drunk on cheap scotch and saturated with the triumph of their selves and their wise ways and the hipness that cloaked and absolved them, when the lip of the dune they'd been sitting on gave way beneath them so that they were rudely plunged into the ice bath of San Francisco Bay, but—and here was the charm—wound up none the worse for it. So all right. The water was rising but he wasn't panicking—he was too humiliated for panic. He was just—concerned, that was all. And amused. Struck between the eyes with the force of his own stupidity—of all the millions of deaths that come raining down each and every day of our lives, how many involve aging novelists trapped under train trestles in canoes?

We fear death because all we know is life, and once you're alive the safest bet is to stay that way. He knew that, subscribed to it as a principle, and it provided his motivation now. What if—experimentally—he were to tip the canoe ever so slightly, purposely letting the water in so he could gain another six inches to free himself and take his chances in the water before the air gave out? He could do that, but then his wallet would be soaked and his clothes ruined, yet what were wallets and clothes when he was so close to joining Lester and Ted Marchant in the Land of the Dead? Nothing, nothing at all. Still, he did take the time to wriggle out of his jacket, shirt, jeans and hiking boots and ball the whole business up in one hand as he pushed hard off the ceiling, found the surge of the water and squeezed into it . . . yes, and Jesus, it was freezing!

A lesser writer than Riley might have said something like "Time stood still," but that wasn't it at all, not even close: time accelerated. One instant had him in the canoe, passively awaiting his death by drowning, and the next saw him flailing his way through cattails and muck, his shirt, shoes and jacket gone but his jeans—and wallet—still clutched sopping in one hand till he reached the high stony embankment some previous generation had erected here in the backwater to carry the locomotive freight. It wasn't easy, his feet battered, the stones slippery, a dense growth of briars and poison ivy impeding his way, but finally, too cold and wet and residually shaken even to curse, he was able to pull himself up by stages and emerge on the tracks, and so what if he was in his Joe Boxers and his shoes were missing? He was alive, alive all over again.

He didn't say a word to anyone, not the old man bobbing in his boat or the two women sitting in lawn chairs at the house across the way. He just limped up the tracks in his bare feet and wet underwear, and here was the dog to greet him, dashing by with its length of chain rapping at the rails, and of course it was inevitable that in the interval yet another train would come hurtling by to rake him with its tailwind, faces pressed to windows, a young girl waving—waving, for god's sake—and he, nothing else for it, waving back.

After the funeral, once everyone had exhausted their praise for the emotional intensity of his eulogy and the tears had dried and the drinks circulated, he bowed out early, pleading a headache. He and Caroline drove back to the rented house on the river, where the dog, its chain reinforced, twisted round and round the steel post Brian had pounded angrily into the ground just that morning, and they spent all of ten minutes throwing their things together and bringing the suitcases down to the car. Then Riley locked up, gave the dog a wide berth and hurried across the lawn to leave the key under the mat at Meg and Brian's before they could get back from the reception or wake or whatever you wanted to call it. The tear-fest. The slog. The canoe had un-wedged itself on the turn of the tide, but Riley hadn't been there to recover it. He didn't leave a note. If Nadine noticed it missing he'd send her a check, no problem, glad to do it, in fact, glad to help out, but no sense in worrying about that now.

Traffic was light and they made good time. Caroline was si-lent most of the way down, but her face was composed and she looked good—better than good—in the black velvet dress and single strand of pearls she'd worn for the funeral. They checked into the Algonquin, the only hotel where he really felt appreci-ated, a homey place, a *writer's* place, and while Caroline went down to see about theater tickets he settled in a chair by the win-dow, high above the crush and grab of West 44th Street. For a long while he gazed out into the grayness, then he picked up the dull book he'd been working his way through, found where he'd left off and started reading.

YOU DON'T MISS YOUR WATER
('TIL THE WELL RUNS DRY)

A light rain fell at the end of the second year of the drought, a female rain, soft and indecisive, a kind of whisper in the trees that barely settled the dust around the clumps of dead grass. We took it for what it was, and if we were disappointed, if we yearned for a hard soaking rain, a macho rain crashing down in all its drain-rattling potency, we just shrugged and went about our business. What were we going to do, hire a rainmaker? Sacrifice goats? There were vagaries to the weather, seasonal variations spurred by the El Niño Southern Oscillation and the Pacific Decadal Oscillation and the Northern Hemisphere Hadley Cell, and certainly the dry years would be followed by the wet in a cycle that had spun out over the centuries, the eons. Daily life was challenging enough—people had to go to the dentist, sit in traffic, pay taxes, cook dinner, work and eat and sleep. It would rain when it rained. No sense worrying over it. Nobody gave it much thought beyond the scaremongers in the newspaper and the talking heads on the television screen, until the third year went by in a succession of cloudless days and no rain came, not male, female or androgynous.

It was that third year that broke our backs. We began to obsess over water, where it came from, where it was going, why there wasn't enough of it. It got to the point where everything that wasn't water-related, whether it was the presidential election, the latest bombing or the imminent extinction of the polar bear, receded into irrelevance. The third year was when it got personal.

For our part, my wife, Micki, and I had long since cut back our usage, so that when the restrictions came we were already at the bare minimum, the lawn a relic, the flowerbeds, once so lush, nothing more than brittle yellow sticks, the trees gaunt, the shrubs barely hanging on. If before we'd resented the spendthrifts with their emerald lawns and English ivy climbing up the walls of their houses, it was all the more intense now. When those people were forced to cut usage by thirty percent, they were dropping to the level at which we'd already arrived, and so our thirty percent cut amounted to a double penalty on us, the ones who'd been foolish enough to institute voluntary cuts when the governor first made his appeal. Not only was it insupportable—it was deeply unfair, the sort of thing that made a mockery of the notion of shared sacrifice. I began shaving dry, with only the spray foam to moisten my beard, and Micki stopped using makeup because she couldn't abide the waste of having to wash it off. When our son came home for spring break (from Princeton, where it rained every other day) Micki taped a hand-lettered notice to the bathroom door: *If it's yellow, let it mellow; if it's brown, flush it down.* Next morning, when he turned on the shower—the very instant—I was there at the door, pounding on the panels, shouting, "Two minutes max!"

He was a good kid, Everett, forthright and equitable, and

if he had a failing, here it was revealed: *He'd actually turned the shower on.* I couldn't believe it. And neither could Micki. She and I bathed once a week—in the tub, together—then used the bathwater to wash the clothes and bedsheets until finally we scooped up the remainder in plastic buckets and hauled it out to moisten the roots of our citrus trees, which were my pride and joy and the very last thing that would go in the vegetative triage that had seen the lawn sacrificed and then the flowerbeds and finally even the houseplants. At dinner that night (a hurried affair, Everett eager to go out prowling the local watering holes—bars, that is—with his cohort of friends who were likewise home on spring break), I tried to smooth things over and deliver a hydrological lesson at the same time. "Sorry if I overreacted this morning," I said, "but you've got to realize it's the whole southwest. I mean, there just isn't any water. At any cost. Anywhere."

The sun was caught in the kitchen window, hanging there like an afterthought. It was warm, but not uncomfortably so. Not yet anyway—all that still lay ahead.

Everett looked up, his fork suspended in mid-air over a generous portion of green curry shrimp and sticky rice takeout. He shrugged, as if to say he was fine with it. "I should have known better," he said, dipping his head to address his food.

"I hear they're recommissioning the desalination plant," Micki put in, hopeful, always hopeful. She had her hair up in a do-rag and was wearing a white blouse that could have been whiter.

"Two years *minimum*," I said, and I didn't mean it to sound like a rebuke, though I'm afraid it did. I was wrought up, all the little things of life magnified now, the things you take for granted during the good times. That was how tense the situation had become. "And something like nine million dollars, not that the money has anything to do with it—at this stage people'll pay anything, double, triple, they don't care—"

"But you can't bleed a stone," my son said, glancing up slyly.

"Or squeeze water out of it either," I added, and we were all three of us grinning, crisis or no.

So we had a sense of humor about it, at least there was that. Or at least at first anyway. Still, as much as I loved my wife and enjoyed seeing her au naturel, two in a tub was a crowd, and I'm sure she must have felt the same though she never said as much. She was a good sport, Micki, and if my knees were in the way and the water felt faintly greasy, she made the most of it, but for me the weekly bath began to feel like a burden. "Remember the old days?" I'd say, soaping her back or kneading shampoo into the long dark ropes of her hair. "You know, when you could just get up with the alarm and step into the shower before work?" And she would nod wistfully, the water sloshing at her armpits and the tender gaps behind her knees, before heaving herself out of the tub to snatch up her thrice-used towel. I'd give her a moment, my eyes averted, then ease carefully out of the water to drip-dry and wield the bucket. Was this good for our sex life? Or was it too much of the usual, her body shorn of mystery so that when we did finally slip between our graying sheets at night, all I could think of was the tub and the soapy slosh of wasted water? I don't know. Maybe. Maybe that was part of the problem, but I found myself reaching out for her less and less, I'm afraid.

Of course, we weren't alone in this. You didn't see couples hugging or holding hands much anymore and at restaurants they sat across the table from each other and as close to the windows as possible. People began to smell a bit off. You especially noticed it on public transportation, which we tried to avoid as much as possible and damn the consequences, because this was all about water, not gasoline, and if we were contributing greenhouse gases to the atmosphere and exacerbating the global warming that was the biggest factor in the drought, then so be it. There was a run on deodorant and various body lavage products for a while there, but eventually people gave up and just lived with their own natural scent. In fact, it became a kind of badge of honor to stink, just as it was to display a lawn as brown as the Gobi Desert.

We were all of us, the whole community, learning to adjust, even the spendthrifts, who were threatened with governors on their intake valves if they exceeded their ration, and I have to admit I took a certain degree of satisfaction in watching their lawns wither and their ivy fade to brown. This was the new normal, and as the days went by I began to feel all right with it, and so did Micki. Then one morning, as I strolled through our modest grove of citrus trees, selecting oranges for fresh-squeezed juice, I noticed something odd. Here were my black plastic drip lines snaking round the root systems of our eight Valencia orange trees, with subsidiary connections for our three lemon, two grapefruit and half a dozen fledgling avocado, but now there seemed to be another line altogether—one that branched off the main line and disappeared under the hard compacted earth of the yard. Which, as I saw now, wasn't so compacted, after all, but seemed to have been disturbed recently. We didn't have a gardener, not anymore—what was the point?—so it wasn't anything he might have done, unless he'd slipped into the yard while sleepwalking. I certainly hadn't put in a new line—again, what was the point?—and unless Micki had been working in the garden, which I doubted, since she'd never shown much interest in anything outdoors aside from maybe the parking lot at the galleria, then this was simply a mystery.

I bent to tug at the hose, but it was held in place by means of a series of metal fasteners, and this just compounded the mystery. What I did then was fetch a hoe from the shed at the back of the house and very carefully scrape the dirt away from the length of the hose, which was clearly newer than the old line, the plastic glistening blackly under the sun. Puzzled, I kept at it, following the direction of it all the way across the yard to the fence that separated our acre and a half from the acre and a half of our neighbors, the Veniers. Where, even more puzzlingly, it seemed to vanish under the fence.

Now, in this community of pricey homes and expansive lots, we kept our distance for the most part, our adjoining properties walled off with six-foot fences of stone, stucco or redwood, and we knew our neighbors in the vaguely familiar way we knew the birds that formerly gathered on the former lawn to peck about for worms and grubs and such. So it was with the Veniers. His name was Bill—or maybe Will—and the wife, a shoulderless blonde in her forties, must have had a name too, but on the few occasions I did encounter her out on the sidewalk, she never once glanced up from her cell phone, and I don't think it ever registered with me. Maybe Micki would know, I was thinking, even as I gripped the top rail of the fence and peered over into their yard.

At first, I couldn't quite comprehend what I was seeing: the Veniers had a virtual oasis back there, shrubs, flowerbeds, trees heavy with fruit crowning a sod lawn as green as creation and stretching all the way across the property to the far wall, on the other side of which lived the Chinese couple (or maybe they were Korean—I never could get that straight). For a long while I just stood there, straining on tiptoe and trying to make sense of the situation. What it looked like to me was that my neighbors—the Veniers, who I'd assumed were decent-enough people with an income level commensurate to buy into the neighborhood—were stealing our water. My next thought was that it couldn't be. Couldn't possibly. Not in this neighborhood. Maybe they had a well or a secret spring or something and they'd run the hose into my yard in a gesture of pure altruism, as a way of sharing the bounty. *Yeah, right,* I told myself, angry suddenly, as angry as I'd ever been, and then I was up and over the fence, my slippers making a telltale indentation in the dense green sod beneath.

Did they have a dog? Not that I knew of—I couldn't recall having heard any whining or barking nor seen either of them out on the street with an animal on a leash. Still, I tensed for a moment, half-expecting the black slash of a Rottweiler or Doberman to come hurtling out of the shadows and make a grab for me. All was still. It was seven-thirty of a Saturday morning. Were they awake, the Veniers? Sitting in their breakfast nook reading the *Times* on their tablets and gazing idly out the window to see an intruder in shorts and bedroom slippers planted in the far corner of their secret lawn? Or sleeping in, their faces slack with the moist compress of their dreams? No matter. The length of hose plunged into the ground and ran beneath the sod to where a dense stand of water-hungry carnations and azaleas crowded the foundation of the house. I could see the faint raised outline of it in the sod and was about to follow it, to rip it up if need be and demand an explanation of Bill—or Will—Venier, but then there was the soft whoosh of a sound I hadn't heard in years and a whole series of sprinklers popped up round the perimeter of the lawn and within moments my slippers were wet.

Fifteen minutes later, after having cut the hose and railed at Micki while her face hardened over this grim evidence of perfidy in our midst, I was standing on the Veniers' front doorstep depressing the buzzer. They apparently didn't have chimes (unlike us), but just a hissing mechanical buzz that reverberated through the house like the sound of an oversized electric shaver. It took a moment, during which I mentally rehearsed various speeches and settled finally on a tone of outraged disbelief, and then the wife was standing there before me, blinking against the light. She was dressed in shorts and halter top, and if she was shoulderless I saw that she was breastless too, and her skin was so pale and leached out she might have been dipped in milk from her toes to her transparent eyelashes and fluff of vanilla hair. "Oh," she said, "hi. You're from next door, right? Jim? Or is it Joe?"

"Actually," I said, "the name's Scooter. But what I wanted to know, I mean, what I'm here for, is this." I brandished a length of the hose, its black plastic aperture gaping raggedly where I'd hacked it off with the garden shears.

She was a liar of the first stripe, this woman (whose name, I was later to learn, was Alta, married to Will, not Bill). She never flinched. Just narrowed her eyes in a look that suggested puzzlement shading into umbrage and maybe even annoyance. "What is that?" she asked, all innocence. "A hose? You want to borrow a hose?"

"I found this attached to the drip line in my yard."

She lifted her eyebrows.

"*Attached*," I said, giving it some emphasis, "and running under the fence to your, your *oasis* back there. How do you explain that, I'd like to know. I really would."

An elaborate shrug. From behind her, in the depths of the house, came the lilt of Debussy's *Images*. Cut flowers decorated a vase on a table just inside the door. I could sense the presence of someone else there, the husband, lingering in the shadows and unwilling to show his face. "It must be some mistake," she said, her hand—beringed, lithe, youthful—already easing the door shut.

"You bet it's a mistake," I shouted, a threat about my attorney—my attorney and the town water board—rattling around in my head, but then the door closed firmly and I was left alone with my complaint.

Summer came early that year and lingered late into fall, the afternoons burned clear and the temperatures toppling records day after day. Everett had planned to come home for summer vacation and take up his former job as lifeguard at the community pool, but the pool had been drained and Micki and I encouraged him to stay back east. "Go to summer school," we said. "Get an internship. Work at

McDonald's." Forgive me if we were both thinking of those showers of his and the extra burden of washing his clothes and dirty
dishes and even of the glass of water he kept on his nightstand. We
missed him. Of course we did. But we told ourselves we'd see him
at the end of the year, at Christmas, when the rains were sure to
come and all this privation would be no more than a memory. As
for the Veniers, I never heard a word from them, either of apology
or denial. I did report them to the water board (if that makes me
a snitch, so be it, because everybody was snitching on everybody
else all across town and god forbid if anybody should actually be
caught wielding a hose) and I made a practice of peeping over the
fence now and again to watch their lawn lose its sheen and their
azaleas wither. I soaped Micki's back. She soaped mine. Our knees
got in the way. And our sex life dwindled down to nothing.

The next development—inevitable, I suppose—was the ap-
pearance of the water trucks. They looked like gasoline trucks—
tankers—but with the difference that their insignia, if they
carried any at all, bore images of waterfalls or huge trembling
blue raindrops. Twice a day, in mid-morning and again after dinner, they began a slow seductive sashay through the neighborhood, dispensing water—with a thousand-gallon minimum—at
prices that redefined gouging. We weren't exactly poor, Micki
and I, but we did have Everett's tuition hanging over our heads
and Micki had recently lost her job, while my hours had been
reduced, and there was no way we could afford what they were
asking. The problem was we both worked in the tourist industry
and the tourists just weren't showing up anymore—they wanted
showers, swimming pools, ice in their drinks—and they began
to discover that the beaches of Washington and British Columbia really weren't so bad after all, not if you factored in rising
sea temperatures and considered that that was actual water flow-
ing without stint from the taps and showerheads of their motel
rooms overlooking Puget Sound and the Strait of Juan de Fuca.

By this point, sad to say, Micki and I had begun to get on each other's nerves. She was home twenty-four/seven now and I was only going in to work sporadically, so we both had too much time on our hands. We bickered endlessly about the pettiest things—who'd used the last clean towel or let the dishwater seep down the drain—and when Micki shaved her head I knew it was only to spite me, though she claimed it was to save her the trouble of washing her hair. She looked ridiculous. Her ears, shorn of their camouflage, stuck out as if they were somebody else's ears altogether, random flaps of cartilage grafted to her head, and I wondered how I'd never noticed just how extreme—and unattractive—they were till now. I made the mistake of commenting on it and we wound up not speaking for a week.

Then one morning she came to me at my desk in the makeshift office I'd set up in the guestroom and finally broke the silence. "You see what's going on next door?" she said, her voice a conspiratorial whisper. The guestroom was on the second floor and from where I was sitting I could just see down into the Veniers' front yard, albeit at a sheared-off angle. Alta Venier was there in the driveway, which was lined on both sides with French lavender in full bloom, and one of the water trucks was just easing in through the gate as she directed it with hand gestures. She was wearing a two-piece swimsuit in the European style that left her all but naked and I could see that her face, even at this distance, was a mask of greed and seduction. Sure enough, as Micki and I watched, she climbed up on the step of the truck and leaned into the window to give the driver—a guy in his thirties with a baseball cap reversed on his head—a lingering kiss, then took his arm as he stepped out of the truck and led him into the house. My wife and I looked at each other and all our animus seemed to dissolve in that instant: we were in league together, in league once again. How long was that driver in the house? Forty-five minutes. I timed it. We both did. He wasn't adjusting his belt or anything like that when he finally emerged, but what had gone on—what sort of bargain had been struck—was clear. He looked round him, and maybe he was smirking, I couldn't say, then paid out his hose, stretched it to the water tank the Veniers had installed at the far side of the house, and began pumping.

Everett did come home for Christmas, but there was no water to greet him. It hadn't rained. Temperatures were above normal, the sun oppressive. There was no snowpack in the mountains, and the Colorado River, from which we'd formerly derived thirty percent of our water via various engineering marvels and pumping stations, was, according to the latest reports, nothing but a muddy trickle. Worse yet, our son, who'd been away so long now, seemed like a stranger to us. In fact, when he walked through the gate at the airport, I didn't recognize him—he seemed taller, heavier, and he'd grown a beard that swelled his face till he looked more like a professor than a student. When Micki rushed forward to embrace him, he seemed to stiffen and even took a step back. "Mom?" he said.

I could see the consternation on his face even as Micki wrapped her arms around him, the slick smooth dome of her scalp flashing an SOS under the glare of the overhead lights. People stopped to stare. One woman, clearly arriving from some wetter place, stood stock-still on the gleaming tiles, working her fingers through her own hair as if to reassure herself. "It's not cancer," I blurted. "Just the drought."

Everett was holding his mother at arm's length now, as if she was somebody else's mother and he'd been wrapped in a counterfeit embrace. Who could blame him if he was confused?

Micki gave him a thick smile, broke away from him, spun out a little pirouette. "It's my new look. You like it?"

Christmas Day came sere and bright, the hot high sun spoiling the pretense of the season, no wreath on the door and the tree from the lot gone yellow with thirst. I tried spraying it with the lawn paint but half the needles fell off and the whole business wound up being more trouble than it was worth. And, of course, season of good cheer or no, the question of water and what to do about Everett's usage soured the mood. I'd sprung for a membership at the local health club, just so I could use the shower, but management was wise to that strategy and installed sixty-second regulators on the showerheads and hired an inflated teenage kid in a pair of board shorts to sit on a stool in the shower room and make sure nobody cheated. I took Everett as my guest, but he did cheat, moving from one showerhead to the next, and the inflated kid reported him and they canceled my membership, so it was back to the tub with Micki for me and a frigid salty dip in the Pacific for Everett. And then Everett returned to school and January came, sans rain, followed by a dry February and drier March, and the fourth consecutive rainless rainy season ended not with a bang but a whimper and we braced ourselves for the long dry year to come.

It was around then—at the beginning of the fifth year—that the Veniers showed up on our doorstep late one afternoon. The winds had been especially bad that day and the yard was all but buried in blowing sand, tumbleweed and the flapping tendrils of wind-whipped plastic bags. I don't know where Micki was—shopping, I suppose, or maybe brooding in the basement. She seemed to do a lot of brooding lately, and whether that was healthy or not I couldn't say, though I did begin to wonder if she might not want to think about seeking professional help. Just for the short term. Till things eased up a bit, I mean.

At any rate, the carillon chimed and I pulled back the door to see my neighbors, the Veniers, standing there hunched against the wind, and a third figure beside them whom I at first took to be a child. Alta was wearing a chador, but she still had her hair, the ends of which whipped around her face in a blond frenzy. Will (at least I presumed this was Will, though I didn't really know him well enough to say one way or the other) was in a hoodie, his face haunted and his eyes as inflamed as a seer's. I saw that he wasn't as tall as I, and it felt good to look down on him, especially considering what he and his wife had done to us—which I hadn't forgotten, not by a long shot. The third figure—I saw now that she was a woman, no more than waist high and with a face so rippled and desiccated it might have been hide—stood there between them with her head bowed and her hands clasped before her as if in prayer. Alta was the first to speak. "Can we come in?" she asked.

I stepped aside, too surprised to respond, the word "effrontery" making a quick tour of my brain as the three shuffled in and I slammed the door against the wind-borne refuse that chased at their heels. We stood there awkwardly in the foyer a moment, the Veniers' eyes scouring me while their companion—she wore ropes of beads over a faded denim shirt and what looked to be a polyester housecoat in a shade of pink so blanched it was almost white—stared down at the floor, until I heard myself say, "Here, let's go into the living room where we can be comfortable."

Custom, manners, the way we respond to and treat one another—these are the first things to go in times of duress, and I have to admit I wasn't very gracious. I didn't offer them anything to drink. I didn't make small talk. I just gestured to the sofa and settled myself wordlessly in the armchair.

Alta stripped back the hood of the chador and shook out her hair. "This may seem like an odd request," she began, "but Will and I are going around the neighborhood taking up a collection, pooling our money collectively, that is"—she paused, snatching a quick glance at the woman, who'd seated herself between her and Will. "For Yoki, I mean. For her fee."

Will spoke up now, his face expressionless, his lips barely moving: "It's a shared responsibility. For all of us. The whole community."

"Fee?" I echoed. "For what?"

Another pause. "She's a—what would you call her, Will?—a rain-bringer. A shaman."

The woman lifted her eyes for the first time and said something then, her voice a dry rasp that rattled in her throat.

"What was that?" I asked.

"She says she can help us." Alta shrugged. "She has powers."

At this point I just let out a laugh. "Good luck with that," I said, rising from the chair and making my way back across the room to the foyer, where I stood waiting with my hand on the doorknob while they exchanged glances and finally, reluctantly, got up and followed me. I held the door for them. The sun blazed on the doorstep. The wind blew. "Just out of curiosity," I said, "how much is she asking?"

They were already out the door. Will hunched his shoulders, swung his head back round. "She doesn't want money."

"What does she want, then?"

Alta turned now too, as did the dwarf woman. "She wants a Mercedes," Alta said.

"450 SEL," the woman put in, her voice as dry as the wind itself. "Verde Brook Metallic. Amaretto interior. And twenty-inch wheels—only the twenty, not the nineteen."

Absurd, right? Effrontery to the nth power? When I told Micki about it she gave me a look of disgust. "How did people like that even get into the neighborhood?" she demanded, as if it had been up to me in the first place.

I shrugged and pointed out to her, as gently as I could, that it was a matter of income. "The people on the west side, in the condos? I'm sure they're even worse."

We were in the kitchen. It was hot. Her scalp glistened with sweat. "Tell me about it," she said, crossing to the sink for a glass of water, then thinking better of it when she saw the yellow tape I'd wrapped around the faucet as a reminder. "And I'll bet they flush their toilets too, don't they?"

Yes, yes they did. And they showered and let the water run while they were brushing their teeth and god knew what else. This was what it had come to, a universal resentment of anyone who used water for any purpose, when it was meant for us— for us and us alone. Here was the lesson of the village green, writ large, but then the village green wouldn't have been there to abuse in the first place if it hadn't rained, would it?

A few days later, when I was out in the yard assessing the condition of the orange trees (there'd been no fruit for two years now and no blossoms either), I heard the thin keening of a voice struggling against the wind and realized, after a moment, that it was coming from the far side of the fence, in the Veniers' yard. Puzzled, I crossed to the fence, went up on tiptoe and peered over. There was the dwarf woman, the shaman, dressed in Indian regalia—feathers, deerskin, a bone breastplate—and doing a slow-motion dance around the faded remnant of lawn the Veniers had been able to keep alive through their illicit means. She was chanting, her voice rising and falling on the wind, and she held a rusted Chock full o'Nuts can in one hand, from time to time dipping her fingers into the mouth of it to extract droplets of the liquid it contained and fling them over her shoulder. The liquid—it was a bright arterial red—stained her fingertips and shone greasily under the assault of the sun. I understood then that it wasn't paint she was releasing into the air and in the same instant felt something open up inside me, a kind of awe I hadn't experienced since childhood. Absurd, yes, but there it was. "Hi, hi, hi-hi," she chanted. "Heya-heya-heya." The sky stood motionless. Nothing moved, not even a bird. I stood there and watched her till the muscles in my calves felt as if they'd been soldered in place.

I'd like to report that it rained the next day, but that didn't happen. Things just got worse. A man whose water had been cut off after he'd exceeded his ration three months in a row attacked the director of the water board as he bent over a bowl of *pasta e fagiole* at a three-star restaurant downtown. Water vigilantes began to patrol the streets. Car washes closed. There was legislation on the table to criminalize golf. On a more personal level, Everett called to say he was getting married and Micki sobbed over the phone for half an hour because there wasn't even the faintest hope we could attend, our credit cards maxed out and our frequent-flier miles long since depleted. Through it all the dwarf woman never stopped chanting. A week went by, then two, then a month, and still she kept at it, her voice a thin plaint that conspired with the trills and whistles of the birds till it passed beyond recognition. The Veniers' lawn grew browner, greasier, the blades of grass gone heavy with coagulated blood. "Hi, hi, hi-hi," the woman chanted. Nights fell. Days broke. Nothing changed.

And then one morning I woke to a presence I couldn't have named, a lightness, a release, as if a band had been stretched beyond capacity till it snapped. Micki was there in bed beside me, snoring softly. The air was fecund, crouching over us like a living thing, daylight just beginning to show at the windows. That was when the sound started in, a sound so alien I didn't recognize it at first. It began as a patter on the roof, and then it quickened, and then the drains *were* rattling, macho, macho as all hell. I snatched my wife's hand and pulled her from the bed and in the next moment we were out in the yard, our faces lifted to the sky as the rain beat down around us and beat and beat again till we were soaked through and fell to our knees laughing in the mud, the glorious mud that clung to us and saturated us and promised everything.

Science, meteorological science specifically, tells us of weather patterns, of hemispheric changes, of cycles of drought and plenitude, but science is cold and disinterested. It models, describes, predicts. All that is small comfort to a community under constraint and a grove of citrus trees stressed to the tipping point. I'm not saying that the Indian woman in the Veniers' backyard knew something the scientists didn't or that superstition is anything but just that, and yet she did get her Mercedes (we even kicked in what we could, though it wasn't as much as we would have liked) and when the rains had gone on for a month and people began to worry about flooding and mudslides and the like there was a movement afoot to bring her back and make it all stop. The water board even did a cost-benefit analysis—what would she have wanted, we wondered, a Jaguar? Two Mercedeses? Her own dealership?—but eventually, in the way of these things, the rains did finally come to an end.

The reservoirs are full now and Micki's growing her hair back. We shower separately, though old habits die hard and we both keep to a two-minute limit, and when I see her wrapped in her terrycloth robe, toweling her hair dry, I just want to reach out and pull her to me, thinking how very, very lucky we are to be alive in this moment on this planet that provides us with such abundance and such everlasting grace.

THE DESIGNEE

THE BOREDOM

What he couldn't have imagined, even in his bleakest assessments of the future, was the boredom. He'd sat there in the hospital while Jan lay dying, holding her hand after each of the increasingly desperate procedures that had left her bald and emaciated and looking like no one he'd ever known, thinking only of the bagel with cream cheese he'd have for dinner and the identical one he'd have for breakfast in the morning. If he allowed himself to think beyond that, it was only of the empty space in the bed beside him and of the practical concerns that kept everything else at bay: the estate, the funeral, the cemetery, the first shovel of dirt ringing on the lid of the coffin, closure. There was his daughter, but she had no more experience of this kind of free fall than he, and she had her own life and her own problems all the way across the country in New York, which was where she retreated after the funeral. A grief counsellor came to the house and murmured in his direction for an hour or two, people sent him cards, books and newspaper clippings in a great rolling wave that broke over him and as quickly receded, but nobody addressed the boredom.

He got up at first light, as he always had. The house was silent. He dressed, ate, washed up. Then he sat down with a book or the newspaper, but his powers of concentration weren't what they once were, and he wound up staring at the walls. The walls just stood there. No dog barked, there was no sound of cars from the street—even the leaky faucet in the downstairs bathroom seemed to have fixed itself. He could have taken up golf, he supposed, but he hated golf. He could have played cards or gone down to the senior center, but he hated cards and he hated seniors, especially the old ladies, who came at you in a gabbling flock and couldn't begin to replace Jan anyway, not if there were ten thousand of them. The only time he was truly happy was when he was asleep, and even that was denied him half the time.

The walls just stood there. No dog barked. The water didn't even drip.

THE LETTER

The letter came out of nowhere, a thin sheet of paper in a standard envelope that bore a foreign stamp (England: Queen Elizabeth in brownish silhouette). It was buried in the usual avalanche of flyers, free offers and coupons, and he very nearly tossed it in the recycling bin along with all the rest, but it was his luck that at the last minute it slipped free and drifted in a graceful fluttering arc to the pavement at his feet. He bent for it, noticing that it was addressed to him, using his full name—Mason Kenneth Alimonti—and that the return address was of a bank in London. Curious, he wedged the sheaf of ads under one arm and pried open the envelope right there in the driveway while the sun beat at the back of his neck and people drifted by like ghosts out on the street.

Dear Mr. Alimonti, the letter began, *kindly accept my sincere apologies for contacting you out of the blue like this but something very urgent and important has come to our notice and we seek your consent for the mutual interest of all.*

His first thought was that this had something to do with the estate, with Jan's death, more paperwork, more *hassle,* as if they couldn't leave well enough alone, and he glanced up a moment, distracted. Suddenly—and this was odd, maybe even a portent of some sort—the morning seemed to buzz to life, each sound coming to him separately and yet blending in a whole, from the chittering of a squirrel in the branches overhead to a snatch of a child's laughter and the squall of a radio dopplering through the open window of a passing car. And more: every blade of grass, every leaf shone as if the color green had been created anew.

The letter was in his hand still, the junk mail still tucked under one arm. When Jan was alive, he'd bring the mail in to her where she'd be sitting at the kitchen table with her coffee and a book of crosswords, and now he was standing there motionless in his own driveway, hearing things, seeing things—and smelling things too, the grass, jasmine, a whiff of gasoline from the mower that suddenly started up next door. *I am Graham Shovelin,* the letter went on, *Operations & IT Director, Yorkshire Bank PLC, and personal funds manager to the late Mr. Jing J. Kim, an American citizen. He died recently, along with his wife and only son while holidaying in Kuala Lumpur, and was flown back to England for burial. In our last auditing, we discovered a dormant account of his with £38,886,000 in his name.*

This is a story, he was thinking, a made-up story, and what did it have to do with him? Still, and though he didn't have his glasses with him so that the letters seemed to bloat and fade on the page before him, he read on as if he couldn't help himself: *During our investigations, we discovered that he nominated his son as his next of kin. All efforts to trace his other relations have proved impossible. The account has been dormant for some time since his death. Therefore, we decided to contact you as an American citizen, to seek your consent to enable us to nominate you as the next of kin to the deceased and transfer the funds to you as the designated heir to the deceased.*

There was more—a proposed split of the proceeds, sixty percent for him, thirty-eight percent for the bank, two percent to be set aside *for expenses both parties might incur (if any) during the transaction.* At the bottom of the page was a phone number and a request to contact the bank if the above-mentioned transaction should be of interest, with a final admonition: *Please also contact me if you object to this proposal.* Object? Who could object? He did a quick calculation in his head, still good with numbers though he'd been retired from the college for fifteen years now: sixty percent of 38,886,000 was 23 million and something. Pounds, that is. And what was the conversion rate, one-point-two or -three to the dollar?

It was a lot of money. Which he didn't need, or not desperately anyway, not the way most people needed it. While it was a sad fact that the bulk of what he'd set aside for retirement had been swallowed up in treatments for Jan the insurers had labeled "experimental" and thus non-reimbursable, he still had enough left, what with social security and his 401(k), to live at least modestly for as long as he lasted. This offer, this letter that had him standing stock still in his own driveway as if he'd lost his bearings like half the other old men in the world, was too good to be true, he knew that. Or he felt it anyway.

But still. Thirty million dollars, give or take. Certainly there were places he'd like to visit—Iceland, for one, the Galápagos, for another—and it would be nice to leave his daughter and his grandson something more than a mortgaged house, funeral expenses and a stack of bills. There were stranger things in this world—people won the lottery, got grants, prizes, estates went unclaimed all over the place, and it wasn't as if he was desperate. A voice warned him against it, but what did he have to lose? The cost of a phone call?

THE PHONE CALL

The phone picked up on the third ring and the first thing he heard was music, a soft trickle of music that was neither classical nor pop, but something in between, and for a moment he thought he was being put on hold before the music cut off abruptly and a deep crisp voice—so deep it surprised him—swelled inside the receiver. "Yorkshire Bank PLC, Graham Shovelin speaking. How may I help you?"

He'd rehearsed a little speech in his head, along the lines of establishing his authority as the person solicited rather than soliciting, but it deserted him now. "Um, I," he stuttered, "I, uh, received your letter?"

There was the faintest tick of hesitation, and then the voice came back at him, so deep he couldn't help thinking of Paul Robeson singing "Ol' Man River" on one of the old 78s his grandmother used to play for him when he was a boy. "Oh, yes, of course—delighted to hear from you. We have your number here on the computer screen, and it matches our records . . . still, one can never be too careful. Would you be so kind as to identify yourself, please?"

"Mason Alimonti?"

"Mason *Kenneth* Alimonti?"

"Yes."

"Ah, well, wonderful. We'll need verification of your identity before we can proceed, of course, but for the moment, since we're just beginning to get acquainted, I am satisfied. Now, what do you think of our proposal?"

He was in the living room, sitting in the armchair under the reading lamp, using the old landline phone his daughter told him he ought to give up since the cell was all anybody needed these days and she really didn't know anyone, not a single soul, who still paid for a landline. But for something like this—an overseas call—he somehow felt better relying on the instrument he'd been using for thirty years and more. "I don't know," he said. "It sounds too good to be true—"

The man on the other end of the line let out a booming laugh, a laugh that scraped bottom and then sailed all the way up into the high register, a good-natured laugh, delighted, a laugh of assurance and joy that proclaimed all was right with the world. "Well, of course, it *is*," the man boomed, and here came the laugh again. "But sometimes we just have to accept the fact that luck has come our way—and be grateful, Mr. Alimonti, kick up our heels and embrace what life brings us, don't you think?"

For a moment, he was confused. He felt as if he'd gone out of his body, everything before him—the love seat, the houseplants, the blank TV screen—shifting on him so that it all seemed to be floating in air. The phone was in his hand. He was having a conversation. Somebody—the man on the other end of the line—wanted something from him.

"Mr. Alimonti—you there?"

"Yes," he heard himself say. There was something odd about the man's accent—it was British, proper British, *Masterpiece Theatre* British, but the syntax was off somehow. Or the rhythm, maybe it was the rhythm. "Why me?" he asked suddenly.

Another laugh, not quite so deep or pleased with itself as the last. "Because you've lived an unimpeachable life, because you pay your debts and you're as solid an American citizen as anyone could ever hope to find. Oh, rest assured we've vetted you thoroughly—as we have each of the nine other final candidates."

Nine other candidates? The receiver went heavy in his hand—molded plastic, but it might as well have been cast of iron.

"Am I hearing surprise on your end of the line, Mr. Alimonti? Of course, you understand, we must protect ourselves, in the event that our first choice doesn't wish to accept our offer for any reason—and I can't really imagine that happening, can you?—but as you *are* the first on our list, the single most qualified individual we've examined to date, we have to say—*I* have to say—that we are delighted you've contacted us ahead of any of the others."

He felt a wave of relief sweep over him. The phone was just a phone again. He said, "What next?"

"Next?" the voice echoed. "Well, obviously we have to make certain that you're the man for us—and that we're the men for you too. Do you have any question about the figures I presented in my letter to you? You agree that a sixty/thirty-eight percent split is equable? You're content with that?"

He said nothing. He was back in himself, back in the moment, but he didn't know what to say—did the man want him to negotiate, to quibble over the way the money would be split?

"Again, let me anticipate you, Mr. Alimonti. You are wondering, no doubt, what's in it for us?" The laugh again, but truncated now, all business. "Self-interest, pure and simple. If this account has not been claimed within a five-year period, the whole of it goes to the government and we receive nothing, though we've been the guardians of the late Mr. Kim's fortune for a quarter century now. We *need* you, Mr. Alimonti, and that is the bottom line. We need an American citizen in good standing, with an unblemished record and absolute probity, to be the designee for your fellow American, Mr. Kim." A pause. "Otherwise, none of us receives a shilling."

"What do I have to do?"

"Oh, nothing really, not for the moment. We'll need banking information, of course, in order to transfer the funds, and our solicitors will have to draw up a contract so as to be sure there are no misunderstandings, but all that can come in time—the only question now is, are you with us? Can we count on you? Can I hang up this phone and check the other nine names off my list?"

His heart was pounding in his chest, the way it did when he overexerted himself. His mouth was dry. The world seemed to be tipping under his feet, sliding away from him. *Thirty million dollars.* "Can I have some time to think it over?"

"Sadly, we have but two weeks before the government accounting office swoops in to confiscate this account—and you know how they are, the government, no different, I suppose, than in your country, eh? A belly that's never full. Of course you can think it over, but for your sake—and mine—think quickly, Mr. Alimonti, think quickly."

A NIGHT TO THINK IT OVER

The rest of the day, he really couldn't do much more than sit—first in the armchair and then out on the deck in one of the twin recliners there—his mind working at double speed. He couldn't stop thinking about England, a country he'd visited only once, when he was in his twenties, along with Jan, in the year between grad school and the start of his first job, his daughter not yet even a speck on the horizon. They'd gone to Scotland too, to Edinburgh and where was it? Glasgow. He remembered he took to calling Jan "Lassie," just for the fun of it, and how one day, leaving a fish and chips shop, she'd got ahead of him on the street and he cried out, "Wait up, Lassie," and every woman's head turned. That was England. Or Scotland anyway. Same difference. And they had banks there, of course they did, London the banking capital of Europe, though he couldn't remember actually having gone into one. He closed his eyes. Saw some sort of proud antique building, old, very old, with pillars and marble floors, brass fixtures, an elaborate worked-iron grate between customers and tellers, but here again, he realized, he was bringing up an image from one BBC drama or another, and what was that one called where they showed the lives not only of the lords and ladies, but the servants too? That had been Jan's favorite. She'd watch the episodes over and over, and sometimes, at breakfast, she'd address him as "My Lord" and put on a fake accent. For the fun of it.

Yes, sure. And where was the fun in life now?

At some point, when the shadows began to thicken in the trees, he went into the house and clicked on the TV—sports, a blur of action, a ball sailing high against a sky crippled with the onset of night—but he couldn't concentrate on it, and really, what did it matter who won? Somebody had won before and somebody had lost and it would happen again. And again. Unless there was a tie—were there ties in baseball? He couldn't remember. He thought so. In fact, he distinctly remembered a tie once, but maybe that was only an exhibition game . . . Or an all-star game, wasn't that it?

It was past eight by the time he remembered he ought to eat something, and he went to the refrigerator, extracted the stained pot there and ladled out half a bowl of the vegetable-beef stew he'd made last week—or maybe it was the week before. No matter: he'd been rigorous about keeping it refrigerated and in any case the microwave would kill anything, bacterial or otherwise, that might have tried to gain a foothold in the depths of the pot. The important thing was not to waste anything in a world of waste. He poured himself a glass of milk, scraped two suspicious spots from a slice of sourdough bread and put it in the toaster, then sat down to eat.

The walls just stood there. But the silence gave way to a sound from the other room, where the TV was, a long drawn-out cheer and the voice of an announcer unleashing his enthusiasm on the drama of the moment, and that was something at least. What was the time difference between here and England? Eight hours? Nine? Whatever it was, it was too early there to call yet. He was thinking he might like to endow a fellowship in Jan's name at the college—maybe in the Art Department; she'd always liked art—and if he gave enough they'd install a plaque, maybe even name a building after her. Or a wing. A wing at least. Maybe that was more practical, really. He saw her face then, not as it was in those last months, but her real face, her true face, fleshed out and beautiful even into her seventies, and he pushed himself up from the table, scraped his bowl over the trash can and set it on the rack in the dishwasher, decided now, his mind clear, really clear, for the first time all day.

In the morning, after breakfast (no rush—he wouldn't want to come across as over-eager), he would settle himself in the armchair, pick up the phone and make the call.

THE SECOND PHONE CALL

Of all days, this was the one he wound up oversleeping, so that it was past eight by the time he sat down with his morning coffee and punched in the bank's number with a forefinger that didn't seem to want to steady itself, as if this wasn't his finger at all but some stranger's that had been grafted on in the middle of the night. This time, there was no music and the phone picked up on the first ring. He was all set to tell Mr. Shovelin—*Graham, can I call you Graham?*—that he'd found his man, that they'd grow rich together, though, of course, as a bank employee, he didn't imagine that Mr. Shovelin would actually get any of the money, but a bonus maybe, there had to be that possibility, didn't there? Imagine his surprise then, when it wasn't Shovelin, with his rich booming basso, who answered the phone, but a woman. "Yorkshire Bank PLC, Chevette Afunu-Jones speaking," she said in a thin weary voice. "How may I help you?"

Again, he drew a blank. This whole business made him nervous. The phone made him nervous. *London* made him nervous. "I was," he began, "I mean, I wanted to—is Mr. Shovelin there?"

A pause, the sound of a keyboard softly clicking. "Oh, Mr. Alimonti, forgive me," she said, her voice warming till you could have spread it on toast. "Mr. Shovelin, who I am sorry to say is away from his desk at the moment, instructed me to anticipate your call. And let me say, from all the good things he's had to say about you, it is a real pleasure to hear your voice."

He didn't quite know how to respond to this so he simply murmured, "Thank you," and left it at that. There was another pause, as if she was waiting for him to go on. "When do you expect him back?" he asked. "Because—well, it's urgent, you know? I have some news for him?"

"Well, I can only hope it's the good news all of us on Mr. Shovelin's staff have been waiting to hear," she said, her voice deepening, opening out to him in invitation. "Rest assured that Mr. Shovelin has given me full details and, in my capacity as his executive secretary, the authority to act on his behalf, though he's—well, he's indisposed today, poor man, and you can't begin to imagine what he's had to go through." Here she dropped her voice to a whisper: "Cancer."

This hit him like a blow out of nowhere. Jan's face was right there, hovering over him. "I'm sorry," he murmured.

"Believe me, the man is a lion, and he will fight this thing the way he has fought all his life—and when he returns from his treatment this afternoon, I know he will be lifted up by your good news, buoyed, that is . . ." Her voice had grown tearful. "I can't tell you how much he respects you," she whispered.

What he heard, though he wasn't really listening on an intuitive level, was an odd similarity to the accent or emphasis or whatever it was he'd detected in Shovelin's speech, and he wondered if somehow the two were related, not that it mattered, really, so long as they stayed the course and checked those other nine names off the list. He said, "Please tell him from me that I hope he's feeling better and, well, that I've decided to take him up on his offer—"

She clapped her hands together, one quick celebratory clap that reverberated through the phone like the cymbal that strikes up the band, before her voice was in his ear again: "Oh, I can't tell you how much this will mean to him, how much it means to us all here at the Yorkshire Bank PLC . . . Mr. Alimonti, you are a savior, you really are."

He was trying to picture her, this British woman all the way across the country and the sea too, a young woman by the sound of her voice, youngish anyway, and he saw her in business dress, with stockings and heels and legs as finely shaped as an athlete's. She was a runner, not simply a jogger, but a runner, and he saw her pumping her arms and dashing through what, Hyde Park?, in the dewy mornings before coming to work with her high heels tucked in her purse. He felt warm. He felt good. He felt as if things were changing for the better.

"Now, Mr. Alimonti," she said, her voice low, almost a purr, "what we need you to do is this, just to get the ball rolling— officially, you understand?"

"Yes?"

"We will need your banking information so that we can begin transferring the funds—or at least cutting you a preliminary check—before the Royal Fiduciary Bureau for Unclaimed Accounts moves on this."

"But, but," he stammered, "what about the contract we were supposed to——?"

"Oh, don't you worry, darling—may I call you darling? Because you are, you really *are* darling——"

He gave a kind of shrug of assent, but nothing came out of his mouth.

"Don't you worry," she repeated. "Mr. Shovelin will take care of that."

THE FIRST DISBURSEMENT

Once the banking details were in place (within three working days, and he had to hand it to Shovelin for pulling strings and expediting things), he received his first disbursement check from the dormant account. It was in the amount of $20,000 and it came special delivery with a note from Shovelin, who called it "earnest money" and asked him to hold off for two weeks before depositing it in the new account, "because of red tape on this end, which is regrettable, but a simple fact of doing business in a banking arena as complex as this." The check was drawn on the Yorkshire Bank PLC, it bore the signature of Graham Shovelin, Operations & IT Director, and it was printed on the sort of fine, high-grade paper you associated with stock certificates. When it came, when the doorbell rang and the mailman handed him the envelope, Mason accepted it with trembling hands, and for the longest time he just sat there in his armchair, admiring it. He was sitting down, yes, but inside he was doing cartwheels. This was the real deal. He was rich. The first thing he was going to do— and the idea came to him right then and there—was help out his daughter. Angelica, divorced two years now, with a son in high school and barely scraping by, was the pastry chef at a tony restaurant in Rye, New York; her dream was to open her own place on her own terms, with her own cuisine, and now he was going to be able to make it happen for her. Maybe she'd even name it after him. Mason's. That had a certain ring to it, didn't it?

That evening, just as he was ladling out his nightly bowl of stew, the phone rang. It was Shovelin, sounding none the worse for wear. "Mason?" he boomed. "May I call you Mason, that is, considering that we are now business partners?"

"Yes, yes, of course." He found that he was smiling. Alone there in his deserted house where the silence reigned supreme, he was smiling.

"Good, good, and please call me Graham . . . Now, the reason I'm calling is I want to know if you've received the disbursement?"

"I have, yes, and thank you very much for that, but how *are* you? Your health, I mean? Because I know how hard it can be—I went through the same thing with Jan, with my wife—?"

The voice on the other end seemed to deflate. "My health?"

"I'm sorry, I really don't want to stick my nose in, but your secretary told me you were, well, undergoing treatment?"

"Oh, that, yes. Very unfortunate. And I do wish she hadn't confided in you—but I assure you it won't affect our business relationship, not a whit, so don't you worry." There was a long pause. "Kidney," Shovelin said, his voice a murmur now. "Metastatic. They're giving me six months—"

"Six months?"

"Unless—well, unless I can qualify for an experimental treatment the insurance won't even begin to cover, which my physician tells me is almost a miracle, with something like a ninety percent remission rate . . . but really, forgive me, Mason—I didn't call you all the way from England to talk about my health problems. I'm a banker—and we have a transaction to discuss."

He didn't respond, but he was thinking of Jan, of course he was, because how can anybody—insurers, doctors, hospitals—put a price on the life of a human being?

"What I need you to do, Mason—Mason, are you there?"

"Yes, I'm here."

"Good. I need you to deposit twenty thousand dollars American in the account we've opened up at your bank, so as to cover the funds I've transferred to you until they clear. You see, I will need access to those funds in order to grease certain palms in the Royal Fiduciary Bureau—you have this expression, do you not? *Greasing* palms?"

"I don't—I mean, I'll have to make a withdrawal from my retirement, which might take a few days—"

"A few days?" Shovelin threw back at him in a tone of disbelief. "Don't you appreciate that time is of the essence here? Everyone in this world, sadly enough, is not as upright as you and I. I'm talking about graft, Mason, graft at the highest levels of government bureaucracy. We must grease the palms—or the wheels, isn't that how you say it?—to make certain that there are no hitches with the full disbursement of the funds."

There was a silence. He could hear the uncertain wash of the connection, as of the sea probing the shore. England was a long way off. "Okay," he heard himself say into the void.

But it wasn't a void: Shovelin was there still. "There are too few men of honor in this world," he said ruefully. "Do you know what they say of me in the banking industry? 'Shovelin's word is his honor and his honor is his word.'" He let out a sigh. "I only wish it were true for the unscrupulous bureaucrats we're dealing with here. The palm greasers." He let out a chuckle, deep and rolling and self-amused. "Or, to be more precise, the *greasees*."

A PROBLEM WITH THE CHECK

Two weeks later, he was on the phone again, and if he was upset, he couldn't help himself.

"Yes, yes," Shovelin said dismissively. "I understand your concern, but let me assure you, Mason, we are on top of this matter."

"But the people at my bank? The Bank of America? They say there's a problem with the check—"

"A small matter. All I can say is that it's a good thing we used this as a test case, because think of the mess we'd be in if we'd deposited the whole sum of $30,558,780, which, by the way, is what our accountants have determined your share to be, exclusive of fees. If any."

He was seeing the scene at the bank all over again, the cold look of the teller, who seemed to think he was some sort of flim-flam man—or worse, senile, useless, *old*. They'd sat him down at the desk of the bank manager, a full-figured young woman with plump butterfly lips and a pair of black eyes that bored right into you, and she'd explained that the check had been drawn on insufficient funds and was, in effect, worthless. Embarrassed—worse, humiliated—he'd shuffled out into the sunlight blinking as if he'd been locked up in a cave all this time.

"But what am I supposed to do?"

"Just what you—and I, and Miss Afunu-Jones—*have* been doing: exerting a little control, a little *patience*, Mason. The fact is, I am going to have to ask you to make another deposit. There is one man at the RFB standing in our way, a scoundrel, really—and I'll name him, why not? Richard Hyde-Jeffers. One of those men born with the gold spoon in his mouth but who is always greedy for more, as if that were the only subject they tutored him in at Oxford: greed."

"He wants a bribe?"

"Exactly."

"How much?'

"He wants twenty thousand more. Outrageous, I know. But you've—*we've*—already invested twenty thousand in him, the greedy pig, and we wouldn't want to see that go down the drain—do you use that expression, 'down the drain'?—or watch the deal of a lifetime wither on the vine right in front of our eyes."

Shovelin was silent a moment, allowing him to process all this. Which, he had to admit, was difficult, increasingly difficult. Nothing was as it seemed. The house slipped away from him again, everything in motion, as if an earthquake had struck. Spots drifted before his eyes. The phone was cast of iron.

"I promise you," Shovelin said, his voice gone deeper yet in a sort of croon, "as I live and breathe, *this* will be the end of it."

THE FLIGHT TO HEATHROW

He'd never been comfortable in the air, never liked the feeling of helplessness and mortal peril that came over him as the great metallic cage lifted off the tarmac and hurtled into the atmosphere, and over the years he'd made a point of flying as little as possible. His most memorable—and relaxing—vacations had been motor trips he and Jan had taken, usually to one national park or the other or just exploring little out-of-the-way towns in Washington, Oregon, British Columbia. The last flight he'd been on—to Hawaii, with Jan, to celebrate their golden anniversary, or was it the silver?—had been nightmarishly bumpy, so much so he'd thought at one point the plane was going down and he'd wound up, embarrassingly, having to use the air-sickness bag. He couldn't help thinking about that as he found his way down the crowded aisle to his seat in economy, both his knees throbbing from his descent down the Jetbridge and his lower back burning from the effort of lugging his oversized suitcase, which he'd randomly stuffed with far too many clothes and even an extra pair of shoes, though he was only staying two nights in London. At the expense—and insistence—of Yorkshire Bank PLC.

In the four months that had dragged by since he'd first received the letter, his expenses had mounted to the point at which he'd begun to question the whole business. That little voice again. It nagged him, told him he was a fool, being taken, and yet every time he protested, Graham—or sometimes Chevette—telephoned to mollify him. Yes, there was graft, and yes, part of the problem was Graham's health, which had kept him out of the office at crucial junctures in the negotiations with Mr. Hyde-Jeffers of the Royal Fiduciary Bureau, but he needed to have faith, not simply in the Yorkshire Bank PLC, but in Graham Shovelin's word, which was his honor, as his honor was his word. Still, Mason had posted funds for fees, bribes, something Chevette called "vigorish," and beyond that to help defray Graham's medical expenses and even, once, to underwrite a graduation party for Chevette's niece, Evangeline, whose father had been run over by a bus and tragically killed the very week of his daughter's graduation (Mason had been presented with an itemized bill for the gown, corsage, limousine and dinner at a Moroccan restaurant that had cost a staggering $1,500). All to be reimbursed, of course, once the funds were released.

It was Graham who'd suggested he come to London to see for himself "how the land lies," as he put it. "After all this time, to tell me that you don't have absolute faith in me, my friend—my friend and partner—is to wound me deeply," Graham had said, pouring himself into the phone one late night in a conversation that must have gone on for an hour or more. "You hurt my reputation," he said in a wounded voice, "and worse than that, Mason, worse than that, you hurt my *pride*. And really, for a man in my condition, facing an uncertain future and the final accounting up above, what else is there for me to hold on to? Beyond love. Love and friendship, Mason." He'd let out a deep sigh. "I am sending you an airline ticket by overnight mail," he said. "You want your eyes opened? I will open them for you."

TWO DAYS IN LONDON

If the walls just stood there back at home, he didn't know it. His life, the life of the widower, of the griever, of the terminally bored, had changed, and changed radically. Graham Shovelin himself took time off from work—and his chemo—to pick him up at the airport in a shining maroon Mercedes and bring him to his hotel, all expenses paid. Of course, there was a little contretemps at the airport, Mason, exhausted from a cramped and sleepless night and at eighty no steadier on his feet than he'd been at seventy-nine or expected to be at eighty-one, had mistaken this heavyset fortyish man with the shaved head and hands the size of baseball mitts for a porter and not the Operations & IT Director of the Yorkshire Bank PLC. But then he hadn't expected him to be black. Not that he had any prejudices whatsoever—over the years he'd seen and worked with all types of students at the college and made a point of giving as much of himself as he could to each of them, no matter where they came from or what they looked like—but he just hadn't pictured Graham Shovelin this way. And that was his failing, of course. And maybe, he thought, that had to do with *Masterpiece Theatre* too, with the lords and ladies and the proper English butler and under-butler and all the rest. So Graham was black, that was all. Nothing wrong with that.

The hotel Graham took him to wasn't more than a twenty-minute drive from the airport, and it wasn't really a hotel, as far as Mason could see, but more one of these bed-and-breakfast sort of places, and the staff there was black too—and so were most of the people on the streets. But he was tired. Exhausted. Defeated before he even began. He found his bed in a back room and slept a full twelve hours, longer than he could ever remember having slept since he was a boy at home with his parents. In fact, when he finally did wake, he couldn't believe it was still dark outside and he had to tap the crystal of his watch to make sure it hadn't stopped.

He lay there for a long while after waking, in a big bed in a small room all the way on the other side of the world, feeling pleased with himself, proud of himself, having an *adventure*. He pushed himself up, fished through his suitcase for a pair of clean underwear and socks. Just then, an ambrosial smell, something exotic, spicy, began seeping in under the door and seemed to take possession of the room, and he realized he was hungry, ravenous actually. Vaguely wondering if he was too late for breakfast—or too early—he eased open the door and found himself in a dim hallway that gave onto a brightly lit room from which the odor of food was emanating, a room he took to be the kitchen.

He heard a murmur of voices. His knees hurt. He could barely seem to lift his feet. But he made his way down the hall and paused at the door, not knowing what the protocol was in a bed-and-breakfast (he and Jan had always stayed in hotels or motor courts). He gave a light knock on the doorframe in the same instant that the room jumped to life: a gas stove, spotless, with a big aluminum pot set atop it; a table and chairs, oilcloth top, half a dozen beer bottles; and someone sitting at the table, a big man, black, in a white sleeveless T-shirt: Graham. It was Graham Shovelin himself, a newspaper spread before him and a beer clutched in one big hand.

THE EXPLANATION

"Really, Mason, you must forgive me for any misunderstanding or inconvenience regarding the accommodations, but I am only acting in your best interest—*our* best interest—in putting you here, in this quite reasonable bed-and-breakfast hotel rather than one of those drafty anonymous five-star places in the heart of the city, which is where Mr. Oliphant, President of the Yorkshire Bank PLC, had urged me to put you up. And why? To save our partnership any further out-of-pocket expense—*unnecessary* expense—until we are able to have the funds released in full. Tell me, have I done right?"

Mason was seated now at the table across from Shovelin, a bowl of stew that wasn't all that much different from what he ate at home steaming at his elbow while a woman who'd appeared out of nowhere provided bread and butter and poured him a glass of beer. She was black too, thin as a long-distance runner and dressed in a colorful wraparound garment of some sort. Her hair was piled atop her head in a massive bouffant and her feet were bare. She was very pretty and for a moment Mason was so distracted by her he wasn't able to respond.

"Just tell me, Mason," Shovelin repeated. "If I've done wrong, let me know and I'll get in the car this minute and take you to the Savoy—or perhaps you prefer the Hilton?"

He wasn't tired, that wasn't it at all—just the opposite, he was excited. A new place, new people, new walls! And yet he couldn't quite focus on what Shovelin was saying, so he just shrugged.

"I take that to be accord, then?" Shovelin boomed. "Happily, happily!" he cried. "Let's toast to it!" and he raised his glass, tapped it against Mason's, and downed the contents in a gulp. His eyes reddened and he touched one massive fist to his breastbone, as if fighting down indigestion, then turned back to Mason. "Now," he said, so abruptly it almost sounded like the sudden startled bark of a dog, "let's get down to business. This lovely lady here, in the event you haven't already divined her identity, is none other than my executive secretary, Miss Afunu-Jones, who is taking time out of her hectic schedule to devote herself to your comfort during your brief stay. She has my full confidence, and anything you feel you must say to me you can say to her and she can handle any and all inquiries . . ." His voice trailed off. "In the event . . . well, in the event I am, how shall I put it?, *indisposed*."

Mason felt his heart clench. He could see the pain etched in the younger man's face and he felt the sadness there, felt the shadow of the mortality that had claimed Jan and would one day claim everyone alive, his daughter, his grandson, this man who'd reached out across the ocean to him and become not only his friend but his confidant.

Shovelin produced a handkerchief, wiped his eyes and blew his nose. "Forgive me for injecting an element of what, *pathos*, into this little party meant to welcome you to our land, and I know it's not professional"—here he employed the handkerchief again—"but I am only human." He looked up at the woman, who hovered behind them. "Chevette, perhaps you will take over for me, and give Mr. Alimonti—Mason—the explanation he's come for—"

Chevette, her eyes full too, pulled up a chair and sat beside Mason, so close their elbows were touching. She took her time, buttering a slice of bread and handing it to him before taking a sip of beer herself and looking him right in the eye. "We will see this business through to the end, believe me, Mason," she said, her voice soft and hesitant. "We will not desert you. You have my word on that."

"About tomorrow," Shovelin prompted.

Her eyes jumped to his and then back to Mason's. "Yes," she said, "tomorrow. Tomorrow we will take you to the central office, where you will meet with our president, Mr. Oliphant, and iron out the final details to your satisfaction." She paused, touched a finger to her lips. "I don't know that all this is necessary, but as you seem to have lost faith in us—"

"Oh, no, no," he said, fastening on her eyes, beautiful eyes, really, eyes the color of the birch beer he used to relish as a boy on family jaunts to Vermont.

"But the explanation is simple, it truly is. What I mean is, just look at us. We are not wealthy, we are not even accepted by many in white society, and I'm sorry to have to repeat it like a mantra, but we are diligent, Mr. Alimonti, diligent and faithful. The fact is, as my—as Mr. Shovelin—has told you, we are dealing with corruption, with thieves, and all the unconscionable holdup in this matter is to be laid at their feet, not ours, Mason, not ours." And here, whether conscious of it or not, she dropped a hand to his thigh and gave him the faintest squeeze of reassurance.

UNFORTUNATE CIRCUMSTANCES

The next day, his last day, and not even a full day at that, as his plane was scheduled to depart at 6:45 in the evening, he was awakened from a dreamless sleep by Chevette, who stood at the foot of his bed, softly calling his name. She was dressed in the sort of business attire he'd envisioned when he'd first heard her voice over the phone, she was wearing lipstick and eye shadow and her hair had been brushed out over her shoulders. "Mr. Alimonti," she said, "Mason, wake up. I have some bad news."

He pushed himself up on his elbows, blinking at her. His knee throbbed. He seemed to have a headache. For a minute he didn't know where he was.

"Unfortunate circumstances have arisen," she was saying. "Graham has had a seizure and they've taken him to hospital—"

He fumbled to find the words. "Hospital? Is he—will he?—"

She made a wide sweeping gesture with one hand. "That is not for me to say. That"—her eyes hardened—"is in the hands of the insurers, who keep denying him the lifesaving treatment he so desperately needs. And we, we are but humble bank employees and we are by no means rich, Mason, by no means. We've exhausted our savings . . . yes, *we*, because now I must confess to you what you must already have suspected—Graham is my husband. We didn't want to have to tell you for fear you might think us unprofessional, but the cat is out of the bag now." She caught her breath. Her eyes filled. "And I love him, I love him more than I could ever put into words—"

He was in his pajamas in a strange bed in a strange place, a strange woman was standing over him and his heart was breaking.

"Please help us," she whispered. "Please?"

THE FLIGHT BACK

He'd given her all he had on him—some eight hundred dollars in cash he'd brought along for emergencies—and written her a check he'd be hard-pressed to cover when he got home. As the expenses had mounted, he'd taken out a second mortgage and depleted his retirement account so that things were going to get very difficult financially if the funds didn't come through soon. But they would, he was sure they would, every minute of every day pushing him closer to his goal. Chevette had tearfully assured him that Mr. Oliphant would see things through, whether her husband survived his emergency operation or not. "Truly," she told him, "he lies between this life and the next."

It wasn't until he'd buckled himself in and the plane was in the air that it occurred to him that he never had gotten to meet Mr. Oliphant, see what an English bank looked like from the inside or even sign the agreement Graham had kept forgetting to produce, and now—he felt his heart seize again—might never be able to. He had two drinks on the plane, watched bits of three or four jumpy color-smeared movies, and fell off into a sleep that was a kind of waking and waking again, endlessly, till the wheels touched down and he was home at last.

ANGELICA STEPS IN

Three months later, after having missed four consecutive mortgage payments and receiving increasingly threatening letters from the bank, letters so depressing he could barely bring himself to open them, he telephoned his daughter to ask if she might be able to help him out with a small loan. He didn't mention Graham Shovelin, the Yorkshire Bank PLC or the windfall he was expecting, because he didn't want to upset her, and, more than that, he didn't want her interfering. And, truthfully, he wasn't so sure of himself anymore, the little voice back in his head now and telling him he was a fool, that he'd been defrauded, that Graham Shovelin, whom he hadn't heard from in all this time, wasn't what he appeared to be. He had hope still, of course he did—he had to have hope—and he made up excuses to explain the silence, excuses for Graham, who for all he knew might be lying there in a coma. Or worse. He could be dead. But why then didn't anyone pick up the phone at the Yorkshire Bank PLC? Chevette, though she may have been grief-stricken, would certainly have had to be there, working, no matter what had befallen her husband, and then there was Mr. Oliphant and whatever secretaries and assistants he might have had.

At one point, despairing, after he'd called twenty times without response, he went online and found a homepage for the Yorkshire Bank PLC, which didn't seem to list the names of the bank officers at any of their branches. He did find a general purpose number and after having been put on hold for ten minutes spoke to a woman who claimed she'd never heard of a Mr. Oliphant, and, of course, he was unable to supply any specifics, not with regard to which branch Oliphant was affiliated with or even what his given name might be. He felt baffled, frustrated, hopeless. He called his daughter.

"Dad? Is that you? How are you? We've been worried about you—"

"Worried, why?"

"I've called and called, but you never seem to be home—what

are you doing, spending all your time at dance clubs or what, the racetrack?" She let out a laugh. "Robbie's starting college in a month, did you know that? He got into his first-choice college, SUNY Potsdam, for music? The Crane School?"

He didn't respond. After a minute, when she paused for breath, he said flatly, "I need a loan."

"A loan? What on earth for? Don't you have everything you need?"

"For the mortgage. I—well, I got a little behind in my payments . . ."

It took a while, another five minutes of wrangling, but finally she got it out of him. When he'd told her the whole story, everything, the thirty million dollars, the disbursement, the bribe money, Graham's treatments, even the two-day debacle in London, she was speechless. For a long moment he could hear her breathing over the phone and he could picture the expression she was wearing, her features compressed and her lips bunched in anger and disbelief, no different from the way Jan had looked when she was after him for one thing and another.

"I can't believe you," she said finally. "How could you be so stupid? You, of all people, a former professor, Dad, a math whiz, good with figures?"

He said nothing. He felt as if she'd stabbed him, as if she was twisting the knife inside him.

"It's a scam, Dad, it's all over the papers, the internet, everywhere—the AARP newsletter Mom used to get. Don't you ever read it? Or listen to the news? The crooks even have a name for it, 419, after the Nigerian anti-fraud statute, as if it's all a big joke."

"It's not like that," he said.

"How much did you lose?"

"I don't know," he said.

"Jesus! You don't even know?" There was a clatter of pans or silverware. He could picture her stalking round her kitchen, her face clamped tight. "All right," she said. "Jesus! How much do you need?"

"I don't know: ten?"

"Ten what—thousand? Don't tell me ten thousand."

He was staring out the window on the back lawn and the burgundy leaves of the flowering plum he and Jan had planted when their daughter was born. It seemed far away. Miles. It was there, but it was shrinking before his eyes.

"I'm coming out there," she said.

"No," he said, "no, don't do that."

"You're eighty years old, Dad! Eighty!"

"No," he said, and he no longer knew what he was objecting to, whether it was his age or the money or his daughter coming here to discipline him and humble him and rearrange his life.

ONE MORE PHONE CALL

The house belonged to the bank now, all of it, everything, and his daughter and Robbie were there helping him pack up. He was leaving California whether he liked it or not and he was going to be living, at least temporarily, in Robbie's soon-to-be-vacated bedroom in Rye, New York. Everything was chaos. Everything was black. He was sitting in his armchair, waiting for the moving van to take what hadn't been sold off in a succession of what Angelica called "estate sales" and haul it across the country to rot in her garage. In Rye, New York. For the moment, all was quiet, the walls just stood there, no dog barked, no auto passed by on the street. He was thinking nothing. He couldn't even remember what Jan looked like anymore. He got to his feet because he had an urgent need to go fetch a particular thing before the movers got hold of it, but in the interval of rising, he'd already forgotten just what that particular thing was.

So he was standing there in the ruins of his former life, a high desperate sun poking through the blinds to ricochet off the barren floorboards, when the phone rang. Once, twice, and then he picked it up.

"Mason?"

"Yes?"

"Graham Shovelin here. How are you?"

Before he could answer, the deep voice rolled on, unstoppable, Old Man River itself: "I have good news, the best, capital news, in fact! The funds will be released tomorrow."

"You're"—he couldn't find the words—"you're okay? The, the treatment—?"

"Yes, yes, thanks to you, my friend, and don't think I'll ever forget it. I'm weak still, of course, which is why you haven't heard from me in some time now, and I do hope you'll understand . . . but listen, we're going to need one more *infusion* here, just to assure there are no glitches tomorrow when we all gather in Mr. Oliphant's office to sign the final release form—"

"How much?"

"Oh, not much, Mason, not much at all."

WARRIOR JESUS

In the first panel of the very first issue you see Him striding across the desert with maybe nothing around Him but sand and the ruins of a shattered village in the distance. He's not wearing a robe and sandals but bike shorts and black lace-up combat boots and a tight black tee and He's not the skinny hippie all the paintings make Him out to be, but buff, as if He's been doing weight training, but of course, like Wolverine or the Hulk, He doesn't really have to sweat anything to be built like that. He just is. And His hair—it isn't that long, actually, just long enough to give Him a topknot like a samurai, and His beard isn't shaggy like some biker's beard, but trimmed close to His rock-hard jawline. His eyes—at first—are calm, and they're not blue like in the paintings either, but green like Asia's (she's my girlfriend). What you see, right off, is that this isn't the sort of hero who'll turn the other cheek or out of some misguided notion of fairness or love or whatever won't use His powers to the very fullest degree. No, just the opposite. Warrior Jesus is the scourge and the whip—the Cleanser—and He's come to wipe up all the slime of the world, the Al Qaedas and Boko Harams, ISIS, the Mexican Mafia and all the rapists and slavers and drug dealers out there, dog abusers, wife beaters, anybody evil who seeks to inflict pain on the weak—they're going to be dust. All of them. Just like what He's walking over in that first panel, the sand grains symbolic of what He's going to reduce them to. No hell, no trial, no punishment: just dust. Or sand. Or whatever.

Saturday night, the place mobbed, and I've got my head down pretty much the whole shift, just trying to keep up with the orders. Stressed isn't really the word for it, just busy, so busy I'm startled when one of the customers—an older woman who comes in on a regular basis—asks me how my drawing's going and the best I can do is rotate the upper half of my body away from the grill, show her some teeth and say, "Great, just great." There must be twenty steaks up and I'm working my tongs like a master conductor waving his baton, only the stage here is a ten-by-three-foot space between the grill and the salad bar and the audience is a snaking line of semi-drunk people with big oval salad-bar plates in their hands, but I'm the main attraction, make no mistake about it. And the meat, of course, sizzling there over the tiny yellow fingers of flame and sending up that authentic mesquite-seared aroma that has them all choking back saliva as they lean over the sneeze guard and fish out cherry tomatoes or avocado slices with the salad tongs. The truth is, on this particular night, I all but blanked on the public-relations aspect of the job until the woman brought me out of my reverie, and that isn't good, because my boss, Mike Twombley, always makes a huge deal of it. *You are representing Brennan's every minute you're standing there at the grill, never forget it. People like to see their steaks go up and they like to see somebody cool, somebody friendly, flipping them, right?* Well, yeah, I get that. But they also like rare rare and medium-rare medium-rare, and if the grillman's busy bending over backwards for everybody—especially on a night like this—then there are going to be fuckups, and what would you rather have, dinners sent back or a grillman who's focused on the task at hand?

Toward the end of my shift, after I've already dumped the grease and taken the wire brush to the grill, Mercy, the cutest waitress, who just happens to drive all the old men at the bar gaga because she's older (thirty-two, divorced, one kid), brings me a late order, party of two, a New York well for the guy, prawn-and-scallop kebab for the girl. Normally the kitchen closes at nine-thirty, after which it's burgers only, flipped in a pan in the kitchen and served at the bar, and it's nine-forty now, but I'm in a good place, really riding high on Warrior Jesus and seeing the panels unfolding in my head as if I've already drawn them, and it's nothing to throw one more dinner on the grill, which will have to be scraped again, but it's not as if it hasn't happened before. The restaurant is in the business of making money and I'm a good employee, a model employee, really, as I try to remind Mike every chance I get, and if it costs me an extra twenty minutes, so what? I'm only going to sit at the bar anyway. Asia's out with her girlfriends—a movie, she said, then barhopping—and there's nothing for me at home except staring at the walls, unless I want to play video games (I don't) or watch TV (I doubly don't).

"I can't see them," I say, "where are they?" My eyesight isn't the best and I don't like to wear my glasses at the grill because they tend to steam up, which means everything out there in the dining room is just a blur.

"Around the corner? Table thirteen?"

"Okay," I say, "okay, great," and why do I always feel so stupid—or awkward, I guess—around Mercy when I've got my own girlfriend and Mercy's too old for me anyway? It's the eternal urge, the mating urge, common to us all, though not Warrior Jesus. He's beyond all that—He doesn't have the time, for one thing. And this isn't Greek mythology, with gods pulling the wires behind the scenes or bickering with each other or coming down to have sex with mortals—this is the One God, the Only God, and He's here for vengeance. "Just tell them we're about to take the salad bar down any minute, so they need to get to it ASAP, okay?"

"I just want to get out of here," she says, giving me a tired grin, and I watch her glide off in her black miniskirt and the low-cut top that adds an extra five dollars to her tip when it's a male paying the bill, which is about ninety percent of the time.

So here they come, the late diners I've gone out of my way to stay open for, a guy and a girl, and the guy's wearing some sort of headgear that flashes white all the way across the restaurant so even I can see it in my semi-blind state. And what is it? A turban? The term *raghead* shoots in and out of my mind, a term I don't think I've ever used because it's not p.c. and Asia's always on me if I make any kind of ethnic reference to anybody, whether in my comics or in person, and then he's there at the salad bar and the girl right beside him (she's mid-twenties, cute, dyed-red hair with black roots showing and a sleeve of tattoos running up her left arm). I can tell they've been dating for a while because he goes ahead of her, flipping a plate off the pile as if he's going to start juggling with it and bending low to dig into the bowl of romaine and pick out the crispest pieces—and he has to bend low, I realize, because he's tall, as tall as me at least, and that doesn't seem right somehow, as if people like him, from wherever he's from, should be shorter than that. He's got a beard, of course, a full beard that just about touches the cracked ice cooling the stainless-steel serving trays, and his skin's not much darker than mine used to get in the summers when I was a lifeguard at the lake. And what is he, a Paki or a Hindu or something? I don't know much about it, one way or the other, though the guy that delivers produce in the mornings is some sort of Arab and there's a Hindu, definitely a Hindu, running the Conoco station. Plus, what do I care? He's just another customer and I probably wouldn't have noticed him at all if he'd come in during the rush.

It's just then that he glances up and gives a little start as if he didn't expect to see anybody there, though even first-time customers seem to get the drill—suck down your cocktail, put in your order, troop up to the salad bar and let the grillman provide the entertainment till you've heaped up your plate and trooped back to your table again. As I say, he was bent at the waist, picking out his toppings, and now suddenly he straightens up and gives me a look. "Oh, hi," he says. "I guess you're our chef, huh?"

"Right," I say, and I'm looking at her too, wondering if I know her from someplace—high school? Pratt?—and what she's doing with him. "You're the New York well."

He lets out a laugh then, which is meant to be all urbane and above it all, and says, "Well, I hope I'm more than that"—and here he gives the girl a sly look—"though for our purposes, that designation suits me just fine." He's got a trace of an accent, which I'm just now picking up—British or something, or maybe Indian. From India.

"It's a crime," I say and watch his grin waver, which gives me just the faintest little tick of satisfaction. He thinks a lot of himself, this guy, this *dude,* and maybe I don't, maybe I take an instant dislike to him.

"What do you mean? What's a crime?"

I glance at the girl and back at him, then turn away to toss his steak on the grill, where it lands with a hiss and sends up a puff of smoke. "Oh," I say, turning back to him now and letting my eyes run first to her, then to him, "the steak. I mean, well-done is kind of like sacrilege. The other grillman—Bobby Reyes?—I've seen him refuse to do well-done." (And once, when he had a buzz on, actually go into the dining room and stand over a party of four, pleading with this woman to at least let him do hers medium.)

The guy in the turban bends down to dig into the artichoke hearts, but when he comes up he's grinning again. "Don't I know it," he says and puts his free arm around the girl. "Jenny's telling me the same thing all the time, right, babe?"

That's when I let my mouth get ahead of me, and I have to attribute it to just being tired at this juncture, that and dehydrated because the heat of the grill really does wring the sweat out of you, no different than if you were sitting in a sauna all day. "I thought Hindus didn't eat meat."

I watch the smile fade and then come up strong again, and he takes his time with me, dipping the ladle for the Roquefort dressing and pouring a half ton of it over everything on his plate. "I'm not Hindu," he says, and then he and the girl are turning their backs on me and heading back to their table.

That's all. That's all there is. Just that little exchange. And I am not prejudiced, or not any more than anybody else, and if you want to know the truth I hardly knew my cousin Bruce— Bruce Tuttle? That ring a bell?—because his family moved out to California when we were still kids and if I saw him more than two or three times over the years that was it. And yes, I did know he was some sort of minor journalist for CBS News—could my mother ever let me forget it?—and I knew he was covering the Middle East and all of that, but I don't know if I felt personally violated when they took him prisoner and then, without even negotiating, went out and beheaded him six days later, and I only watched the video once, on YouTube, but I felt something, let me tell you. I felt sick, sad, shocked, confused, angry, of course I did—who wouldn't? It didn't matter who they were doing this to—that video is the purest expression of evil that's ever come into my life. But that doesn't excuse what happens next, once the guy in the turban and his girlfriend disappear round the corner, and I don't feel good about it, but you have to understand how I was feeling that night, not only because of Asia, who might or might not have been lying to me about who she was going out with, but because I was tired and maybe a little fed up and I'd been listening to my mother go on about Bruce over and over for the last six months till I was either going to have to build a shrine to him in the backyard or go out and shoot myself in the head.

I flip the steak. Press down hard with the tongs till the juices sizzle and the flames jump up, then I put the girlfriend's kebab on, and all the while I'm working this ball of phlegm in my throat—I've got the cold to end all colds and the Dristan I took at four is wearing off. So he gets his steak, cooked through till it could have come right from the tannery, and if it has a nice translucent glaze on it, I just feel it's the least I can do for him.

The second panel shows Him coming into this burned-out village, which is still maybe a hundred yards off, and you can see figures there now, shadowy, wreathed in smoke, and in the third panel He's there and the people—civilians, victims, little kids, old women in head scarves—are all looking flabbergasted at Him as if they're wondering what next, expecting the worst, only the worst. That's when your eye jumps to panel four and you see the bad guys, all dressed in black with black ski masks and AKs and grenade launchers slung over their shoulders. One of them has a knife, and not one of these seven-inch Ka-Bar things like they used in the video, but a huge blade, curved like a scimitar—do they still use scimitars?—and it shines against his all-black clothes, or maybe it's a robe he's wearing, a black robe, till it definitely focuses your eye. Panel five is the knife, foregrounded, and just beyond it are the victims, a skinny kid and his father, kneeling in the sand with hoods over their heads. You wonder, What have they done to deserve this?, and the answer is nothing, they just had the bad luck to live in a godforsaken place where the bad guys have sway over everything, stealing their cars, their houses, their food, their wives and daughters and mothers. Maybe the father's the village mechanic, maybe he owned the burned-out service station you can see in the distance, maybe he tried to stop them when they dragged his twelve-year-old daughter into the back room and shut the door. No matter. The knife's already in the air, already coming down, and we cut away to just the head, the father's head, in the sand.

That's when Warrior Jesus comes on the scene, just striding ahead, taking His time. The guards see Him coming and they give Him a curious/hostile look, but He's got nothing in His hands and His shorts and tee are so tight He couldn't be concealing anything like a suicide vest or a gun or even a box cutter, so though they level their AKs on Him, they're hardly worried. At worst—or best, depending on how you look at it—He'll be the next victim, once they get done with the boy. Warrior Jesus doesn't say a word. And this is something that separates Him from the other superheroes out there—He doesn't need to talk, only act. Plus, another thing about this character is His power is absolute. He doesn't have a nemesis, no Lex Luthor or Professor Zoom or Red Skull, and He doesn't rocket around like Neo or Superman or the Flash. He doesn't need any of that: He just is. He has immanence. And no one can threaten Him.

The executioner is raising the blade over the boy's head when Warrior Jesus lifts His finger, just one finger—His index finger—and points it. In that instant the scimitar clatters to the ground because there's no one holding on to it, no one there, in fact: the executioner is gone, converted, as you see in closeup, into a knee-high pyramid of dust. The others, the henchmen, that is, open up with their rifles and the bullets are depicted hanging there in the air (think *The Matrix*) but they never reach their destination because they dissolve like vapor and the weapons themselves vanish too, along with the henchmen, who form their own piles of dust, even as Warrior Jesus frees the boy and restores the father's head, perfectly, just as it was before (which is tricky, but if the old Jesus could raise the dead, why not?). No sutures, no scars, no operating room, just a dip into the immediate past, a time warp that fixes everything. Except for the executioner and the henchmen, that is. They are dust forever.

One more thing, because this is just the introductory episode and the readers won't really know what they're getting into yet, what the rules are, I mean—the village springs back up around the astonished onlookers as if it's a stage set, every building, every storefront, even the burned-out service station instantly recreated, only better than before, with trees, lawns, a glittering fresh-water stream emerging from the place where the father's blood saturated the sand, maybe a KFC franchise—or no, Subway, which is way healthier. The people look around them—and they're all wearing new clothes and their wounds are healed, even their dogs are back—and they're wondering who this savior is. Or where He is. Because the next panel shows the village from afar over the squared-up shoulders of Warrior Jesus, who, we see, is already on to His next adventure. Or not adventure, that's not the right word, though there's plenty of adventure in the book—call it correction, His next correction. What's changed? Word is out now and all the psychopaths and murderers and dictators are in for a rude surprise.

And cheats, cheats too.

The next day's my day off and I wind up sleeping in, which means I blow off my date with Asia for a late breakfast at the brioche place before she goes into work at noon (irony of ironies, she's the hostess at Cedric's, our rival steak house on the other side of town, a place that's pricier than ours and a whole lot less fun, the waiters strictly in jacket and tie—no waitresses—and a bar scene that's pretty well dead no matter the hour; plus, if you want a salad, the waiter's going to go into the kitchen and bring it out to you). The minute my eyes open I reach for my phone and text her, but she doesn't text back and I figure I'll try again later, when she's at work and so bored she's going to be checking her messages every ten seconds. Her job, like any hostess's, is to look great, open up her megawatt smile and lead diners to their tables, which doesn't leave much room for creativity or job satisfaction, but like me she's two years out of college (with a degree in art history) and trying to make ends meet any way she can.

There's not a whole lot in the refrigerator beyond a couple of bagels as hard as horseshoes and a take-out box of mistakes from the night before (you might think it sounds cool having all the filets, New Yorks and lamb chops you want, but that gets old fast), and so I just pour myself a glass of orange juice and sit at the window awhile, looking out on a bleak February day with a crust of grimy snow on the lawn and a cold drizzle fuzzing the windows. The place I'm renting is a spare room, with full bath and private entrance, in a tract house like the one I grew up in, but it's my own to do anything I want with and it has a big picture window with a southern exposure, which gives me the kind of afternoon light I like for my work. Am I hungry? Not really. I'm still dogged by the cold, stuffed up when I get out of bed and then sniffling to the point where I'm going to have to go out and buy more toilet paper at some point, and maybe that has something to do with why I overslept and why I'm not hungry, or at least not hungry enough to get in the car and go out and pick something up. At any rate, before I can think about it, I'm at my desk (a Martin drawing table, actually, which my mother got for me two birthdays ago) and I'm deep into Warrior Jesus, inking the first couple of panels and letting the story come to me, no speech bubbles yet, but a couple captions running through my head just to set things up so people aren't confused (Is this Syria, or what? He can replace a severed head? Really? What about donor heads? What about all the heads already lopped off in all the other villages?). It doesn't take much. The way I see it, if the drawings don't tell the story, or ninety-nine percent of it anyway, you're dead in the water.

It's two-thirty on the dot when she calls, off work now till they reopen for dinner at five, and finally remembering she has a boyfriend, me, that is, who got shut out the night before and must have called her a dozen times and even, at one a.m., tried her at her parents', though admittedly he—I—hung up after the third ring because the last thing I wanted was for her mother to see the caller ID and answer in that spooky accusatory voice she has.

"Hey," I say.

"Hey."

"Sorry I missed you this morning. I guess I overslept. This cold's a real bitch, you know?"

She doesn't say anything, or if she does—my ears seem to be stuffed up too—it's "Yeah," which isn't much more than a space filler (Yeah, she knows? or Yeah, it's too bad? or Yeah, I'm at the dentist having my teeth drilled?).

"How was the movie?"

"What?"

"You know, the movie you guys saw—Stephanie and who-all? What was it again?"

"Oh, that," she says, her voice dropped low and clogged up, as if she's the one with the cold. "We wound up not going. It was Steph's birthday, did I tell you?"

"No, you didn't mention it. And you didn't answer your phone or your messages either. I even tried your parents' at like one—"

"What can I say, Devon—girls' night out, okay? I guess I just didn't feel like checking my phone—I mean, it's not like we're Siamese twins."

I let that hang a minute, then I'm irate, and I'm sorry, because this isn't the first time and I know something's going on, *I know it.* "Shit, you don't have to jump down my throat—I'm not the one that didn't call. I'm the one that had to sit at the bar and get shit-faced till Tonio shut out the lights and locked the door, and *still* you wouldn't answer."

"I'm not going to argue," she says.

"No," I say, "me neither. If you want to know the truth I'm working, really working for the first time in like months, and you—this call?—you're interrupting me, you're *distracting* me, okay?"

Another pause. And then, her voice dwindled down to practically nothing, she says, "What is it—Warrior Jesus?"

For some reason, this sets me off even more, and yes, I've told her all about the concept, talked it up for weeks, but right now, in the mood I'm in, I can't abide the idea of her horning in on it, of getting between me and my character, which is a kind of intimacy I never asked for. I don't know what comes over me, but I shout into the phone as if I'm shouting across the street at her. "Fucking A!" I yell. And then repeat myself, even louder: "Fucking A!"

The next scene He enters isn't all that much different from the first, though it's a matter of degree. We're in a city now, not a village, a big city like Ramadi, which is where they think Bruce was killed, though the backdrop of the video was so generic—dirt, rocks, rubble—nobody could really be sure. I've downloaded a ton of pictures to give me an idea of what it's supposed to look like, which is no different, really, than what you see in photos of

WWII or Vietnam and, it goes without saying, in all the apocalyptic comics and graphic novels, as if it's a genre, *Shell Cities*. I do try to make it my own, give it a little originality, but you don't want to go overboard—it's a bombed-out city, that's all you need to know. Anyway, there's a whole lot more of it than what you got of the village, so in the splash you see Warrior Jesus' head in profile and the city, with all the rubble and one-sided storefronts rolling out to the gutter on all four sides. Where is He? You see that in the next panel, when He walks up to a towering mosque-like edifice decorated with all these wedding-cake curlicues around a pair of big reinforced double doors, which can only mean He's heading up the stairs of the palace where the big guy, the caliph himself—al-Baghdadi—is holding court. Or hiding. Or whatever.

There are guards, of course, hundreds of them, ranged up and down the street and perched on the roofs of the buildings that are still standing, but Warrior Jesus never even bothers to give them a glance—He's after bigger game. Up the steps He goes, completely ignoring the shitstorm of bullets and rockets and grenades blasting all around Him, which even if they're direct hits, just fall harmlessly to the ground. He doesn't have to open the doors: they swing open automatically and in He steps, which is when we cut away to the deepest hold in the deepest subbasement of the place, where all the drone strikes in the world couldn't even begin to penetrate, and here's the big guy, looking scared—he's heard the rumors—and his minions are strapping suicide vests on two little girls, retarded girls (all right, *Asia*: mentally challenged), which are his last line of defense. Then back to Warrior Jesus, inside this big glittering palace-like place with maybe a few shell holes in the roof and the far wall, and here come the girls, hurrying up the steps to take Him out, whether they know what they're doing or not.

But that doesn't happen. That's the point: it *can't* happen.

There's no kryptonite in this universe, no Mist or Magneto or Dr. Polaris: Warrior Jesus is all-powerful. And, as we see now, merciful too. He doesn't lift His finger to annihilate the girls, but just winks one eye and the suicide vests are gone—and better, the girls are instantly cured, which you can see in their smiles and the way their eyes radiate intelligence. Then it's al-Baghdadi's turn. He's cowering in the subbasement with its bomb-proof walls and three-foot-thick tungsten-steel doors and all the rest, but it's not going to do him any good. Warrior Jesus just steps right through the steel door as if it's made of paper like in manga or the old samurai movies. And then He lifts His finger, and the big guy is dust.

I wind up working all day, just on fire, really, and the funny thing is I keep seeing Bruce in flashes, as if there's something in this that's for him, as if I'm doing this for him, when really, as I say, he was nothing to me. To my mother, maybe—he was her sister's only child, taken from her in this incredibly senseless barbaric way, and how could people be like that, et cetera—but I wouldn't even know what he looked like if my mother hadn't taped him every time he did a story from one dusty outpost or another. To me, he was like any other reporter or TV personality, completely disembodied, as unreal as the image itself flickering there in a haze of pixels, and if I felt any emotion at all it was disgust, especially with the bland smugness of his face as he mouthed the words nobody was listening to and nobody cared about, palm trees waving in the background and him going through the whole battery of facial tics they taught him in broadcast journalism school. But still, as the day wears on and the light goes bad and I'm working under my lamps, I keep seeing him, scenes from ancient times shuffling in a loop over and over in my brain. An example, a thing I hadn't thought of in years, is the time his mother, my aunt Marie, took him and me to the Central Park Zoo when I must have been five or six, I guess, and we both broke away from her and ran up to the leopard's cage. It was summer. Or no, spring. I remember I had a jacket on, and the colors, I remember the colors, everything concrete-gray and the black bars of the cage cutting the backdrop in neat rectilinear sections and then this cat, this huge muscle-rippling cat, that stood out as if he'd been dipped in Day-Glo. Bruce was older than me, faster and taller, and he got there first so I arrived at the moment the leopard let loose with a sudden soul-stripping roar that scared the living shit out of us because this thing wasn't a stuffed toy and we both knew it could hurt us beyond repair, that it *wanted* to hurt us. One of us cried, I remember that too.

Anyway, though I never did get hold of Asia, which really irritates me (did that earlier conversation qualify as a fight, in her mind anyway?), I nonetheless get in the car come nine and go to pick her up at work, which is what I usually do on my day off. She's got her own car, but over the past couple of months, it's become a ritual for us to meet at the bar at Cedric's, which might be a mortuary, but it's convenient and they pour a killer drink. We have maybe two, on her employee discount, and then go out to get something to eat or hit a late movie or just go back to my place, where the most essential thing is—the bed—because with her living at home it's pointless to go to her place. Unless her parents take off on a cruise, which they did last month and we had the whole house to ourselves, with the bed the size of a life raft, the Jacuzzi and the Samsung forty-inch TV and a freezer full of frozen entrées like Stouffer's lasagna and Bistro sesame-ginger salmon bowl.

The bar is separate from the dining room at Cedric's, unlike at Brennan's, where you can sit at the bar while you're waiting for your table and see people eating, which, in theory, gets you to drink more. At Cedric's, you come into a vestibule where you can stomp the snow off your boots and hang up your coat. The swinging doors straight ahead lead into the dining room and the ones to your right open directly on the bar. On this night—it's starting to freeze up outside, the drizzle whitening under the headlights until it's suspended there like in a Japanese print—I don't bother with my coat and just push through the doors and step into the bar, which isn't as dead as usual, three or four older couples getting raucous at the bar and a scatter of people at the tables, and I don't at first see Asia, which isn't unusual, because sometimes she's in the kitchen or still out in the dining room, depending on the dinner crowd. But then—and this is the strangest thing, like something out of the Believe It Or Not! strip—I spot the white turban floating there in the candle gloom like a seagull, and it's the non-Hindu from last night and his girlfriend right beside him and I'm thinking he's either a restaurant critic or he must really like steak. I hear Asia before I see her, this distinctive machine-gun laugh she's got—*ack, ack, ack*—and now I'm really confused because she's sitting right next to the guy in the turban and laughing at something he obviously just said.

There's no room at the bar—some guy I've never seen before has his stool pushed right up against hers and he's laughing too, all of them part of some joke or routine and all of them, I realize, smashed. So what *is* going on here? I don't have a clue. But I push my way in and slip my arm around Asia's waist, which causes the guy next to her (weasel face, long black hair) to practically jump out of his seat, and I say, "What's up?" and Asia turns around and gives me a look like she doesn't even recognize me.

"Oh, hi," she says, after a minute, and the turban guy turns his head too, like this has anything to do with him. She pauses, everybody does, as if in freeze-frame, then says, "I didn't think you were coming. I mean, after—"

"After what?"

"When I called? And you yelled at me?"

The new guy—he's so close I can smell the old-fashioned

limey aftershave he's got on—is just looking at her now, studying her, as if she's some kind of experiment he's been working on, and then the turban guy, in his fruity tones, says, "Hey, don't I know you?" And all of a sudden he slaps his head and comes on with a big lemon-sucking grin. "From last night, right—you're the chef." The grin goes wider. "So what's this, a busman's holiday?"

I am full of Warrior Jesus, the whole dividing line between how intense work was and this moment here as confusing as if I'm just now waking up from a dream, and I don't know what to say—don't, in fact, want to say anything. These people are nothing to me. And they're drunk, way ahead of me, and even if I started throwing down shots I'd never catch up to them. What I say, and I don't even glance at anybody but Asia, is "Time to go." And because that might sound maybe too abrupt or harsh, I add lamely, "I've got a cold? And I'm really wiped from working all day."

Asia gives me a steady look. "I'm not ready," she says. There's half a drink in front of her and a full one backing it up, which somebody obviously bought her—a mai tai, which she only drinks when she's in interplanetary space, which is where she is now.

"Yeah," I say, and both guys are watching me, one from the left, one from the right, and the tattooed girlfriend too, "but maybe you didn't hear me. I said, *it's time to go.*"

Asia doesn't like to be told what to do, nobody does, really, but I have certain rights here—she's my girlfriend, not theirs—and when she says, for the second time, "I'm not ready," something just goes loose in me and I say, "The fuck you're not," and the Turban starts in with, "Hey, hey, now, no need for that," but there is a need, every need in the world, my need, and before I know what I'm doing, I'm stalking out the door and into the cold, cold night.

Which is where I see the Mercedes parked at the curb, two

cars down. It's an older model, a classic, I guess, the sort of thing your parents might hand down to you once you get your license and they go for an upgrade. It's a mustard yellow, more gold where the streetlight hits it, and everything else bordered in the black of the night so it stands out as if it's the only car on the street. And didn't I see this very car in the lot at Brennan's just last night? One of the last cars there and the Turban and his girlfriend lingering at their table over after-dinner drinks? Maybe. Maybe so. It doesn't really matter at this point—and it only takes me a minute to extract what I need from the trunk of my car, and yes, I do occasionally tag around town, very distinctive, eyeless faces usually, with my own DD insignia underneath, and I will not apologize for it because it's public art, at least the way I do it. Nothing so exacting as that tonight, though. Tonight it's just one word, in black, dripping right down the driver's side door. Can you guess what it is? I'll give you a hint: seven letters, starting with *R*.

The scene changes for Warrior Jesus, no more desert, no more ISIS and Al Qaeda. He's in the tropics now, palm fronds stirred by a gentle breeze, butterflies hanging like mobiles in the air, and the place He's approaching is in a block of storefronts, a glitter of windowpanes, white stucco, red-tile roofs gone dark with night. Out front a sign that says *Cantina*. Who's in there? The narcos and their minions, some of them out-of-uniform *federales* even, everybody bought and sold and every business on the street—in the whole city—paying the extortion tax. We see them partying in a tier running down the right side of the page, tequila bottles, cocaine, video games, and their whores hanging all over them, women they've forced into prostitution because it's either that or die, and some of the girls as young as thirteen, though obviously I can't show all of that without getting into some serious back-

story. Just let the drawings give you the picture and you can fill
in the rest from general knowledge. The point is, these are bad
guys, very bad guys, and at the center of the action, just like in
Ramadi, is their kingpin, a kind of El Chapo figure, only bigger,
the way El Chapo would be if he was younger and pumped iron.
They look menacing, armed to the teeth, and yet for all that they
don't stand a chance—we've already seen Warrior Jesus in action and they are half a beat from being reduced to dust. Or at
least that's what you think.

But—and I had to backtrack here, trying to dredge something
up from all those years I went to church with my mother as a
little kid—a new element enters the picture, and it's so obvious I
have to slap myself for not having thought of it earlier. Of course
there's a nemesis—what was I thinking? It's Lucifer, the Devil
himself, Satan, the original nemesis, the one that ruined Adam
and Eve and tempted the old Jesus in the desert. All this evil, what
they did to Bruce, the mass killings, all of it—it's got to be coming from someplace, and here it is, evil incarnate. Anyway, he's
lounging in back, just behind the kingpin, and he doesn't have
horns or a pointed tail or anything like that, but you can see from
the way he's built and from his eyes—slit yellow eyes, like a
goat's—just who he is and what he thinks of himself.

That's when Warrior Jesus comes through the door and the
whole room freezes. We see Him run His eyes over the narcos
and corrupt cops and the whores and then the kingpin before
coming to rest on Satan, who you see in closeup in the next
panel is sporting a mercury tattoo that reads EL ÁNGEL CAÍDO,
just in case you're not getting it. Right. And though this part
isn't really worked out yet, you see Warrior Jesus raise His finger and point it right at Satan and nothing happens. The whole
room is one big smirk, the joke's on Him. What comes next
is the fight scene, the two antagonists, with all their powers,
locked together in a Manichean struggle as if the forces of good

and evil neutralize each other all the way down the line. You see fire, radiation, suns exploding, and they wrestle over the oceans and the continents and all the way out into deep space, way beyond the glittering satellites and even the spacecraft of aliens we haven't even dreamed of to this point, and then the panel goes black, as if we're in a black hole and all the energy's been sucked out of the universe.

The next day I'm at work, the lunch crowd heavier than usual, and more demanding too—one clown even wants me to Pitts a steak for him (cover a filet in fat, prop it three inches above the grill on kebab skewers and incinerate the outside while leaving the middle all but raw). The meat goes on the grill. The exhaust fans suck back the smoke. I'm sweating, dehydrated, I still have a cold. And I'm upset about the night before, my second night in a row back at home with nothing to do but draw, and she hasn't texted or called so I have no idea what the resolution of that little gathering at the bar turned out to be, whether she's fucking one of them or both of them or if she's going to start wearing a turban now or what. So I put my head down and lose myself in work, and when I look up it's two-thirty and time for my break, at which point I make myself a burger and a salad, sit down at one of the tables in back and dial her number.

I count four rings, five, and just when I think she's not going to pick up, she's there saying, "What do *you* want?"

"What do you mean, what do I want? I want to talk to you."

"Well, I don't want to talk to you."

"Don't give me that shit, because I want to talk to *you*, hear me?"

She doesn't answer.

"All right, fine—I don't want to talk to you either," I say, but still she doesn't say anything and it takes me a minute to realize the phone's gone dead.

A spread now. You see Him way in the distance with all the turmoil and quasars and all the rest diminishing behind Him till He's back in the scene out front of the cantina and stepping through the doors all over again, and for a minute you think nothing's changed, the panel almost identical to the one two pages back, until you realize Satan, with his goat's eyes and mercury tattoo, is gone. And then you realize that the rest of them, everybody in the room, though they draw their weapons and start blazing away, are doomed, just like bad guys everywhere. Warrior Jesus points His finger, the narcos vanish and their weapons clatter to the floor. There's nobody left in the room now but a bartender, a couple waitresses and the whores, maybe fifteen or twenty of them. These are innocents, the whores, that's what we're thinking—forced into the trade, sold into it—and He will free them from their chains and restore them to what they once were, sisters, daughters, mothers, just like He took the burden of retardation off the two Syrian girls.

We're wrong, though. The whores are beyond redemption, we can see that in their faces, cheaters, sinners, betrayers, riddled with every kind of STD known to man, and we linger on them in a panel that takes in the whole scene. The one in the middle, the prettiest one, I give her Asia's face, and I don't need a photograph to work from, just the implant in my memory, and I give her Asia's green eyes too, though I shade them more toward olive so as to take nothing away from His eyes. It's a moment of tension. He lifts His finger, but the whores don't turn to dust—no, that would be too easy. What happens is they begin to melt, like wax, and we see the one in the middle screaming out her pain with every waxy drop of her flesh that sizzles on the floor beneath her. Then a full-page spread: Warrior Jesus' face in closeup, so huge it bleeds off the edges of both pages, and for the first time since He's come on the scene, He's smiling. It's not a happy smile, that wouldn't work, not at all—He's still got a job to do—but more rueful, as if He's just about to shake His head in a go-figure kind of way. And then the final image, and I'm still not sure about this, though it could work as a branding icon and I could see it on a line of tees, easily, you get a closeup of His finger, just His finger, pointed right at you.

So what do you think? Is it a go?

THE FUGITIVE

They told him he had to wear a mask in public. Which was ridiculous. It made him feel like he had a target painted on his back—or his face, actually, right in the middle of his face. But if he wanted to walk out the door of the clinic he was going to walk out with that mask on—either that or go to jail. Outside it was raining, which made everything all that much harder, because what were you going to do with a wet mask? How could you even breathe? Here, inside the office, with the doctor and his caseworker from health services, there was no sound of the rain, or if there was, he couldn't hear it—all he could hear was the rasp and wheeze of his own compromised breathing as he sucked air through the fibers of the mask.

The doctor was saying something to him now and Marciano watched him frame the words with his hands before they both looked to the caseworker, a short slim woman with a big bust and liquid eyes he would have liked to fuck if he wasn't so sick. She was named Rosa Hinojosa, and he kept saying her name in his head because of the way it rhymed, which somehow made him feel better.

"You understand what the doctor is telling you?" she asked in her clipped north-of-the-border Spanish he could have listened to all day under other circumstances. But these were the circumstances and until he got better he would have to play their game, Dr. Rosen's game and Rosa Hinojosa's too.

He nodded.

"No more lapses, you understand that? You will report here each morning when the clinic opens at eight for your intravenous medication, and"—she held up two plastic pill containers—"you will take your oral medication, *without fail,* every night at dinner. And you must wear your mask at all times."

"Even when I'm alone?"

She looked to the doctor, said something to him in English, nodded, then turned back to Marciano, her breasts straining at the fabric of her blouse, a pink blouse that made her look even younger than she was, which, he guessed, was maybe twenty-four or -five. "You have your own room in this house"—she glanced down at the clipboard in her lap—"at 519 West Haley Street? Is that right?"

"Yes."

"There are other roomers there?"

"Yes."

"All right. When you're alone in your room, you can remove the mask, but only then and never if you're in the common area, in the kitchen or the living room or even the bathroom, except to brush your teeth and wash your face. You're highly contagious and if you were to cough without the mask on, the bacteria could get into the air and infect your roommates, and you wouldn't want that, would you?"

No, he agreed, he wouldn't, but now the doctor was saying something more, his tone harsh and hectoring, and though Marciano didn't register what he was saying, or not exactly, he got the gist of it: this was his warning, his final warning, and now there could be no appeal. He watched the doctor's eyes that looked at him as if he were less than human, something to step on in the street and crush, angry eyes, hateful, and what had he done to deserve this? He'd gotten sick, that was all—and couldn't anybody get sick?

Rosa Hinojosa (her lips were fascinating—plump and adhesive—and he wanted desperately in that moment to get well if for no other reason than to kiss them or even for the promise of kissing them) told him what he already knew, that because he'd stopped taking his medication a year ago, his case of tuberculosis had mutated into the multi-drug-resistant form and his life was at risk because after this there were no more drugs. That was it. They didn't exist. But more, and worse: if he did not comply fully—no lapses—Dr. Rosen would get a court order and incarcerate him to be sure he got the full round of treatment. And why? Not out of charity, entertain no illusions about that, but to protect society, and at a cost—did he even have any idea of the cost?—of as much as two hundred thousand dollars for him alone. She paused. Compressed her lips. Looked to the doctor. Then, as if she were tracking the drift of the very microbes hanging invisibly in the air, she brought her eyes back to him. "You agree?" she demanded.

He wanted to say yes, of course he did—he wanted to be cured, but he was already feeling better, much better, and this whole business was so cold, so hard, he honestly didn't know if he could go through with it, and wasn't that the problem last time? He'd taken the medicine, which was no easy thing because it made him sick to his stomach and itch as if there were something under his skin clawing its way out. They said he'd have to stay on the regimen anywhere from six to thirty months, but within three months he'd felt fine, his cough nearly gone and his arms and chest filling out again, so he started selling the pills be-cause he didn't need them anymore and then he stopped coming to the clinic altogether and that would have been fine until the disease returned to shake him like a rat in a cage and he spat up blood and came back here to their contempt and their antiseptic smells and their masks and dictates and ultimatums. He wanted to say yes, and he tried to, but at that moment the cough came up on him, the long dredging cough that was like the sea drawing back over the stones at low tide, and the inside of the mask was suddenly crimson and he couldn't seem to stop coughing.

When finally he looked up, both the doctor and Rosa Hi-nojosa were wearing masks of their own and Rosa Hinojosa was pushing a box of disposable surgical masks across the desk to him. He couldn't see her lips now, only her eyes, and her eyes—as rich and brown as two chocolates in the dark wrappers of her lashes—didn't have an ounce of sympathy left in them.

Before he got sick the second time, he'd been working as part of a crew that did landscaping and gardening for the big estates strung out along the beach and carved out of the hills, a good job, steady, and with a *patrón* who didn't try to cheat you. One of his jobs was to trap and dispose of the animals that infested these places, rats, gophers, possums, raccoons and whatever else tore up the lawns or raided the orchards. His *patrón* wouldn't allow the use of poison of any kind—the owners didn't like it and it worked its way up the food chain and killed everything out there, which to Marciano's mind didn't seem like such a bad proposition, but it wasn't his job to think. His job was to do as he was told. The gophers weren't a problem—they died under-ground, transfixed on the spikes of the Macabee traps he set in the dark cool dirt of their runs—but the possums and raccoons

and even the rats had to be captured alive in Havahart traps of
varying sizes depending on the species. Which raised the question of what to do with them once you'd caught them.

The first time he did actually catch something—a raccoon—
it was on a big thirty-acre estate with its own avocado grove and
a fish pond stocked with Japanese koi that cost a thousand dollars
each. It was early, misty yet, and when he went to check the cage
he'd baited with a dab of peanut butter and half a sardine it was
a shock to see the dark shadow compressed inside it, the robber
itself with its black mask and tense fingers grasping the mesh as if
it were a monkey and not a *mapache* at all. In the next moment he
was running down the slope to where the *patrón* was assembling
the sprinkler system for a new flowerbed, crying out, "I got one,
I got one!"

The *patrón*, big-bellied but tough, a man who must have been
as old as Marciano's father yet could work alongside the men on
the hottest day without even breathing hard, glanced up from
what he was doing. "One what?"

"A raccoon."

"Okay, good. Get rid of it and reset the trap. Is it a female?"

A female? What was he talking about? It was a raccoon, that
was all, and what did he expect him to do? Flip it over and inspect
its equipment?

"Because if it's a female, there'll be more."

Breathless, excited, the microbes working in him though he
didn't yet know it, he just stood there, puzzled. "Get rid of it
how?"

"I thought you were a trapper?"

"I am, it's just I want to be sure to do things the way you
want them, that's all."

A steady look. A sigh. "Okay, listen, because I'm only going
to tell you once. Take one of those plastic trash cans lined up

there behind the garage and fill it with water, right to the top, you understand? Then just drop the cage in and it'll be over in three minutes."

"You mean drown it, just like that?"

"What are you going to do, take it home and train it to walk on a leash?" The *patrón* was grinning now, pleased with his own joke, but there was work to do and already he was turning back to it. "And do me a favor," he added, glancing over his shoulder. "Bury it out in the weeds where Mrs. Lewis won't have to see it."

Why he was thinking of that, he couldn't say, except that he missed the job—and the money—and as he walked to the bus in the rain, the box of face masks tucked under one arm, he wanted to be back there again, under the sun, working, just that, working. They'd scared him at the clinic, they always scared him, and he was feeling light-headed on top of it. The blood was bad, he knew that, he could see it in their eyes. Thirty months. He was twenty-three years old and thirty months was like a lifetime sentence, and even then, there were no guarantees—Rosa Hinojosa had made that clear. He was sick from the intravenous. His arm was sore. His throat ached. Even his feet didn't seem to want to cooperate, zigging and zagging so he was walking like a drunk, and what was that all about?

The sidewalk before him was strewn with the worms that were coming up out of the earth because if they stayed down there they'd drown, whereas up here, in the rain, they'd have a chance at life before somebody stepped on them or the birds got to them. He liked worms, nature's recyclers, and he was playing a little game with himself, trying to avoid them and hold in the next cough at the same time, watching his feet and the pattern the worms made on the pavement, loops and triangles of pale bleached-out flesh, and when he looked up he was right

in front of the bar—Herlihy's—he'd seen from the bus stop but
had never been inside of. It was just past ten in the morning and
he wasn't working today—his new job, strictly gardening, was
with an old white-haired *campesino* who booked the clients and
sat in his beater truck and read spy novels while Marciano did all
the work—and his ESL class at the community college wasn't
till five, so there really wasn't anything to do with himself but sit
in front of the television in his room. That had something to do
with it. That and the fact that his new boss—Rudy—had just
paid him the day before.

He didn't go directly in, but walked by the place as if he was
on an errand elsewhere, then stripped off the mask and stuffed
it in his pocket, doubled back and pushed open the door. Inside
were all the usual things, neon signs for Budweiser and Coors,
a jukebox that might once have worked, the honey-colored bottles lined up behind the bar and the head of a deer—or no, an
elk—jammed into one wall as if this was Alaska and somebody
had just shot it. There were three customers, all white, strung
together on three adjoining barstools, and the bartender, also
white, but fat, with big buttery arms in a short-sleeve shirt.
They all turned to look at him as he came in and that made him
nervous so he chose a stool at the far end of the bar, rehears-
ing in his head the phrase he was going to give the bartender,
"Please, a beer," which made use of his favorite word in English
and the word wasn't "please."

The bartender heaved himself up off his own stool and came
down the bar to him, put two thick white hands on the counter
and asked him something, which must have been "What do you
want?" and Marciano uttered his phrase. There was a moment
of ambiguity, the man poised there still instead of bending to the
cooler, and then there was a further question, which he didn't
grasp until the man began rattling off the names of the beers
he stocked, pointing as he did so to a line of bottles on the top

row, ten or twelve different brands. "Corona," Marciano said, unfolding a five-dollar bill on the bar, and all at once he was coughing and he put his hand up to cover his mouth, but he couldn't seem to stop until he had the bottle to his lips, draining it in three swallows as if he were a nomad who'd just come in off the desert.

One of the men at the end of the bar said something then and the other two looked at Marciano and broke out laughing, and whether it was good-natured or not, a little joke at his expense, it made him feel tight in his chest and the cough came up again, so severe this time he thought he was going to pass out. But here was the bartender, saying something more, and what it was he couldn't imagine, because it wasn't illegal to cough, was it? But no, that wasn't it. The bartender was pointing at the empty bottle and so Marciano repeated his phrase, "Please, a beer," and the heavy man bent to the cooler, extracted a fresh Corona, snapped off the cap and set it before him.

He sipped the second beer and watched the rain spatter the dirty windows and run off in streaks. At some point he saw his bus pull up at the stop across the street, a vivid panel of color that made him think of what was waiting for him at home—nothing, zero, exactly zero—and he watched it pull away again as he tried to fight down the scratch in his throat. He was scared. He was angry. And he sat there, staring out into the gloom, drinking one beer after another, and when he coughed, really coughed, they all looked at him and at the wet cardboard box of face masks, then looked away again. Nobody said another word to him, which was all right with him—he just focused on the television behind the bar, some news channel, and tried to interpret the words the people were saying there while the backdrop shifted from war-planes and explosions to some sort of pageant with models on a runway looking raccoon-eyed and haughty and not half as good as Rosa Hinojosa. The bloody mask remained in his pocket, and the box of masks, the new ones, stayed right where it was on the stool beside him.

All that week he went into the clinic at eight as instructed and all that week he felt nauseous and skipped breakfast and went to work with Rudy anyway, and the only good thing there was that Rudy didn't like to start early—and he didn't ask questions either. Still, Marciano was lagging and he knew it and knew it was only a matter of time before Rudy said something. Which he did, that Friday, TGIF, end of the week, the first week of his new life with the new cocktail of antibiotics running through his veins and making him nauseous, one week down and how many more to go? He did a quick calculation in his head: fifty-two weeks in a year, double that and then add twenty-six more. It was like climbing a mountain backwards—no matter how many steps you took you never got to see the peak.

They were on their third or fourth house of the day, everything gray and wet with the fog off the ocean and the sun nowhere in sight. His chest felt sore. He was hungry, but the idea of food—a taco or burger or anything—made his stomach turn. "Jesus," Rudy said, startling him out of a daydream, "you're like one of the walking dead. I mean, at that last place I couldn't tell whether you were pushing the mower or the mower was pushing you." The best Marciano could do was give him a tired grin. "What," Rudy said, staring now, "late night last night?"

Rudy was helping him lift the mower down from the back of the truck, so he couldn't avoid his eyes. He just nodded.

"Youth," Rudy said, shaking his head as they set the mower down in the driveway of a little mustard-colored house with a patch of lawn in front and back and a towering hedge all the way round that had to be clipped every other week, and this was that week, which meant hauling out the ladder too. "I used to be like that, burn the candle at both ends, drink till they closed the bars and get up for work three hours later." Rudy sighed, paused to give him a look. "But no more. Now I'm in bed before the ten o'clock news on the TV—and Norma's already snoring."

He'd heard all this before, twenty times already, and he didn't say anything, just leaned into the mower to push it up the driveway, but the mower didn't seem to want to budge because he felt weak all of a sudden, weak and sick, and here came the cough, right on cue. He really hacked this time, hacked till he doubled over and tears came to his eyes. When he straightened up, Rudy was watching him and his smile was gone.

"That doesn't sound too good," he said. "You ever go to the clinic like I told you?"

"Yes," he said. "Or no, not really—"

"What do you mean, *not really*? You sound like your lungs are shot."

He paused to catch his breath, because he couldn't really cough and talk at the same time, could he? Not even Rudy would have expected that of him. He lifted one hand and let it drop. "It's just a cold," he said, then turned and pushed the mower up the drive.

They were waiting for him when he got home, a cop in uniform and Rosa Hinojosa, who looked so fierce and grim she might have been wearing somebody else's face. He'd run into her at the clinic the day before and she'd asked him if he was sticking to the regimen and he told her he was and she flashed a smile so luminous it made him feel unmoored. *Good,* she said, *good. Do it for me, okay?* But now, here she was, and at first he didn't understand what was happening, and he saw her before he saw the cop, the crisp line her skirt cut just above her knees, her pretty legs,

the heels she wore to work, and for the briefest flash of a second he wondered what she was doing there and then he saw the
cop and he knew. Rudy had just dropped him off, already pulling
away from the curb, and Marciano wanted desperately to climb
back into the pickup and go wherever Rudy would take him, but
everything was in slow motion now like in the outer space movies where the astronauts are just floating there on their tethers
and the ship slides away from them in a long smear of light and
shadow.

Before he decided to run, he pulled a mask from his pocket—a
dirty one, to show it had been used—looped it over his ears and
snapped it in place, as if that would make him look better in
Rosa Hinojosa's eyes, but her face showed only disappointment
and something else too, anger. He'd let her down. He'd had his
warning, his final warning, and he'd been caught out, but how
had she known? Had somebody informed on him? Some sneak?
Some enemy he didn't even know he had?

The cop, he could see at a glance, wasn't a real cop, more
some sort of health services mule, and he was old and slow and
his head was like a big *calabaza* propped up on his shoulders,
and Rosa Hinojosa, for all her youth, was no runner, not in
those shoes. So he ran. Not like in the track meets at school
when he was a boy, because his lungs were like wet clay and he
was weak, but still he put one foot in front of the other, hustling down the alley between his house and the one next door,
to where the fence out back opened onto the dry streambed and
the path through the weeds he sometimes used as a shortcut to
the corner store. He got as far as the fence before he gave out,
and, he had to admit, both Rosa Hinojosa and the *calabaza*-head
were quicker than he would have thought. He was just lying
there, pathetic, humiliated in front of this woman he wanted to
prove himself to, and he watched them pause to snap on their

own masks before the cop bent to him and encircled his wrists with the handcuffs.

The next sight he saw was the hospital, a big clean white stucco box of a building that had secondary boxes attached to it, a succession of them lined up like children's blocks all the way out into the parking lot in back. He'd been here once before, to the emergency room, when he'd nearly severed the little finger of his left hand with the blade of the hedge trimmer, and they'd spoken Spanish to him, sewed and bandaged the wound and sent him on his way. That wasn't how it was this time. This time he was wearing a mask and so was Rosa Hinojosa and so was the mule, who kept guiding him down the corridors with a stiff forefinger till they went through a door and briefly out into the sunlight before entering an outbuilding that looked like one of the temporary classrooms you saw when you went by the high school. What was funny about it, or maybe not so funny, was the way people made room for them in the corridors, shrinking into the walls as they passed by in their masks.

When they'd arrived, when he'd had a chance to take in the barred windows and the heavy steel door that pulled shut behind them with a whoosh of compression, Rosa Hinojosa, cold as a fish, explained to him that he was being remanded to custody as a threat to public safety under the provisions of the statutory code of the state of California, and that he would be confined here temporarily before he could be moved to the Men's Colony in the next county, which was equipped with a special ward for prisoners with medical conditions. He felt sick, sicker than ever, and what made it worse was that there was no smell to that room, which might as well have been on the moon for all it seemed to be attached to this earth. He saw a sterile white counter and a man in thick-framed glasses and some sort of hospital scrubs stationed behind it. Rosa Hinojosa was doing all the talking. She had a sheaf of papers in one hand and she turned away from him to lay them on the counter. There was a flag of the U.S. in the corner. A drinking fountain. Black-and-white tiles on the floor. "I didn't do anything," Marciano protested.

Rosa Hinojosa, who was conferring with the man behind the counter, gave him a sharp glance. "You were warned."

"What do you mean? I took my medicine. You saw me—"

"Don't even give me that. We have you on the feed from the security camera at the 7-Eleven making a purchase without your mask on—and there was testimony from the bartender at Herlihy's that you were in there without a mask, *drinking*, and on the very day you gave me your promise, so don't tell me. And don't tell me you weren't warned."

"I'm an American citizen."

She shrugged.

"Look it up." This was true. He'd been born in San Diego, two years old when his parents were deported, and so he'd never had a chance to learn English or go to school here or anything else, but he had his rights, he knew that—they couldn't just lock him up. That was against the constitution.

Rosa Hinojosa had turned back to the counter, riffling through the stack of forms, but now she swung angrily round on him, a crease of irritation between her eyes. She wasn't pretty anymore, not even remotely, and all he felt for her was hate because no matter what she said, when it came down to it she was part of the system and the system was against him. "I don't care if you're the president," she snapped, "because you're irresponsible, because we bent over backwards and now you've left us no choice. Don't you understand? The order's been signed."

"I want a lawyer."

He saw that she had a little dollop of flesh under her chin—fat, she was already going to fat—and he realized she was nothing to him, and worse, that he was nothing to her but one more charity case, and what he did next was born of the sadness of that realization. He wasn't a violent person, just the opposite—he was shy and he went out of his way to avoid confrontation. But they were the ones confronting him—Rosa Hinojosa and the whole Health Services Department, the big stupid-looking mule who'd clamped the handcuffs on him and had made the mistake of removing them after they stepped through the door, and the man behind the desk too. Marciano took as deep a breath as he could manage and felt the mucus rattling in his throat, the bad stuff he kept dredging up all day and spitting into a handkerchief until the handkerchief went stiff with it. What he was about to do was wrong, he knew that, and he regretted it the instant he saw it before him, but he wasn't going to any prison, no way. That just wasn't in the cards.

So he was running again, only this time they weren't chasing him, or not yet, because mask or no mask they were all three of them frantically trying to wipe his living death off their faces— and good, good, see how they like it, see how they like being condemned and ostracized and locked up without a trial or lawyer or anything—and he didn't stop spitting till he had the door open and was back out in the sunlight, dodging round the cars in the lot and heading for the street and the cover of the trees there. His heart was pounding and his lungs felt as if they'd been turned inside out, but he kept going, slowing to a stiff-kneed walk now, down one street, then another, the windshields of the parked cars pooling in the light like puddles after a storm, birds chattering in the trees, the smell of the earth and the grass so intense it was intoxicating. He patted down his pockets: wallet, house key, the little vial of pills. And where was he going? What was he doing? He didn't have any money—no more than maybe ten or fifteen dollars in his wallet—and there was nobody he could turn to, not really. There was Sergio, the only one of the other roomers he was close to, and Sergio would loan him money, he was sure of it, but Sergio probably didn't have much more than he did. The only thing that was for certain was that he couldn't stay around here anymore.

He hadn't seen his mother in two years, hadn't really given her a thought, but he thought of her now, saw her face as vividly as if she were that woman right there slipping into the front seat of her car—she'd nursed him through the measles, whooping cough and the flu and whatever else had come along to disrupt his childhood, and why couldn't she nurse him through this too? She could, if he was careful and took his pills and wore the mask every single minute of every day because he wouldn't want to infect her—that would be the worst thing a son could do. No matter what the doctors said, his mother would save him, protect him, do anything for him. But how was he going to get to her? They'd be watching for him at the bus station and at the train depot and the airport too, even if he could scrape up enough for a ticket, which he couldn't . . . But what about Rudy? Maybe he could get Rudy to drive him as far as Tijuana—or no, he'd tell Rudy he needed to borrow the truck to help one of his roommates move a refrigerator, or something big anyway, a couch, and then he'd do the driving himself and get somebody to bring the truck back, pay somebody, make promises, whatever it took. That was a plan, wasn't it? He had to have a plan. Without a plan he was lost.

He kept moving, breathing hard now, the sidewalk like a treadmill rolling under him, but he had to fight it, had to be quick because they'd have the cops after him in their patrol cars, all-points bulletin like on TV, and they weren't going to be gentle with him either. Up ahead, at the end of the street, was a park he'd gone to once or twice with Sergio to drink beer and throw horseshoes, and there were bushes there, weren't there, along the streambed?

Pushing through the park gate—kids, mothers, swings, a couple of bums laid out on the grass as if they'd been installed there along with the green wooden benches—he tried to look casual, even as the sirens began to scream in the distance and he told himself it was only just ambulances bringing people to the emergency room. He went straight across the lawn, looking at nobody, and if he had to pause twice to let the cough have its way with him, there was nothing he could do about that, but then he was in the bushes and out of sight and he dropped to the ground and just lay there till his heart stopped hammering and the burning in his lungs began to subside. It would be dark soon and then he could make his way back to the house, borrow somebody's phone, call Rudy, pack a few things and be gone before anybody could do anything about it.

Paranoia was when you felt everybody was after you even if they weren't, but what would you call this? Common sense? Vigilance? Wariness? They'd come to his house and handcuffed him and put him in that white room and he hadn't done anything. Now they'd charge him with escaping or resisting arrest or whatever they wanted to call it—and assault too, assault with the deadly weapon that was his own spit. It didn't matter—the result would be the same, thirty months in a sterile room with the fans sucking in and the warders wearing masks and gloves and pushing a tray of what passed for food through a slot in the door and coming in twice a day to stick the intravenous in him. He'd rather be dead. Rather be in Mexico. Rather take his chances with his mother and the clinic in Ensenada where at least they spoke his language and wouldn't look at him like he was a cockroach.

He was thirsty, crazy thirsty, but he forced himself to stay

where he was till it was dark, then slipped back into the park
to get a drink at the faucet in the restroom. Only problem was,
the door was locked. He stood there a long moment, rattling the
doorknob, feeling disoriented. There was the steady hiss of cars
from the freeway that was somewhere behind him in the intermediate distance. The trees were shrouds. The sky was black
overhead and painted with stars and it had never seemed so close.
Or so heavy. He could almost feel the weight of it, all the weight
of the sky that went on and on to infinity, outer space, the plan-
ets, the stars, all of it pressing down on him till he could barely
breathe. Desperate, he went down on his knees in the grass and
felt around till he located one of the sprinkler heads. At first it
wouldn't budge, but he kept at it till the seal gave and he was
able to unscrew it and put his mouth to the warm gurgling flow
there, and that made him feel better and pushed the vagueness
into another corner of his mind. After a while he got to his feet,
eased himself down into the streambed and began working his
way back in the direction of the house.

It wasn't easy. What would have taken him ten minutes out
on the street took an hour at least, his feet unsteady in a slurry
of mud and trash, stiff dead reeds knifing at him, dogs barking,
the drift of people's voices freezing him in place—and what if
somebody sipping a beer on their back porch decided to shine
a flashlight down into the streambed? What would they think?
That he was a fugitive, a thief, a drunk, and before he could even
open his mouth they'd be dialing the police. He was breathing
hard. Sweating. His shirt was torn at the right elbow where he'd
snagged it on something in the strange half-light of the gulley,
and he was shivering too, sweating and shivering at the same time.

He didn't really know how far he'd gone or where he was
when he emerged, scrambling up a steep incline and into the
yard of a house that was mercifully dark, not a light showing
anywhere. There were lights on in the houses on both sides of it,

though, and the black humped shape of an automobile parked in the driveway. He moved toward the car and then past it and if he was startled by a voice calling out behind him, a single syllable he would have recognized in any language—*Hey!*—he never hesitated or turned round or even looked over his shoulder, but just kept going, down the driveway and straight across the street to the sidewalk on the far side where he was just another pedestrian out for a stroll on a cool night in a quiet city.

When he got to his own street he made himself slow down and scan the cars parked on both sides of the road, looking for anything suspicious, the police or the health services, Rosa Hinojosa, though that *was* being paranoid—Rosa Hinojosa would be at home with her parents at this hour, or maybe her husband, if she had one, absorbed in her own life, not his. He took his time, though he was feeling worse by the minute, shivering so hard he had to wrap his arms around himself, his shirt sweated through and too thin against the night and the temperature that must have dropped into the mid-fifties by now. And then, steeling himself, he slipped across the street and into the dark yard of the rooming house where they'd come for him once and would come for him again.

He ducked in the back door, tentative, all the blood in his brain now, screaming at him, but there was nobody in the hall and in the next moment he was in his room, the familiar scent of his things—unwashed laundry, soap, shampoo, the foil-wrapped burrito he'd set aside to microwave for dinner—rising to his nostrils in the ordinary way, as if nothing had happened. The cough was right there waiting to erupt, but he fought it down, afraid even to make the slightest sound, and though he was tempted to turn the light on, he knew better—if anyone was out there, this was what they'd be watching for. He found his jacket thrown over the back of the chair where he'd left it that morning and wrapped himself in it, then went to the window and opened the blinds so that six thin stripes of illumination fell across the bed. That was when he remembered his pills—he had to take his pills no matter where he was or what happened, that was the truth of his life, whether he ever saw Rosa Hinojosa again or not.

He went to the sink for a glass of water, shook out two of the little white pills and swallowed them. Then—and he couldn't help himself—he lay down on the bed and closed his eyes, just for a minute.

The knock startled him out of a dreamless sleep, the knock at the front door that thundered through the house as if the wrecking ball had come to reduce it all to splinters. But who would knock? Everybody who lived here had a key so there was no need for knocking, not unless you were immigration or the police. Or health services. For one fluttering instant he pictured Rosa Hinojosa in police blues with a cap cocked over her eye, a nightstick in one hand and a can of mace in the other, and then he was pulling the door softly shut and fastening the latch, as if that would save him—and what was he going to do, hide under the bed? Coughing now—he couldn't help himself, really dredging it up, the weakness squeezing him like a fist, then letting go and squeezing again—he slammed round the darkened room in a panic, thinking only to get away, far away where they'd never find him, where there was sunshine and he could stretch out in the hot sand and bake the microbes out of him. He didn't know much, but he knew they'd be at the back door too, just like in the movies when they nailed the gangsters and the pimps and the drug lords and the whole audience stood up and cheered . . .

No time for his backpack, no time for clothes, his toothbrush, for the change he kept in a pickle jar in the top drawer, no time for anything but to jerk up the window in its creaking frame while the knocking at the front door rose to a relentless

pounding and the voices started up there, Sergio's and somebody else's and a dog barking, and then he was down in the grass
and scrambling hunched-over for the next yard and then the
next one after that. It took everything he had. Twice he tripped
in the dark, going down hard on somebody's patio, all the little
sounds of the neighborhood amplified now, every TV turned up
full-blast, motorcycles blaring like gunfire out on the street,
even the crickets shrieking at him, and that dog, the ratcheting
bark of that dog back at the house, a police dog, the kind of dog
that never gave up, that could sniff you out even if you sprouted
wings and flew up into the sky.

Where was he? Some dark place. Some citizen's backyard
with its jade plants and flowerbed and patch of lawn. A cold
hand went down inside him, yanking at his lungs, squeezing
and bunching and pulling the meat there up into his throat so he
couldn't breathe. He went down on his hands and knees, shivering again, sweating again, and there was no plan now but to
find the darkest corner of the yard, the place where nobody had
bothered to cut the grass or trim the shrubs, where the earth was
real and present and he could let the blood come up and forget
about the pills and Rosa Hinojosa and his mother and Rudy and
everybody else.

Time leapt ahead. He was stretched out in the dirt. What was
on his shirt was hot and secret and wet. He closed his eyes. And
when he opened them again, all he could see was the glint of a
metal trap, bubbles rising in the clear cold water and the hands of
the animal fighting to get out.

T.C. BOYLE is an American novelist and short story writer. Since the mid-1970s, he has published sixteen novels and more than 150 short stories. He won the PEN/Faulkner Award in 1988 for his third novel, *World's End,* and the Prix Médicis étranger (France) for *The Tortilla Curtain* in 1995, as well as the PEN/ Malamud Award for Excellence in Short Fiction in 1999. *The Harder They Come* was a *New York Times* bestseller. In 2014 he won the Rea Award for the Short Story, and he was the editor of *The Best American Short Stories* (2015).